MYSTERIES OF THE OZARKS,

VOL. I

Nineteen New Short Stories

Edited by Ellen Gray Massey

Copyright 2003 by Skyward Publishing, Inc.

Publisher: Skyward Publishing, Inc.
               17440 N. Dallas Parkway, Suite 111
               Dallas, Texas 75287
               (972) 490-8988
               E-mail: info@skywardpublishing.com
               Web Site: www.skywardpublishing.com

Library of Congress Cataloging-in-Publication Data

Nineteen new short stories / by Ellen Gray Massey, et. al. ; edited by Charlotte Harris.
        p. cm. — (Mysteries of the Ozarks ; v. 1)
    ISBN 1-881554-36-8 (alk. paper)
    1. Detective and mystery stories, American—Ozark Mountians. 2. Short stories, American—Ozark Mountains. 3. Ozark Mountains—Fiction. I. Massey, Ellen Gray. II. Harris, Charlotte. III. Series.
PS648.D4 N57 2004
813'.08720897671—dc22
                                                    2003022574

Printed in the United States of America
Cover Design by Jim and Peggy Thomas

TABLE OF CONTENTS

FOREWORD

In August 2001 five writers and I formed a nonprofit organization in the state of Missouri called Ozark Writers, Inc. (www.ozarkwritersinc.com). In March 2003 we received 501(c)3 status from the United States Treasury, Internal Revenue Service. Our purpose is to encourage and promote writers from the Ozarks in publishing their work and to educate and expand the reading public to the literature of the region.

To encourage writers in southern Missouri and northern Arkansas, in groups or individually, we have conducted four daylong writing workshops, an Elderhostel in Branson, and given over forty talks. To expand the reading public to Ozark literature, in addition to Missouri and Arkansas, we have presented programs in Illinois, Connecticut, Washington, D.C., and Seattle, Washington.

With the publication of *Mysteries of the Ozarks, Volume I*, we are beginning our goal to make available to the world the work of the fine writers of the area. We sent out invitations to well-known and lesser-known published writers with strong ties to the Ozarks for family-reading short stories.

The stories in this edition vary in length, style, and approach. Some are historical, portraying the ancient Bluff Dwellers and the unique position of Missouri during the Civil War. Some have romances, fantasy, supernatural beings, humor, and adventure. All take place in the Ozarks; all have a mystery to solve.

The six directors of Ozark Writers, Inc. thank the writers for taking time from their busy schedules to write new stories specifically for our anthology. We also want to thank our readers for pausing during their busy days to join us in these mystery tales of the Missouri and Arkansas Ozarks. It was my pleasure to work with so many talented writers.

Ellen Gray Massey

Directors of Ozark Writers, Inc.

Vicki Cox, Lebanon, Missouri
Jane Hale, Buffalo, Missouri
Betty Henderson, Monett, Missouri
Ellen Gray Massey, Lebanon, Missouri
Shirleen Sando, Kennett, Missouri
Carolyn Gray Thornton, Nevada, Missouri

What do wind chimes, a parakeet named Mr. Peepers, and a long-stemmed rose have to do with his mother's death, Andy wonders, except to make him feel her presence.

AVENGING ANGEL

by Jory Sherman

Andrew Duncan stood on the empty porch. The board beneath him was still creaking. That was the one that always groaned when he stepped on it, and now he let the sound reverberate in his mind like some tuning fork of memory stirring up rhythms of his past when he had lived in the house, first as a boy, then as a man. He turned at the melodic sound of his mother's wind chimes and chills sprouted on his arms in the form of goose pimples that made the small hairs stiffen and stand straight up.

"When you hear the chimes," his mother had said to him, "it may not always be the wind. It could be the spirit of a loved one who has passed, stopping by to say hello and give comfort."

His mother was dead. She had died in the Boone County Hospital in Harrison, Arkansas, only a week ago. He was still shaking inside from the memory of hearing that tragic news. And, from other things that had happened since. Things he did not want to think about right now.

Andy walked over to the porch swing and sat down. From there, he faced the wind chimes hanging from a beam at the end of the porch.

"Is that you, Mother?" he asked. The chimes tinkled melodiously in just a faint whisper of wind.

The hackles rose on the back of his neck. The swing groaned under his weight and the chains anchored to the porch ceiling creaked, much like that familiar board he had stepped on a few moments before.

Tears welled up in his eyes as he thought of his mother. She died all alone because his stepfather was out of town. And he, Andy, had been staying over in Diamond City on a fishing trip with friends on Bull Shoals Lake.

"I should have been here," he said aloud. "Maybe I could have saved you, Mother."

Andy fought back the tears that began welling up in his eyes. He knew that once he started crying, he would be unable to stop. He sat there, trying to summon up the courage to go inside the house, knowing it would be empty. Empty, but resonant of his mother's presence. He drew in a breath as if to shut off the tears and gain composure before he got up and entered the hollow house.

Moments snailed by, and it seemed he could hear the house ticking. Houses did that. Wood expanded and contracted with the temperature, with the wind, with the whispers of ghosts. The house ticked, like an erratic clock, but time seemed to hold its breath, as if suspended by some unseen force, like a clock waiting to be rewound.

Tick, tick, tick.

Then, in the deafening silence as the house settled, Andy heard someone's voice, coming from inside.

"Hello, Tommy."

His mother's voice, very low and sounding far away. Andy stiffened.

"Come here, Tommy. Come here."

Andy stood up, shaken from hearing his mother's voice. Mr. Peepers. His mother's pet parakeet. The bird sounded uncannily like his mother, and hearing her voice come out of nowhere like that sent cold ripples up his spine.

He took out his keys and unlocked the front door. He walked inside the living room and stopped, listening. He heard his heart pounding and his temples throbbed with the rush of blood through his veins.

"Hello, Andy."

Again the hackles on the back of his neck rose stiff as cactus spines and vibrated like miniature tuning forks.

He heard a fluttering as if someone were shuffling through a deck of cards. A whirring sound, he thought. The hallway seemed more narrow than he remembered, and it was dark enough to give him shivers all over again.

"Andy's home. Andy's home." The mindless parroting of his mother's voice was unnerving, still, as it had been the day his mother died, when he had come to her house after being away, teaching college classes up in Springfield, Missouri.

His throat constricted and he quickened his pace, hurried down the hallway, stepped through the dining room and into the kitchen. Freshly washed plates were still standing in the drying rack on the counter, along with glasses, cups, saucers, and silverware. They were dry, but their surfaces gleamed in the light that came through the window. Smells lingered in the room and he looked at the stove. It too had been cleaned up, like the counters and dishes. He couldn't isolate the aromas still clinging to the walls, ceiling, and floors, but it smelled as if his mother had cooked lunch only a few moments before. Funny, he thought, how a closed-up house can retain all its smells.

He looked at the large trash container at the end of the counter. A long box stuck out as if it had just been tossed there. He smiled, recognizing it. The box bore the legend: Lou's Nursery, Osage, Arkansas. Lou Spetaza was always bringing his mother flowers and vegetables he grew in his greenhouses. As if he were squiring his mother, a married woman. Now, Andy knew better, and the knowledge was bitter in his mind. The deceit, all the little deceptions that had gone on while he was away, living on his own up north.

He heard a slight cheeping sound and resurfaced from his almost dazed reverie.

He almost collapsed with relief when he saw the parakeet in its cage.

"Mr. Peepers, you're a naughty bird," he said, walking over to the cage, which hung on a standard in one corner of the room. He looked inside the cage and saw that the bird had food and water. He pushed a fingertip between the bars. Mr. Peepers hopped along its trapeze bar and pecked at Andy's finger. Its beak clacked on his fingernail.

"You sound just like Mother, Mr. Peepers."

He had always been amazed at the bird's mimicry.

He breathed a sigh of relief, then walked back out toward the living room. He paused in the dining room to look at the table. There were two place mats there, salt and pepper shakers. In the center on a colored doily, there was a vase sprouting a single, long-stemmed rose. Someone had cleared the table, but had left the two place mats. And, the rose. Mother must have had company for lunch, he thought.

There was so much of his mother's presence in the house, and very little of his father's. But, he had always accepted that. His stepfather was away on business most of the time, and the house might have been his castle, but it was his mother's nest. Over the years she had decorated it, filled it with flowers and colorful furniture, carpets, drapes, and knickknacks that suited her artistic temperament. Yet she loved her husband dearly and all that she did was for his comfort, as well as her own sensibilities.

Andy walked back into the living room, taking the vase with him, wondering that he had missed it a week ago, wondering why the rose still seemed fresh. His mother always put that vase back on a folding table where she kept it except when she brought it to the dining table. He looked around the room as if to piece together his mother's last moments in the house.

Nothing looked out of place. There were doilies on the arms of the chair and couch and on the back of the couch. He almost laughed. Nobody made or used doilies anymore. Except his mother. She even had them in her bedroom. His stepfather hated doilies and throw pillows and anything that smacked of lace or filigree. But, his mother was old school. She loved lacy things, curtains, bedspreads, blouses, curtains, and throws. And doilies.

The room was smothering for those few moments as he felt his mother's presence. He could smell her scent in the room and he became gripped with an overwhelming sadness. He knew she was no longer there, but she was there, in his mind, in his rapidly beating heart. He fought back the tears that threatened to well up in his eyes, and he gasped, gulping in air to clear his head, to make his body function normally.

That's when he heard the humming sound of a car coming up the drive. The sound startled him as it jarred him out of that solitary place of sadness. It took him more than a moment to comprehend that there was another world beyond the windowpanes, that people were moving about and going places while he was standing still, his world stopped in its tracks like a movie stuck in the projector.

He saw the black car drive to the front of the house and stop. There was a shield on the door panel bearing the words, "Carroll County Sheriff." Puzzled, he went to the door, opened it, and stepped outside onto the porch. A man stepped out of the car. He wasn't wearing a uniform, but he had a pistol strapped on, and the military shirt he wore, gray, with epaulets, gave him a kind of official presence.

"Mr. Bailey," the man said. He was a slender man, wiry, with pale blue eyes that were as vacant as a doll's eyes, with weathered wrinkles at their corners, creases

in a tanned complexion. He wore a baseball cap embla-
zoned with the name of a farm implement company. A
small notepad and pen stuck out of his left shirt pocket.

"The name's Andrew Duncan. Bailey's my stepfather," Andy said.

"And Georgia Bailey was your mother."

"That's right."

That had been a week ago, when Carroll County
Sheriff Lonnie Yost had driven up, inspected the house,
and told Andy that he, along with his stepfather, Tommy
Bailey, and Lou Spetaza, were suspects.

"Suspects in what?" Andy had asked.

"We believe your mother was murdered," Yost said.

"Murdered? How?"

"Poison. Some kind of poison. Coroner's conducting
an autopsy even as we speak."

When Andy had seen his mother in the hospital, she
had been in a coma. She died a few moments after he
arrived. Nobody there had mentioned that his mother
had been poisoned.

That's when Andy decided that he had to find out
who had murdered his mother, and why.

He recalled the morning following his mother's
death when Sheriff Yost had come over to question him
again. That's when he heard the full story of his mother's death from the coroner himself.

"I've got a couple more questions," Yost had said.

Andy snorted, shook his head.

"When that woman at the hospital called you," Yost
said, "Charlotte whoever, where were you?"

"I was out on a boat, fishing. On Bull Shoals."

"You have a cell phone?"

"It's in the car. Yes."

Yost pulled out his notepad and jotted something
down.

"You were gone a week?"

"About that. I'm off from teaching for the summer."

"And your father. Your stepfather. He was also supposed to be gone for a week?"

"About that. Why?"

More jotting. Yost didn't reply.

"Sheriff, I think you're barking up the wrong tree," Andy said.

"We'll see. We'll wait for the others to arrive. I left a deputy and a detective at Lou's Nursery," Yost said. "They should be bringing your father over directly, along with Lou Spetaza."

They waited. Andy fumed. Yost started rocking the swing. He hummed some tuneless melody as if he were mulling something over in his mind. Finally, they heard the sound of car engines.

"I hear two cars," Andy said.

"The other would be the coroner and possibly an assistant D.A. I told the medical examiner to stop at the nursery first and make sure my deputy brings the other two suspects out here when he came."

"This is beginning to sound like an Agatha Christie mystery," Andy said.

"Who's Agatha Christie?"

"Never mind."

"Oh, you mean the mystery writer."

Andy shook his head, exasperated.

A sheriff's car pulled up with four people in it. Thomas Bailey and Lou Spetaza sat in the back seat. Behind that car, one bearing a Boone County official seal pulled up with two men in it.

"Ah, they're here," Yost said.

"You're very observant, Sheriff," Andy said, his tone laced with sarcasm.

"This isn't the time to be cute, Andy."

Still another car drove in, with two people in the front seat.

"Crime Scene Unit," Yost said. "Forensics team."

"Are you sure you don't need an army?" Andy said. "I think you might need a warrant too, Sheriff."

"We got that." Yost got up from the swing and walked to the center of the porch, stopped just above the top step.

One man got out of the sheriff's car, carrying two sheets of paper, while another stayed with Lou and Thomas.

"Lonnie," the man said, handing the papers to the sheriff. "CSU got something at the nursery."

"Thanks, Billy. Billy, this is the son, Andy Duncan. Andy, say hello to Billy Ray Milam. He's a lieutenant. Boone County detective."

"Mr. Milam," Andy said, his voice as cold as frozen iron.

"That's three suspects right handy," Milam said, his wide grin showing a gap in his teeth, which gave him the look of an idiot, Andy thought.

"Well, we might be able to narrow the short list down," Yost said. "Let's see what Cooper has to say."

The coroner and his assistant, an Oriental man, both left their car and walked up to the front porch.

"This the young 'un?" Cooper said.

"He's Andy, the stepson of Thomas. Mrs. Bailey's natural son."

"Son, I want to talk to you," Cooper said. He was dressed garishly in a checked shirt and orange trousers. His rounded belly hung over an old, worn belt. His face was florid, the blue veins vivid on his high cheekbones and threaded like highway routes on a map. "Name's Horace Cooper and I'm the Boone County coroner. This is my assistant, Ng Tranh, a criminalist. Ng, you go on inside the house and start looking around."

Tranh nodded. He was carrying a square leather case. He was a small man in his twenties, with large brown eyes, thin lips, and a rounded, almost chinless face. His skin was the color of lightly creamed coffee. Yost stepped aside to allow the young man to enter the house.

"Where can we talk?" Cooper asked.

"You and Andy go sit on the swing yonder. I'll listen in."

Cooper walked to the swing and sat down. He pulled out a soggy bandanna and wiped his sweaty forehead. "Sit, son," he said, patting the place next to him. Andy sat down. Yost leaned against the porch rail, facing them.

"Horace," Yost said. "Did you do the autopsy?"

"I sure did, Lonnie." Cooper looked at Andy, a sympathetic expression on his face. "Son, what I got to tell you ain't pretty, but you got to hear it."

"I'm listening," Andy said, his voice lacking conviction.

Cooper looked briefly at Yost, shook his head, as if about to apologize for what he had to say to Andy.

"Andy, may I call you Andy? Good. Your mother was tortured. She took a long time to die. A week, I'd say. I'm sorry."

Andy hung his head. He began to sob. Cooper reached over and patted him softly on the back.

"Should I go on, son?" Cooper asked.

Andy lifted his head and nodded.

"She was poisoned. Probably every day for that week's time. Now, if you were here . . ."

"He wasn't," Yost said. "He was off fishing."

"Or your father . . ."

"Could be," Yost said.

"Well, someone had to be here and feed her that stuff."

"What stuff?" Andy asked.

"Mushrooms," Cooper said. "Poisonous mushrooms."

Andy sat in stunned silence as Cooper paused to assess his reaction.

"You folks eat wild mushrooms?" Yost asked. "Morels?"

"Yeah," Andy said. "We picked them every spring out in the woods."

"You pick any this year?"

Andy nodded. "We ate them all, though. I'm sure of that."

"Ever get sick from any mushrooms you picked?" Yost asked.

"Never."

"Well, your mother did," the coroner said. "An autopsy revealed that she had ingested a large amount of *Amanita Virosa*, a deadly mushroom sometimes called Destroying Angel. We also found some *Amanita Bisporigera*, better known as Death Angel. Somebody wanted to make sure your mother died from these deadly mushrooms. Lonnie, we found both varieties growing in Lou's Nursery. They come from North Carolina. Here, I'll show you what one of the Destroying Angels looks like."

Cooper plucked a white mushroom from his coat pocket and held it in the palm of his hand.

Andy and Yost leaned over to look at it.

"You can see it's got a white cap," Cooper said. "The gills are white too and not attached to the stalk like an edible mushroom, or a morel. But, the gills are very close to the stalk, so they can fool you. Stalk's white too. This one's center will soon turn to a tan-colored white as it ages. I just picked it a few minutes ago from a bed Mr. Spetaza had underneath the shelving in his greenhouse. This stalk is still pearly, but it could be like fuzzy cotton, and some of the others I found were like that. Doesn't look deadly, does it?"

Yost shook his head. Andy drew away from the mushroom and drew in a deep breath.

"How bad was it for my mother?" Andy asked.

"You want it straight?"

Andy nodded. Yost did the same.

"Your mother started showing symptoms from six to twenty-four hours after she ate them. She would have had severe abdominal pains, diarrhea, and vomiting for a period of about six to nine hours. Then, she may have stopped having symptoms for another day or so. But, during that time, the toxins were attacking her liver. When she was brought to the hospital in Harrison, this had already occurred."

"Lou took her to the hospital," Andy said. "He said he came over and saw that she was in distress. He was trying to save her life."

"That could be. But, it was too late. Your mother began having gastrointestinal bleeding soon after she was brought in. Then, she went into a coma. Her kidneys failed, and she died."

Andy broke into tears. His face contorted as if he were in pain.

"We're trying to find out who did this," Yost said. "So far, you're in the clear. But, Thomas Bailey and Lou Spetaza were here."

"Tommy was out of town, I thought," Andy said.

"We don't know where he was just yet."

Yost turned to the detective in the car and motioned for him to bring Bailey and Spetaza up to the porch.

"Andy, this is a crushing blow," Bailey said as he mounted the porch steps. "A shock to all of us." He wore a cream polo shirt and light tan slacks, Adidas jogging shoes. His face was clean-shaven, his sandy hair neatly combed. He looked, Andy thought, as if he were going to play a round of golf, which was unsettling under the circumstances.

At least, Andy noted, neither his stepfather nor Lou were in handcuffs.

"It's a tragedy," Lou said in his deep silky voice.

As usual, Lou was wearing a green ball cap with the Lou's Nursery emblem on it, a light green gardening smock, blue jeans bought at the Gap, lace-up work boots. His fingernails, as usual, were embedded with black soil.

Andy noticed that Yost was observing the three of them like a cat watching three mice in a cheese factory. But then, he too was looking at Lou and Tommy as if seeing them for the first time. They looked as if they were more than good friends, and that was odd, because Andy had always thought of Lou as his mother's friend, not Tommy's.

The police made no arrests that week, but Andy had been thinking hard after Tommy came home and tried not to look sheepish about it. Both men avoided talking about Georgia. Andy had found out from Sheriff Yost that Tommy hadn't gone to St. Louis on business, as he said he was when he left, but had been staying at Lou's Nursery. Andy had asked why, and Yost had said he wondered the same thing and was working on it.

Then, something happened the day after Tommy had come home. That was when Andy knew who had killed his mother. He still didn't know why, even though Yost had told him Tommy carried a large insurance policy on his wife. The day before his mother's funeral, Tommy left, telling Andy he was going to look at some paintings in Berryville.

Andy followed Tommy, almost hating himself for his suspicions, but telling himself he had to know. Tommy didn't drive to Berryville. He drove straight to Lou's Nursery. Andy drove his Buick into an old road nearby, got out, and snuck up to the nursery with a pair of binoculars he had brought with him.

Tommy spent most of the day at Lou's and Andy made a suggestion that night at supper, when Tommy was home.

"After Mother's interment, Tommy," Andy said, "I'd like to have you and Lou over for lunch. I'll fix it. You know I'm a great cook."

"Why, that would be nice. And, yes, your mother always bragged about your cooking. She said she taught you all she knew."

Andy forced a laugh at that.

"The funeral's going to wring every last ounce of grief out of all of us, and I thought we'd just eat a nice meal and talk about Mom," Andy said.

"A little private wake, eh?" Tommy said.

Andy sat through the funeral wracked with almost unbearable grief. He doubled over when the procession passed by his mother's casket, weeping uncontrollably. He left without talking to anyone and hurried home to prepare the noon meal.

During lunch Tommy and Lou talked about what a good woman Georgia had been. But Andy only nodded. He was fuming inside, struggling to disguise his anger. He took some satisfaction in watching Lou and Tommy devour the food he had prepared.

"A bit spicy," Tommy said.

"Good, though," Lou said, his throaty voice grating on Andy's nerves like a rasp drawn across a piece of tin.

As soon as they were done eating, Tommy drove Lou back to the nursery. When they were gone, Andy called Sheriff Yost.

"I think you ought to come right out," Andy said. "It's about my mother's murder . . . and some others."

"Did you say 'others'?"

"You heard me."

"I'll leave here about five. I'm buried in paper-work."

"That'll be fine," Andy said.

Andy spent the rest of the afternoon washing the dishes, cleaning the kitchen, and strolling through the house, knowing there wasn't much time left. He thought of Lou and Tommy and ground his teeth together as he looked at his watch every few minutes.

Andy waited on the porch for Sheriff Yost. Dusk was coming on like some spectral portent creeping onto the swing. The porch threw a long wide shadow on the front lawn. It was quiet for a few moments, then a breeze wafted out of the woods and the wind chimes sounded.

"Soon, Mother," Andy said, in a breathy whisper.

Andy had moved Mr. Peepers and his cage into the living room and left the window open.

"I love Lou," the bird rasped. It was the same phrase that Andy had heard two days after his mother had died. The same voice that had startled him then.

"Did you know, Mother?" Andy said. "Did you know about Lou? And Tommy?"

The wind chimes tinkled a tapestry of melodic notes.

Andy's lips curled in a faint smile, and then he heard the purr of Yost's car as it wound up the lane.

"You figured it out, Andy?" Yost said, as he crossed the porch, stepping on the creaking board.

"Yeah. You?"

"Pretty much. Want to tell me about it? You mentioned other murders. What's that all about?"

"That's why I called you out here, Sheriff Yost. I thought we might compare notes."

"Just call me Lonnie. Everybody else does."

"Okay."

Yost pulled his notepad out of his pocket and clicked the ballpoint pen so that the tip emerged.

"Shoot," Yost said.

The parakeet was muttering.

"Mr. Peepers," Andy said, leaning toward the open window behind the swing. "Where is Lou?"

The sheriff's eyebrows arched.

"I love Lou," Mr. Peepers said. "I love Lou."

"Did you hear it, Lonnie?"

"Yeah. I heard that bird before, remember? Sounds like your mother, you said."

"Most of what Mr. Peepers says imitates my mother's voice, but not that phrase."

"Come to think of it, the voice is deeper. Whose is it?"

"Tommy's," Andy said.

"That's odd, isn't it?"

"Better write that down, Lonnie. That's what gave me the idea that there was something between my stepfather and Lou."

"These things happen, I guess." Yost seemed uncomfortable.

"I saw them. Tommy and Lou. I spied on them the other day."

"And?"

"First, let me tell you what I've done, Lonnie. I broke into Lou's Nursery yesterday and found some of those Destroying Angels. They were growing in a storm shelter out back. I guess Cooper didn't check there the first time."

"No, I guess not. More poisonous mushrooms?"

Andy nodded.

"I chopped them all up, very fine, and put them in a quiche I made for our lunch. I made the dish very spicy. If you looked at it, you couldn't tell the mushrooms were in it. You saw spinach and cheese and ground beef. The three of us finished eating about six hours ago."

Yost stiffened. "You did what?"

Andy smiled. "I fed us all those mushrooms, Lonnie. I'm a murderer too."

"But, you ate them also?"

"Yes. I don't care about myself. I wanted to avenge my mother's death. And, I did. I figure Lou and Tommy will start getting sick pretty soon. And, so will I. In fact, I'm feeling some spasms now."

"Are you crazy? Why?"

"I saw them, Lonnie. Lou and Tommy. Only Lou is Louise. I heard them too. Over at her place. They both planned my mother's murder. Lou—Louise—knew my stepfather before and came here disguised as a man to be close to him. She lured him away from my mother and . . ."

"We pretty much tagged them for the murder," Yost said. "And, we knew Lou was living a double life. Real name's Louise Porras and we think she's done this before. She was an actress when Tom Bailey met her, a Shakespearean actress who played both men's and women's roles."

"That voice of Mr. Peepers when it said, 'I love Lou,'

was Tommy's. He taught the parakeet to say it, I guess. Perverse of him, wasn't it? Arrogant too."

Yost swore under his breath. He put the notebook back in his pocket.

"Andy, I'd better get you to the hospital. If you ate those . . ."

"So you can arrest me?"

"If you live, maybe yes. But, why did you do it?"

"Why? Think of me as an avenging angel, Lonnie. But I'm a criminal too. I committed a crime and I know there's a penalty to pay. I loved my mother, and I chose my own punishment so that I could be with her again. Ironic, isn't it? I teach poetry and write poetry myself. The myth is that the good poets die young. Maybe I'm one of those. Or maybe I'm just another criminal. Anyway, I've made my peace with the world and my maker. I'll pay for my crime. But maybe the punishment won't last long. I won't go to prison, at least, but I'll pay for my crime. And, I'll be with my mother soon."

Andy smiled. He looked at the wind chimes as they swayed and rang out in the wash of the evening zephyrs. Then, he doubled over in pain as his stomach spasmed.

"Have them put me in the same bed where my mother died," he said after he recovered. His face was drained of color.

In the distance, down by the creek that ran through the property, Andy heard the frogs croaking, and he felt the hills rise up in the looming darkness like magical fortresses. He thought of the deep hollows filling up with night and drew comfort from the land he and his mother had loved so much, those gentle Ozark hills so green and vibrant, the woods and the streams.

He was not afraid of death. Nor had his mother feared dying. "Death is just a continuation of life," she had told him, "a pause at a crossroads. We give up our breath and partake of light, one form of energy exchanged for another."

Andy thought his mother was very wise.

The shadows thickened on the porch and the lawn turned dark. Fireflies began to flash golden messages above the grasses in the field beyond the fence. Venus winked on in the pale blue sky, like a lighthouse at the edge of a vast ocean, like a beacon marking a farther shore at the end of a long sea.

The wind chimes sounded like distant church bells in Andy's ears.

Mr. Peepers was silent.

JORY SHERMAN BIOGRAPHY

Jory Sherman began his literary career as a poet in San Francisco's famed North Beach in the late 1950s, during the heyday of the Beat Generation. His poetry and short stories were widely published when he began writing commercial fiction. He has won numerous awards for his poetry and prose and was nominated for a Pulitzer Prize in Letters for his novel, *Grass Kingdom*. He won a Spur Award from Western Writers of America for *The Medicine Horn*. He has also won a number of awards from the Missouri Writers Guild. He lived in the Ozarks for over twenty years, last making his home in Branson. His writing regularly appears in *The Ozarks Mountaineer* and his latest collection of Ozark pieces are in *The Hills of Home*, published by Hardshell Word Factory. He now lives on a lake in northeast Texas.

The McGuires were an odd bunch even for the town of Possibility. But what the sheriff and his buddies found . . . that was far beyond odd.

MISSING PETE MCGUIRE

by C. J. Winters

The usual bunch of us was sitting at the big table in the back of Luanne's Cafe having coffee when someone asked if anybody had seen Pete McGuire for a while. Everybody shook his head except Matt Forrester, who took off his Family Hardware cap and scrubbed one hand over his freckled scalp.

"Musta been three, four weeks ago. Come in the store, bought a spool of wire, a portable drill, and a batch of batteries."

"Wonder why he ever come back to Possibility anyway," said Terry Johnson. The town used to be called No Possibility, but a few years back the business owners got a petition going to officially rename it.

Matt snagged another packet of sugar. "His wife died a long time ago, and their boy in Vietnam. Said he wanted to get back to his roots."

Sounded one board short of a load to me, all his local folks being dead too.

"Even so," persisted Terry, "you'd think after sixty years of city life, living raw in that old house without plumbing and TV be tough on an old guy."

"Got to be eighty if he's a day," I said.

"That's not so old," Ernie Bledsoe said. "My daddy's older'n him. He says the two of them used to hunt squirrel and rabbit for supper when Pete wasn't no bigger'n a minute. He says the McGuires was an odd bunch."

"Still," put in Dan Halstead, our county sheriff, "we need to keep a lookout of these older folks—'specially when they live alone out in the timber like that."

We all nodded somberly, thinking how Jean Mather laid under her kitchen table for over a week before folks started wondering why she didn't show up at church.

Dan pushed back his chair. "Any of you want to ride out to Pete's place with me?"

"I will," I said, shoving back. "Give me time to tell Lori and the boy where I'm headed. They run the store better without me anyway."

"Might as well tag along," Ernie said. "Not much going on to the agency the girls can't handle."

Terry nodded. "I'll follow you out. It's on the way. I need to get home and tack some new shingles on the garage. The wife fusses, says the leak isn't doing the Mustang finish any good."

We all laughed at that. Terry's pride and joy is his restored '64 Mustang, and everybody hereabouts knows what happened in it got him to get married in the first place. *He* is now a doctor in Cincinnati.

So it was near noon before the four of us headed out to Farm Road 1020 and the cutoff to the red gravel track to the four-room house that's been in the McGuire family more than a hundred years.

When we got there, Dan hoisted himself out of the patrol car, his forehead creased like one of the limestone bluffs around here. I followed, but my gut was churning like I'd eaten a bowl of Mexican chili beans. There wasn't one sign of life on the place, and Pete's '94 Olds, parked under an oak near the house, looked like every bird for miles around had dumped on it.

Terry pulled up behind us and got out of his pickup. "Don't like it," he muttered. "Place looks like a calendar called *Ozarks Revisited.*"

Situated in the middle of the Mark Twain Forest, the house set empty, except for an occasional summer renter, since Pete left for the city sixty years ago. There were holes in the roof big enough to throw a cat through. Somebody, though, had cut deadwood and stacked it by the door.

"Yo, the house!" shouted Dan. "Pete, you in there?"

I'd have been mighty surprised if anybody answered, and sure enough, nobody did.

Dan pushed open the front door, his right hand near his revolver. "Pete, it's Dan Halstead, the sheriff. I come to see you're okay."

Wind ruffled the leaves of nearby maples. Otherwise it was quiet. Even the birds had shut up.

Dan stepped cautiously into the front room of the little house. "You wait here," he said over his shoulder. "I'll check the bedrooms."

He was back in half a minute, looking puzzled. "Nobody there. Not even a bed." Then he stepped into the kitchen. "Well, I'll be damned!"

We moved up to peer over his shoulder. There wasn't a stick of furniture in the kitchen, unless you call a dry sink furniture. The cabinet doors hung open, the shelves empty.

"He's disappeared," I said and promptly felt foolish for voicing the obvious.

Ernie crowded up close. "And taken the kitchen furniture with him. Now *that's odd*."

Terry said, "You reckon whoever took Pete, took the furniture too? I mean, no bed, no table, no chairs?"

Dan held up a hand of authority. "Anybody been here since he came back to know there was furniture?"

Terry nodded. "Yep. I told the wife he'd moved back here and she sent over a casserole and a loaf of home baked bread. I didn't see the bedrooms, but there was a table and two chairs in the kitchen." He backed up a few paces and glanced over the front room. All we saw there was a little table, a couple of oil lamps, a wood bench with a moldy plaid cushion, and a three-legged stool. "There was a rocking chair, but it's gone too."

Ernie said, "Somebody robbed the place, that's for sure."

We tagged Dan out to Pete's car, which wasn't locked. He checked under the floor mat, found the key, and opened the trunk. In it were a spade, an old hand-saw, a hammer, portable drill, box of canned food, a few kitchen utensils, packs of fresh batteries, cleaning equipment, bug spray, and a suitcase containing toi-letries and an envelope with thirty-nine dollars and loose change. No clothing, no bedding, no papers, no wallet.

Dan unhooked the cell phone from his belt, then put it back. "Before I call this in as a missing person, sup-posing we take a look around. Everybody go in a differ-ent direction, check the area, say for ten minutes. Okay?"

Of course we all agreed. Dan checked that the cement well cover around the pump was secure, and he gave the handle a few pumps, turning out yellowish water. Then he pointed each of us in a different dir-ection and we fanned out into the surrounding timber of oak, cedar, hickory, maple, underbrush, and poison ivy.

I checked the privy, leaning like the tower of Pisa, and figured it hadn't been used recently. From there I angled uphill behind the house, slipping and sliding on loose pebbles and thin soil slimed by last night's rain, the dampness emphasizing the smells of vegeta-tion and mold. Like always, I kept a sharp eye out for snakes. It was a pretty June day, and any other time I'd have enjoyed the little excursion, but now my stomach wouldn't settle down. Every time a squirrel stomped on a leaf, I jumped. Frankly I was looking forward to get-ting back to town and letting Dan and his team get on with their business. I felt pretty sure we weren't going to find Pete McGuire safe and sound.

My ten minutes were almost up when I heard a shout down the hill to my right.

Terry kept hooting until the three of us puffed up to where he squatted, waiting. I was the last one to get there, having twisted my ankle in a sprawl as I hustled back downhill.

I'd never been on the property before, and I was surprised to see six fairly fresh-dug holes inside a little fence made of a heavy chain looped between metal posts. Once it had been painted white. Scraps of damp, rotted wood were scattered around. "What the *hell*?"

Dan said patiently to me, "This is a family plot. You know, a *graveyard*." He shot a look at Ernie and Terry, who looked kind of pasty. "Leastways, it *was*."

I stood there, digesting that. I'm a newcomer, having bought the 4-Korner Konvenience Store just three years ago. Lori and I came from Oklahoma. Right then I wished I was back there.

Ernie's eyes were big and round. He said to Dan, "You think maybe it's *witchcraft*? Grave robbing for . . . whatever those folks do?"

Dan pulled out his cell phone for real this time. When he got through telling his deputy what to do, he said to us, "Boys, you can stay or go. I got to wait here."

Ernie and I glanced at Terry, our only other means of transportation. "I'll wait," he said. "Either of you can take the pickup if you need to get back. I can ride with the sheriff."

Of course Ernie and I said we'd wait too—and help out if we could.

Dan poked around in an incinerator made of cement blocks, the ashes cold and wet from the rain. After fishing out a couple of buttons and a hunk that might've been leather, he said, "I best leave this to forensics. They don't like us amateurs mucking around in their muck."

Fifteen minutes later Dan's two deputies showed up, having left the dispatcher to run the office. Now there were six of us to search the timber as far as we could walk and return in an hour. Dan passed around a bunch of little yellow flags so we could mark any spot that looked disturbed or suspicious and leave a trail so we could find the place again.

An hour later we met back at Pete's house, grubby and disgusted because we hadn't found a single clue. Dan said, "I got to get back to town and decide who to call to help search. Probably the Highway Patrol."

I had an idea, but being the new boy, so to speak, I said hesitantly, "Ernie, you suppose your daddy might know some place Pete could've disappeared to? I mean, if they hunted here in the old days, he must know every ditch."

"If he *remembers*," said Ernie. "Hell, must've been seventy-five years ago."

"Worth a try," said Dan. "Let's you and me go ask him." He gave us his stern cop-eye. "Now you-all keep quiet about this, you hear? Gossip gets around we maybe got grave robbers, all hell will break loose . . . people trampling all over the place. Can't have that. Maybe have to get search teams with dogs in here."

Just by looking at our faces you could see the idea of grave robbers and witchcraft spooked us some. I said, "Somebody's bound to ask if we found Pete. What'll we say?"

Dan scratched his jaw with a stubby finger, thinking. "Say . . . he wasn't home, that I'll check back later . . . and change the subject."

So Terry went home to shingling his garage, and the rest of us went back to town.

Obeying Dan's orders, I didn't even tell Lori what we hadn't found at Pete's place. But was I nervous! Visions of spread-out entrails of butchered chickens and worse kept coming into my mind while I checked some kid's ID before selling him cigarettes or listened to a long-winded opinion of how the world was going to hell in a handbasket mostly because most everybody in these parts had to work three jobs just to keep bread on the table, or how a combination of onions, garlic, and talcum powder did wonders for so-and-so's arthritis.

Maybe I'm not cut out to run a convenience store, because later when Dan stuck his head in the door and beckoned, I dumped a customer's change in his hand, told Lori to look after things and lit out like a chicken after a bug.

"Figured you might like to come along," Dan said. "Ernie's already in the car. Seems his daddy remembers a place the boys used to go play. Thought I'd check it out before I put out a call for more searchers."

So the three of us took another ride out to Pete's place. We had to wait there for another guy the sheriff had called. He turned out to be Matt Forester's nephew, Brian Frey, a school teacher who teaches scuba diving over at Branson in summer. Brian and the sheriff dragged a bunch of gear out of Brian's car and distributed it among the four of us to carry.

This time the sheriff took off west of the house like he knew where he was going, with Ernie, Brian, and me following.

Dan led us to the opening of a spring that at first glance didn't look like anything but a six-foot wide green pond at the base of a bluff. There was, however, an opening about two-and-a-half feet high above the water surface. "According to Ernie's daddy," Dan said, "the boys used a dinghy and rowed in under the bluff. He claims it opens up and after about ten yards bends to the right, where there's a shelf big enough for the boys to play like they were hiding out from the Osages. He doesn't know how deep the water is in there, so we're going to tie Brian to a tree," he indicated a nearby scrub oak, "so he can find his way back."

Dark caves give me the creeps, and the idea of swimming into one made the hair on my neck stand up and freeze. I said to Brian, "I thought you guys always work in pairs."

"We do. Diving in caves and caverns is dangerous. Normally I'd wait for a buddy, but I've got a new group starting in the morning, so I have to get back to Branson tonight. It would be the weekend before I could make it back here."

"Don't take any chance at all," ordered Dan. "You get the least little bit nervous, you get out. We'll call Branson or Springfield and get a couple of guys in here. Anything happens to you, I won't get reelected next year."

Brian laughed. "You just hang onto the line and watch for any signal from me. If it snarls I'll cut loose and come out. No farther than I'm going, there'll be a little light from the opening."

We watched Brian strip down to his swim trunks and then start piling on his gear. All I knew about scuba diving came from *National Geographic Explorer* shows. First he zipped himself into a thin body shell, then a short rubber suit and booties. Next he strapped a knife to his inner left calf. After that he strapped an inflatable vest to the air tank, attached the breathing apparatus to the tank, checked valves, and wriggled into the life vest that had a flashlight attached by a coil. Then he tied a nylon line to the tree, clipping the hook on the other end of it to his belt. Lastly he pulled on fins, a mask, and stuck one of two mouthpieces in his mouth.

As he stepped into the pool, I shuddered, half expecting him to disappear beneath the surface, but outside the cave the water was only knee-deep. By flattening out and using his hands to propel himself over the rocky pond bed, he made his way into the cavern. Dan carefully played out the coiled nylon line a yard at a time, using his arm to measure.

He'd counted up to fourteen when he felt two jerks on the line and started drawing on it, hand over hand.

Brian emerged from under the bluff, got to his feet, spat out his mouthpiece, pulled off his mask and said, *"You got to see this!"*

Dan sent me back to his car for his camera and more flashlights while he, Brian, and Ernie inflated the rubber dinghy Brian had brought along. Brian said it would be a tight squeeze, but with him swimming along beside it, the three of us could fit in it as long as we ducked low to get under the bluff. There was plenty of headroom inside, he said, so the most we'd get wet was our feet trailing over the side.

Right then I kind of wished I'd liked running a convenience store too much to leave it.

If I live to be two hundred and can't find my way to the bathroom, I don't think I'll ever forget the next fifteen minutes. Inside the cavern the air was dank and chilly. The spring feeding the pond is a sluggish one, so we didn't have any trouble making it into the cavern. I slopped over the balloon edges of the dinghy so the three of us could keep our butts inside it while Dan paddled with the only oar. Brian, kicking in the water, helped shove us along. With every foot of progress it got darker. By the time we made it to the bend to the right, the cavern seemed to swallow us up in blackness. All I could think of was how Jonah must've felt when he went down into the belly of the whale. Then we rounded the bend.

Brian looped one elbow over the edge of our dinghy and aimed his flashlight at a little wooden dinghy bobbing upside down in the water. There was a jagged hole in the bottom of it. Then he directed the beam of light to the ledge where two little boys used to play.

Dan, Ernie, and I stared open-mouthed at the tableau mounted there.

A family grouping of skeletons, their bones strung together by wire, included two adults and one youngster seated at a kitchen table, an adult in a rocker holding another youngster, and an infant in a cradle. The seventh figure, an elderly naked male, lay on the bare springs of a bed, a bullet hole in its head, a pistol beneath its trailing, decomposing hand.

C. J. WINTERS BIOGRAPHY

C. J. Winters, Blue Springs, Missouri, was always more interested in Tomorrow than Yesterday. Then she discovered the American Past offers a wealth of backgrounds for some of her offbeat story ideas. Combined with her fascination for the extra-normal, the discovery led to time-travel romances *Moon Night*, *Sleighride*, and *Right Man, Wrong Time*. To come are more paranormal books—*A Star in the Earth* (sequel to *Moon Night*), a cozy mystery anthology *Show-Me Murder*, and the *Autumn in Cranky Otter* series, as well as C. J.'s only non-paranormal novel, *Mae's Ties*. All books are published by Hard Shell Word Factory in multi-electronic formats and paperback.

Although she lives in the Kansas City area, C. J. prefers rustic settings for her stories. Creating intense relationships and helping them unfold through intriguing, subtle, or whimsical interplay is her idea of fun. She says, "Story plotting is like weightlifting for the brain. You collect puzzle pieces and then find places to fit them." Her website is www.cjwinters.com.

Historical facts and Dusty's imagination spin this tale, which starts four hundred years ago.

DE SOTO'S LEGACY

by Dusty Richards

Twenty miles south of Fayetteville, Arkansas, interstate traffic roars over a ten-story tall bridge and soon the highway tunnel in the side of Owl Mountain swallows those clacking eighteen wheelers and speeding cars. Underneath this thoroughfare, Black Burn Creek still joins Hess Creek, a half mile west and in times of flow spills southwest into Lee's Creek and eventually the Arkansas River above Fort Smith.

Tucked beneath those sandstone bluffs west of I-540 in the Boston Mountains is a seam of low grade salt much like a gold vein. This source of life's precious mineral was crudely mined throughout the years back to ancient times. If this reddish rim rock could tell stories they would begin with the earliest aborigines who slashed and burned small plots along the creek bottoms each summer, raising a species of dwarf corn, as well as squash, melons, and beans. These Stone Age people hunted the deer, elk, and even an occasional buffalo for meat and clothing.

Thin smoke from their cooking fires swirled around the hide-covered lodges on the flat below the salt deposit. Five-foot-two, the village's leader Red Hawk stood six inches taller than his wife, Flower. He watched her working on her knees with a stone to grind some of last year's corn into meal for hoecakes. The honeycomb he found the day before would sweeten them. The thoughts of such a treat drew a rush of saliva into his mouth.

Despite the stings of the angry bees, he had eaten handfuls of their comb, until he made himself sick. Amused by his memory of the incident, he hitched up his elk skin shirt and, spear in hand, walked to the spring hole in the creek for a drink. His eyes and ears were always open for anything amiss, for there were many enemies about the land. A man and his people lived by their wits. When the corn was ripe they would move away from the salt source. By then the women would have boiled off enough of the grey white granules to trade with others as well as keep what they needed for their own use. Hawk knew of many good places to camp that were less traveled and where they would be safer.

He had seen the spiked-haired Osage warriors come this far south to take women slaves and kill the men and children. Roaming bands of other braves on the warpath came from the west and preyed upon his kinsmen who were widely spread about in small groups across the mountains. He had no name for his tribe—they were simply, "The People."

He always carried his lance and a stone hatchet in his belt. The alternative to being aware was certain demise. This darkness called death came often enough to his small band. A young mother who was bitten while weeding the corn died from the venom of a rattlesnake. The old man of the camp went to the other side only a moon before, after he complained how his chest felt like he had been struck by a stone ax. Three babies had expired since the last snow. Each time a great fire soared through their tiny bodies and they swiftly went to the spirits' place.

"I am hungry for fish," his wife said, busy preparing the skin that she would parboil the cornmeal in. "When can we go downstream and have a feast?"

"Soon," he promised her, knowing farther west at the junction of the creek, the potholes were deeper and bigger fish resided in them. By sinking green walnuts hulls in an old hide full of holes, he could bring up more fish than the camp could eat at one sitting.

A sharp scream shattered the canyon's solitude. A noise like Hawk had never heard before caused him to look around for the source. The other men in camp bounded to their feet and reached for their lances. Everyone went on alert. Women silenced and quickly gathered children to make their way to the salt mine above them. The men shared stern nods with one another and then as a precaution began to hurry everyone up the steep slope for the protection of the large rocks and rim rock over them.

Red Hawk stood at the hardest part for them to climb across, pulling the women and small ones by their arms over the jumbled talus. With a quick check over his shoulder, he saw nothing, then he followed the last ones to the entrance. In the gap he stopped and looked back.

His eyes blinked at something so bright that when the sun hit it, the skin shone like a colorless fish in clear water. This shiny figure rode atop a black dog—the largest dog he had ever seen with a great mane—and the creature snorted out his nose. Behind this stranger-than-life object came a whole herd of hairy black dogs that rooted up earthworms and roots, which they quickly gobbled down. They made snuffling sounds out of their tough snouts and were quarrelsome with each other. Several Indians armed with thick sticks herded these smaller dogs and struck them hard when they would not mind. Their actions caused more of the screams that had alerted the camp. The herders, dressed in skins, were careful the smaller dogs did not disturb the clan's food plot for which Hawk was grateful.

"Will they kill us?" Flower whispered from behind him.

Hawk shrugged. The black dog that the Fish Man rode looked ferocious—bigger than any stag elk he had ever seen, and his club feet were not split like a deer or any game he knew about that size.

The invaders stopped at the base of the debris. Then one of the red men came forward and began making sign language with his hands.

"He speaks of peace," Blue Deer said, from his place of observation on top of the huge rock beside Hawk.

"I see that," Hawk said, feeling upset and suspicious with their presence. "But we don't know these men. It could be a trick. They are well armed and have no women with them. I fear they are a war party."

"What should we do?"

"Keep your lances ready. I will go see what they want."

"Don't go too close to that big black dog. He might eat you."

Hawk nodded he had heard the man's warning. Choosing his way carefully down the steep rock slide, he blinked in shock when the rider on the dog stepped off. Then he removed his head. Hawk's breath caught in his throat for the beast without his top on looked like a turtle—except, he had a wooly-covered face and a paleness about his skin that Hawk had never seen before. He renamed him Turtle Man.

"Who sent you?" Hawk asked the translator in sign language. Standing on two large rocks above the man, Hawk waited for the answer with his spear ready in his right hand.

"De-so-toe."

The word meant nothing to Hawk. He only wished these weird intruders would move on and leave him and his band alone. Those crazy dogs they drove and that Turtle Man must have come from the spirits' world.

"Mon-sewer." Sign-Giver bowed and then spoke some other unfamiliar words to the Turtle Man. Then this one doing the translating waved for Hawk to come over to his leader.

Closer to him, Hawk discovered the biggest dog had a strong musk different than the small hairy ones that they held back with the threat of their sticks. Cautiously, Hawk stepped toward Turtle Man. A mouth opened in the hair and a strange language came forth. He ended with Sign-Giver's word again. "De-so-toe."

Whoever that is must be their great spirit, Hawk decided. He worried the entire time if that herd of hairy dogs ever got loose, they'd devour in a flash all his people's hard summer's work. The thoughts of his village going hungry in the winter made his stomach cramp. Perhaps if he could help these strange ones, then they would move quickly away.

The Turtle Man held some tiny stones in his hand, red, blue, and yellow. He motioned for Hawk to come take them. With care he picked up one and examined it. A hole went through it. Then Turtle Man indicated he wanted him to take the rest of them. Hawk did so.

Soon the other men from his clan came down and they too looked amazed at the bright stones with holes in them. Then Sign-Giver said with his hands how they would kill a hairy dog if Hawk's people would supply the green corn, beans, and squash for a big feast.

Hawk looked at his men for the answer. They agreed. He turned back and made signs that they would do that.

Then the women and children came down. They made big cooking fires to heat the stones that they would drop in the skins to boil their vegetables. It would require many for such a feast. Hawk gave Flower his small treasures, and she nodded in pleased approval as she hurried off to work with the others.

One of the hairy dogs was slaughtered and Turtle Man's crew shared the raw liver and sweet meats from butchering with Hawk's men. A couple of clan women took the intestines to wash them out, and later they stuffed them with pemmican. Soon the dog's meat was roasting over the fire.

Hawk did not like the way Turtle Man kept staring at his wife as she moved about. He could see evil in this one's eyes. Besides such actions were considered bad manners to look so openly on another's woman. Flower was very pretty, but she was his mate.

Soon Sign-Giver came over to Hawk and with his hands asked, Would-he-trade-her-for-a-hairy-dog?

Hawk shook his head.

Would-he-trade-her-for-many-small-rocks-with-holes-in-them?

Hawk said, "No." He grew angry. Flower was his woman. Two other wives had died. She was healthy. Why would he trade her for such trivial things? A sound wife was worth much more than rocks or dogs.

Some pieces of the meat were soon brown enough to eat. To hold the cooked chunks in their hands, men shifted the hot pieces back and forth from palm to palm to cool them. One brave took the first bite and, despite the pain, grinned in pleasure over the flavor. Good. Soon others were chewing on the meat, then nodding at each other in approval and talking out loud about the rich taste. So the two parties mixed and mingled, eating until they were so full they fell upon the ground to moan or vomit and then, as if pulled by an unseen hand, went back for even more.

Sign-Giver brought a cup of red blood-like material to Hawk who stood aside from the activities, overseeing things in the event of any trouble. A-special-drink-for-a-chief. It-will-make-you-a-very-strong-man.

Hawk drank the contents of the small vessel. Though it tasted bitter, he thanked the man to be polite. In a short while, his legs lost their strength, and he was forced to sit down with his back to an oak. Then his entire body ceased to function. His muscles turned to stone, no words went past his lips. He felt no pain–but was helpless to move. Still his ire rose when he watched

Sign-Giver roughly lead his Flower away. He could do nothing—not even lift a finger. This must be the land of the shadows where people went when they died, he decided.

After the feast, Turtle Man took Flower with him when he, his men, and their dogs left the camp.

With much wailing and sorrow, the villagers buried Hawk under the rim rock in the dust of the cave floor. But even deep in his grave, he could make out their voices talking. He heard their moans when they died with their bodies covered all over with small sores, a horrific plague that no doubt Turtle Man had cast upon them.

Then one day, many, many winters after the last one in his village cried out in death's throes, the powdery dirt was scrapped aside. Soon Hawk could see light and the familiar roof of the overhang. He looked into the face of a man with lots of hair on his face, dressed in a blue skin with straps on both shoulders. Turtle Man had come back. But this time, he only looked at Hawk's shriveled body parts for a quick take, then he ran away.

Soon others came and his petrified body was carefully laid in a symmetrical thing and the top closed of him. When he felt them moving him, he heard them speak a familiar word. "De-so-toe." Then sounds of a large animal's purring surrounded him, but he could not see anythng as he rocked back and forth in his new home.

Next he rested on a flat rock in a large cave with strange torches for light. Many came and poked at his remains. Some made lots of bright flashes at him that even blinded his vision for a short while. But unlike the many winters he had endured underground in the cave, he found in this new land he no longer wanted more skins to cover up with to keep warm.

Many came by to look at Hawk after they put him in an even larger lighted cavern. There were black faces, white ones, even red ones. Some stared hard at him, others acted afraid that in the blink of an eye he could jump up and strike them like a rattler. Once even a white-skinned woman with fiery red hair and the greenest eyes looked close at him.

Though he never understood the meaning of their words, he could recite what many said aloud when they came to stand over him, "A mummified Indian found under a bluff near West Fork. University of Arkansas, Old Main Building."

At every sunrise, he prayed to his gods to come and free him, so he could go and be at last with all of his kinsmen in the dark world. Even DeSoto was on that prayer list. Hawk was hopeful he would send Turtle Man on his great black dog to ride up again and take him away to be with his own people.

The mummified Indian is on exhibit at Old Main on the University of Arkansas campus, Fayetteville, Arkansas. In 1960, writer Dusty Richards and his partners, Sumner and Monty Smith, bought the seven hundred acre ranch west of Winslow that contained the salt vein bluff. The previous owner took them to the site on their first visit. Through older residents in the area, they learned that some time in the 1920s or 1930s, the University of Arkansas made an extensive archeological dig under the rock overhang, assisted by a previous landowner, Black Gill Center. During that operation, they exhumed the corpse, preserved for centuries because of the extreme dry conditions existing under the cliff.

Many references have been made about DeSoto's men exploring the Ozarks. Escaped swine from the herd that they drove with them as a food supply supposedly were the source of the original razorbacks.

DUSTY RICHARDS BIOGRAPHY

Rancher, auctioneer, and rodeo announcer, Dusty Richards and his wife, Pat, live on Beaver Lake in northwest Arkansas. Author of more than sixty western novels under his own name and pseudonyms, he teaches fiction writing at many writers' conferences and short courses across the country. He is past president of Ozark Writers League and Ozark Creative Writers at Eureka Springs, Arkansas. He has been awarded a lifetime membership to Oklahoma Writers League. His novel about rodeos, *The Natural*, won the fiction book of the year in 2003 at Oklahoma Writers Convention. You can visit his web site at www.dustyrichards.com. His latest series is *Burt Green, U.S. Marshal* from Pocket Books. Watch for titles, *Deuces Wild*, *Aces High*, and others; also two trail drive novels in the Ralph Compton series, *Trail to Abilene* and *Trail to Fort Smith*.

On a cold, wet, and windy night Mindy knocked on Anna's door. She wanted to go home to tell people it was her fault. Then she left. Who was Mindy? Where did she go? What was she talking about?

WHERE'S MINDY?

by Velda Brotherton

The rattle against the front door sounded like an animal trying to get in out of the rain. Curious, I laid down my book and padded in sock feet to peer through the glass.

A girl hunched in the glow from our porch light. Wet mist clung to strands of her brown hair and gleamed on the shoulders of her oversized sweater— one of those high school letter sweaters that was too big and made her slight body appear even smaller. A sudden gust of wind whipped her long skirt to reveal muddy, bare feet.

What was she doing out this late in such weather?

Through sleepy eyes I studied her, trying to assess the danger she might represent, and then pushed the door open.

She darted a frightened look at me. "Please, I need help."

Dark corners of the yard appeared menacing, as if something terrible hid there. I shivered. Too much television and an overactive imagination defeated my common sense. Small towns like Sycamore, Arkansas, seldom shelter gangs. The girl was just what she seemed—lost, abandoned, and terrified. I stepped aside.

"Come on in and get dry."

She gave me another of those frantic glances, then sidled inside as if she expected someone to jump out and grab her.

"It's okay, take off that wet sweater and sit down. I'll get you a towel."

She let me take her sweater, which I hung on the coat rack by the door. In the light, I saw she wore an off-the-shoulder dress with a wilted corsage, as if she'd been to a dance. A gold locket hung around her neck. A feeling of misgiving rippled through me. Like I might be doing something really dumb by taking this girl in, but I brushed it away. What danger could she possibly pose? Even so, I found myself hoping that when I returned from the linen closet she would have vanished, leaving behind only a puddle on the floor.

But she remained where I'd left her, dripping water on the shiny parquet. I held out the towel. "Can I call someone for you?"

Paying no attention, she hunched forward and shivered, allowed me to dry her long dark hair and pat her face dry. In silence, she sat when I guided her to the couch.

Since she hadn't answered my first question, I asked another. "What are you doing out at this hour? It's nearly midnight." To my surprise, my words came on angry notes. I have little patience with those who run away and refuse to face up to their problems.

"It wasn't his fault," she said so low I barely heard her.

"Whose fault? What?" Still that harsh tone in my voice. I'm afraid I still didn't trust her. There was something ethereal about her appearance and, more than that, she looked out of place.

"You have to tell them he didn't do it. I did. Tell him I love him and ask him to forgive me so I can go home." She twisted her hands together in her lap. "I need to go home."

The plea wrenched at my heart. "We'll get you home. But you're not making sense. Who didn't do what? Who should I tell?"

"My . . . uh . . . a friend. Could I call my mother? And if she's not there . . . well, then, could you take me home?"

Even as she spoke, I knew she was lying. The girl already knew her mother wouldn't be at home to come for her, and all that babbling was a coverup. She was probably taking drugs, and she was certainly unstable. Why had I let her into my house, with my children asleep in the next room?

"Where do you live?" I asked and picked up the telephone.

Her eyes followed my movement, as if I held a snake. "Cedar Cove."

I knew the town. It was nearly forty miles to the north, a secluded community off the main highway and far back in the hills. How had she gotten to Sycamore? I shook my head, handed her the cordless.

Puzzled, she studied it.

"Would you like me to do that?" I took the instrument, turned it on, glanced up. "What's the number?"

Despair flared in her chocolate brown eyes. "I'd pay you to take me home."

"I can't, honey." Switching off the phone, I waited for the next lie.

Shoulders slumped, she glanced around the room again, taking in the plastic basket filled with the kids' toys and the stack of books beside my chair, then dragging her forlorn gaze back to meet mine. What I wanted was to put her in a tub of hot water, bed her down, and kiss her good night. Show her someone cared. I certainly wasn't going to drag Amanda and Daniel out of bed to drive forty miles in the pouring rain. "How old are you?"

"Sixteen." I couldn't tell if the prompt reply was truthful or a lie. For sure, it was a challenge to my earlier inclination to baby her.

So, I took another tack. "My name's Anna Webber, what's yours?"

A slanted look telegraphed her intention to dredge up another falsehood. "Mindy. Uh, Mindy Lane."

"Well, Mindy. We have a problem here. You're underage, and I've got two babies asleep in the other room. I'm going to call the sheriff, and he'll find your mom, see you get home. That's the best way."

Her eyes grew wide, pooled with tears.

God, why are things so complicated? Why doesn't the law allow for the intentions of the good guys? I could get in deep trouble following my heart and helping this child.

Mindy leaped to her feet. "You're going to call the law on me. I have to go."

I resisted the urge to grab her, pull her to me, and hug away the irrational fears. I didn't. I dared not touch her, or later it could become abuse, violence, indecent approach, or whatever she might wish to call it in her haste to justify herself to a mother who didn't care where her child was at midnight.

So, instead, I picked up the phone again.

"Do what you want," I told her as I dialed. "I wish you'd stay. They'll help you. They truly will."

She bolted, fumbled with the door, and was gone. My shouted, "Wait," following her into the stormy night.

As I told my story to a voice on the other end of the telephone, I saw the girl's wet sweater hanging on the hook beside the door.

Exhausted, I went to check on my kids. Watching Amanda sleep, arms flung above her chubby face, I couldn't help but imagine her at sixteen. Suppose she were lost, asking for help, and there was no one?

I shook away the illogical anxieties and covered Daniel, who'd outgrown that baby look to take on features that reminded me of my sweet Randy. After smoothing his auburn hair, I went to bed, but not to sleep. All night I tossed and turned, trying to get comfortable while thinking of that small, frightened girl alone out there in the dark somewhere. Surely there must have been more I could have done for her.

The next morning a deputy came by to tell me he couldn't find Mindy or a family named Lane in Cedar Cove where she'd said she lived. And that should have been the end of it. But I couldn't forget her sorrowful features and the lost look in her dark eyes. And her plea, "I need to go home." The words were branded in my soul. I had to do something.

Besides, it was a beautiful Saturday morning, the sky a rain-washed cobalt blue and the green hills sparkling. The laundry piled in the utility room could wait. Mom was always begging to have the kids so I could get my chores done, so it took little to convince me to spend the day searching for Mindy. Where to start or what I would do if I found her, I had no idea.

After breakfast, I gathered up the kids and started out the door. At the last minute, I grabbed the damp sweater from the coat rack. Maybe somebody in Cedar Cove would recognize it.

An hour later, having enjoyed a short visit over coffee with Mom, I was on my way north. I hadn't told her about my midnight visitor or of my somewhat foolish quest. She tends to worry things to death, more so now that Randy was gone. He'd been not only my anchor but also hers, and it was difficult to say who had loved him more.

Pushing away memories of my lost love, I rolled down the window and breathed deeply of the honeysuckle-scented wind. No place in the world is prettier than the Ozarks, especially in the springtime.

That notion made me laugh. I knew no other place, for I'd been here all my life except when our senior class went to Six Flags in Dallas. However, I could imagine nothing more beautiful or peaceful than this two-lane highway winding through a thick growth of oak, hickory, and sycamore trees, following the meandering of a cheerful, rocky-bedded creek.

Taking my time, I eased through a sharp curve and saw at the side of the road a small white cross covered in bright purple plastic flowers. It occurred to me that this was the perfect place to die, and the thought so startled me in its morbidity that I slammed on the brakes and sat there for a long while before moving on. What a horrible notion. And one I hadn't entertained in several months. Randy's death seven months ago had hit me hard and recovery came grudgingly.

Shaking away the urge to curl into a ball and cry, I drove on and soon saw a green and white sign that read, "Cedar Cove 11 Miles." Anticipation suppressed the bad memories as the highway climbed and coiled into all that remained of Cedar Cove. Like many settlements in these hills, it had dwindled over the years until all that was left were a few empty buildings, an outdated but still functioning grocery store and service station, and scattered houses that looked on the verge of being abandoned.

I pulled in to the station, parked out of the way of the two pumps, and went inside. It smelled of old grease and gasoline and tires. On the walls hung radiator hoses, hubcaps, fan belts, and other parts I couldn't identify. They'd been hanging there a good long while.

"Help ya, ma'am?" A gangly, coverall-clad man came through the door from the garage, wiping his hands on a greasy rag. Bright blue eyes studied me from his sun-wrinkled face, as if he were amused.

"I hope so. I'm looking for a family that's supposed to live around here. The Lanes?"

He scratched tufts of graying hair, shook his head. "No, don't recall 'em."

"They have a daughter. Mindy?"

"You know, I don't. But you might go into the store there and ask my wife." He grinned and his eyes sparkled. "She knows everything about everybody, and then some."

When I left the station, it occurred to me that the woman might recognize the sweater, so I grabbed it out of the car before crossing the lot to the store. Three cars and an old pickup with a hound dog in the back were nosed up to the glass front. The windows were filled with hand-lettered signs announcing the prices of pork 'n' beans and cabbage and Oxydol.

On a rack beside the door were a few flats of strawberries with a sign, "Arkansas Strawberries— $1.50 a quart." I picked up two quarts and pushed through the screen. Their sweet tangy smell blended with the ancient odor inside the old building. It was as if I had stepped into another era, far removed in time and space from the Wal-Mart over in Huntsville where I shop.

A young man in overalls unpacked cans of green beans from a cardboard box and lined them on a shelf. He glanced up when the bell over the door jingled.

"Help ya, ma'am?"

I grinned. He sounded and looked like a younger version of the man in the gas station.

"Yes, I'm trying to find a family named Lane. The man in the station said his wife might know about them."

"That'd be my ma." Before I could reply, he turned toward the back of the store and bellowed, "Ma."

The boy glanced at the sweater folded over my arm, said nothing. But his eyes flickered in recognition.

Before I could question him further, a tall, thin woman, in a shapeless, colorless dress with streaked silver hair done up in a bun, approached.

"Lannie, I've asked you not to shout so. It's unseemly." To me she smiled. "Could I help you find something?"

"Somebody. Oh, I do want these berries, though."

She nodded, took them and walked toward the counter on which sat an old cash register. "Anything else?"

"No. I mean, yes." I repeated again my desire to find the Lane family or the girl, Mindy.

"Why?" she asked, ringing up my purchase, her smile replaced by twin furrows between her eyes.

"Why?" I felt a bit silly echoing her question, but I wasn't sure I understood.

"Stranger comes around asking after someone, we don't know but what they might want to cause them harm. I reckon I'd have to know why you're looking for the Lanes."

"Then you do know them?"

"Didn't say I did or didn't. That'll be three dollars and eighteen cents." She glanced straight into my face. She wasn't nearly as friendly as her husband and son. "For the berries," she added.

I dug the money from my jeans pocket, considered telling her the story of Mindy's appearance, then thought better of it. This woman wouldn't give me the time of day. I'd have to go elsewhere, and there wasn't much elsewhere in Cedar Cove.

When I returned to my car, the young man who'd been in the store was waiting for me, backed up against the hood.

"Hi," I said and set the berries on the seat through the open window.

He nodded. "Ma'am."

"Do you know where this sweater came from?" I asked.

A sheepish look crossed his narrow face. "Not that one in particular, no. It's old."

I studied the garment. "Doesn't look old to me."

"No, didn't mean that. Meant, it's from when we had a school here. I've seen 'em. Old man Christensen has one. Said he played on the 1968 football team. Cedar Cove Panthers. Said they barely had enough boys to make up a team in those days, but said they was one hell of a team." He laughed.

My heart fluttered. "But where would someone get this, then? When did your school close?"

"Nineteen and eighty-five, when they consolidated with Mountain Ridge. That's where I go. Reason I noticed the sweater is I got me one from the Mountain Ridge Cougars, only I play basketball. See here?" He pointed to the football on the left front of the purple and gold sweater I held. "This'n's a football letter sweater. The kind you give your girl, if you've got one." He grinned and his youthful face lit up. "Jocks always got a girl."

The young man looked like anything but a jock, but considering the baggy clothes he wore, it was hard to tell what shape he was in.

"And this 'old man Christensen.' Where could I find him? He might know who this sweater belongs to." The feeling that passed over me was unsettling. I had begun to feel like I really had been dragged into the past.

The boy shuffled his sneakered feet out toward the highway and pointed. "See that white house yonder?"

"That's where he lives?"

"No, that's where you turn. Go off to your right and up that rise. At the top is a mailbox. Turn at it and go . . . oh, a quarter mile or so. You'll see his place."

After thanking the boy, I followed his directions, almost reconsidering when the drive at the mailbox turned out to be two narrow ruts puddled by last night's rain with grass growing tall and thick in the middle. I eyed it with misgiving, glanced again at the sweater, and remembered the look in Mindy's eyes. I had to find out what was going on. Where the girl had come from and where she had gone. And what her cryptic message might mean to someone. Without knowing the answers, I wouldn't have a moment's peace. And I was afraid she wouldn't either.

With a great deal of care, I guided my ten-year-old Taurus along the lane, weeds scraping at its bottom. If I hit a rock and tore something up, I couldn't afford to have it fixed. Living expenses and trying to finish my college courses took up every penny I earned working at the nursery in Huntsville.

I rounded a curve and saw a small house nestled in a thick growth of trees. A new pickup sat out front. The yard was a thick tangle of wild daisies and sweet-smelling roses, but a walk had been cleared up to the porch. A large black dog ran from out back and stood at my door barking. I waited in the car, fearful of getting out until someone came.

Maybe no one was home and I'd wasted my time. I was about to drive away when a man emerged from the shadows under the roof and came down the steps. The sunlight caught his sandy hair, and I could see he couldn't be "old man Christensen." He was closer to my age than that of a man who had graduated high school in the late sixties.

"Shep, cool it. We don't bare our teeth at visitors." He leaned down and smiled. A nice smile that put dimples in his cheeks. "Are you lost?"

"I hope not. Is this . . . I mean, I'm looking for a Mr. Christensen."

"Well, I'm Dell Christensen, but from the look on your face, it must be my dad you came to see. I hate to tell you, but he passed away last night. I'm just up here getting some papers together."

"I'm sorry to bother you at such a time. I didn't know." In view of this man's loss, my errand seemed less important, yet he didn't seem devastated.

"It's all right. We weren't close. Sometimes . . ." A brief sadness dimmed his eyes, then was gone. "Could I help you with something?"

Looking at the sweater once again, I felt foolish. "I don't . . . I'm not sure."

"Well, it can't be that hard. Where'd you get that?"

"From a girl. A girl named Mindy. Did you know the Lanes? They have a daughter named Mindy?"

"I knew a Mindy, but her name wasn't Lane."

"There's a chance she was lying to me, but she came to the house last night during the storm, wearing this. Small girl with beautiful long dark hair. About sixteen or so? She ran off before I could get help for her."

He leaned down and studied my face. "Is this a joke?"

"Most certainly not. I didn't come all this way to play a joke. I have better things to do." Yeah, like the laundry, I thought.

"Well, the Mindy I know didn't come to your house last night. She's been dead for twenty years. So it must have been someone else. You sure you have the right town? Maybe she said Cedar Grove. That's over in eastern Arkansas."

I could do nothing but stare at him, dumbfounded. It was almost as if I'd known. That she was dead, I mean. Well, not exactly that. Just that she'd come from another place or time. Her being dead hadn't occurred to me. Suddenly I felt foolish considering either possibility. Time travel or the dead making house calls were both pretty dumb ideas.

"Why did you come to see Dad? Did this Mindy mention him?"

"No, the boy in the store in town sent me out here."

His fingers curled over the window frame. A man's strong fingers. Like Randy's. Laced through mine.

I swallowed hard to keep back the tears. "I guess this was a bad idea. I'm sorry I bothered you."

Turning the key in the ignition, I stared blindly through the windshield, wanting only one thing. To forget all about Mindy and leave this place and this man whose very presence was disrupting my hard won stability.

"Wait. Why don't you come inside. Dad has yearbooks from Cedar Cove High up until it closed. Maybe we can find this Mindy."

The car was in park and I left it there, shut off the engine, and climbed out when he opened the door. Granted, I didn't want to do this, but it was as if I couldn't help myself. Bad dreams haunted me as it was. It wouldn't do to add a lost girl to the list.

The sweet fragrance of wild roses filled the warm spring air, reminding me of promises kept and dreams lost.

"By the way, you haven't told me your name," he said.

Odd, I couldn't remember his, though he'd told me earlier.

"Anna, my name is Anna Webber. And I'm sorry, I've forgotten yours."

"Dell," he said, placing a hand under my elbow to steady me as we climbed the three slab steps onto the shadowy porch littered with tools.

Inside the house was dark and cool. The musty smell of mementos long kept permeated the room. Boxes and an open trunk filled most of the small living room, and here and there were piles of old magazines and newspapers. A table was littered with cards and photos.

"Sorry about the mess. I'm having to go through everything. I found a five hundred dollar bond hidden between the pages of a magazine. No telling what all is stuck away like that." He moved some books out of a chair. "Here, sit down. I saw those yearbooks in this trunk when I was looking for Dad's birth certificate. Do you want a glass of lemonade or a cup of coffee? This could take a while."

"Yes, lemonade would be good. Thank you." The chair was a bit lumpy, and I grinned at the accumulation of junk lining the walls of the room. Dad had obviously lived alone for some time. Men liked to keep their belongings around them, and without a woman to organize things, their junk soon closed in. Randy had been like that. The fond memory coaxed a bittersweet smile.

Dell returned from the kitchen with a glass of iced lemonade and set it on the table beside my chair. He carried a cup of coffee, which he sipped from before putting it down and digging around in the trunk.

The lemonade was good, not too sweet, and I drank deeply. "Show me the Mindy you knew."

"But I told you, she's dead. She couldn't have—"

"Humor me, then." God help me, I knew before he pulled out the book and turned to the page with her picture that it would be the girl who had stood in my living room, dripping on my floor only the night before. A very alive, very frightened girl.

"Oh, there, that's her." My finger trembled touching the sweet, smiling face.

"That's Mindy Richardson. You must be mistaken." But his voice had lost some of its resolve as he stared first at the picture, then at me.

"Tell me how she died." The words would barely come out, and my voice trembled so I marveled he could understand me. I have been frightened in my life before, but never as terrified as this. Though the death of a loved one is difficult to deal with, it is a state with which we can eventually come to terms. But this phenomenon was entirely out of the realm of understanding. Yet, studying her picture, I knew beyond any doubt I had talked with this girl.

"I was ten or eleven, I suppose, so I don't remember it as clearly as Dad would. But it was a tragedy for this small town." He gazed at me in the gloom of the closed-up room, dark eyes catching a sliver of light from the shaded window. "The kids had a dance at the school gym after graduation. That was before they had to have these fancy balls for prom night. In those days they graduated on the football field, then went inside the gym, decorated earlier by the juniors and sophomores, where they would dance the night away. It was fun. Like I said, I was just a kid, but I saw them, all seventeen of them, get their diplomas. Hung around shooting hoops at school till almost dark so we could watch them return dressed in their gowns and suits."

He took a sip of coffee, glanced at the open page, and went on. "Mindy was a pretty girl, popular, and I suppose I had a crush on her in my kid-like way." Cocking his head, he grinned in his engaging manner. "I didn't have a chance. Though she was only a junior, she was a cheerleader and going with Aaron Wells, football quarterback and quite the hero. I used to see them kissing out behind the school. God, poor Aaron."

When he didn't go on, I prodded him. "So, what happened?"

"The next morning Dad came in all white-faced. Mom was alive then and she was fixing breakfast at the stove. Out there in the kitchen." He glanced that direction as if he expected to see her there.

"When she asked him what happened, Dad stood there, big tears running down his cheeks, and I just stared at him. Dad never cried. I figured it must be something awful. I could tell Mom thought the same. She poured him a cup of coffee and got him to sit down before he'd even say a thing.

"He told her then. About how Aaron and Mindy had left the prom about eleven o'clock. Nobody knew why, but they were on their way to Huntsville and out on Highway 6, about a mile north of Sycamore, they ran off the road. Mindy was killed instantly. Aaron was in the hospital, but they didn't know if he'd live or not." Dell shook his head, then caught sight of my own expression.

"What is it?"

"She died on Highway 6 about a mile north of . . .? My God, that's practically in my front yard."

"Oh, now, this is getting spooky."

"I can't help that. You explain it, if you can."

"I guess I can't. A series of coincidences, I suppose."

"No. I won't buy that."

He nodded, looking even more perplexed. "Okay. So let's leave it at that for now. I hadn't thought about the accident in a long while, but it sure shook up this little community. And everyone said it was Aaron's fault. He always drove too fast. Had been warned, I don't know how many times, that he was going to kill himself or someone else. But he never cared. Wild, they said he was. So I suppose it was natural for them to blame him. Everyone loved Mindy, and her folks, well, you can imagine how they felt."

There was nothing I could say. It was as if my throat had closed and my heart stopped beating. "'It wasn't his fault, it was mine,' she'd said. And then, 'You have to tell them he didn't do it, I did.'"

Fingers clamped over my mouth, I stared at the sweet child in the picture. "Oh, I'm so sorry, so sorry," I sobbed and covered my face with both hands.

He let me cry for a while, then stood and put a hand on my shoulder, awkwardly, the way men do when they aren't sure what to do with a bawling female. "You gonna be okay?"

"She said I had to tell them it wasn't his fault," I managed.

His sigh filled the room. "Surely you don't believe . . . I mean, maybe you read about the accident somewhere and you fell asleep last night. Dreamed this whole thing."

"I might buy that except for the wet sweater hanging on my coat rack, the one out in my car. You saw it."

"And so you think Mindy came back to life and sought you out for what purpose? And why you? And why wait all these years?"

"I don't know. That's what has me so upset. Why me, and why now? I barely got my life back together after . . . after . . ." Again, I covered my mouth, this time filled with an awesome knowing.

"My . . . my husband . . . Randy." I swallowed hard. Never had I said one word about how I felt about this to anyone, not even Mom. "Seven months ago, on a foggy night in October, Randy crossed the median out on the interstate and hit a car head-on. A young woman in that car died. The family sued his estate for wrongful death. I . . . we settled and I lost everything. My kids and I, we . . . Do you know what it's like to resent someone you love with all your heart? To blame him for the hardships, even though he's dead?"

"But it was an accident, wasn't it?"

"A witness said he was driving erratically prior to the accident, and the ME could find no cause, like a stroke or heart attack or anything. Careless . . . reckless . . . that's what they said."

He patted my shoulder again. "And so you think Mindy . . .? My God, that stretches . . . I mean, even if you believed in ghosts. It seems too coincidental." He thought about that a while, then asked, "Would you like to meet Aaron?"

"He's alive?"

"If you can call it that. But it might help if he could hear what you've told me." Dell held up a hand. "Not that I believe Mindy actually came back, but, well, what could it hurt to tell him what happened? He's had a rough go of it because of that wreck. I don't think he ever forgave himself. He did love that girl so." He tried out a grin on me, but I was in no mood.

He pressed on. "It might help you to sort out your feelings too. And what could it hurt?"

"Show me his picture first. I don't know if I should do this. Maybe he'll think I'm crazy too, like you do."

He turned a few pages and pointed at a handsome, muscular young man with an impish grin. "I don't think you're crazy. Well, not exactly. I think you had a very vivid dream, but the sweater, well, I'm still trying to work that part out."

"Okay, let's go see Aaron. I mean, that is, if I'm not taking you away from your chores here."

"I'm tired of wading through old junk. It might be nice to take a drive, and I wouldn't mind seeing Aaron again. He was always nice to me, but then he was always nice to everyone. A good kid, even if he was wild."

We went outside into the warm May afternoon and walked through sunlight splashing down through the giant oaks in the yard. Shep came along, as if he expected to go.

"And what about you? What were you like?" I asked.

All the way to Aaron's we chatted amicably, as if we'd been friends for years. I learned that Dell had been married for a short time, had been in the Army for three years, and was now going to college and studying architecture while working for a contractor in Joplin.

We talked about Amanda and Daniel and my struggle with courses in landscaping and exterior design. Surprising how our occupations overlapped. Even more surprising how at ease we were with each other.

On the other side of Cedar Cove, he pointed out the old school, empty now and growing quite dilapidated. "Aaron lives just a ways down this road," he said, turning onto a gravel lane. The tidy white house sat on the side of the hill, the front porch high off the ground. We parked out back and walked along a wooden, slatted ramp to the door. It opened before Dell could knock.

My heart thumped as I caught first sight of the boy who had loved Mindy. He sat in a wheelchair. The impish grin was gone and around the eyes, lines traced a deep sorrow.

"Hi, Aaron, I'm Dell Christensen. You may not remember me, but—"

"I do, come on in. Good to see you again. I just heard about your dad. I'm sorry. Is this your wife?"

My laugh was self-conscious, Dell's, I couldn't read.

"No, sorry. This is Anna . . . I guess I don't know your last name."

"Webber," I supplied, and we both stepped inside.

Everything in the kitchen was built to accommodate the man in the chair, and it was neat as a pin. He still cared about something, for those who don't respect themselves are content to live in a disorganized mess. Those were my father's words, but I believed them.

"Would you like some coffee or iced tea?"

I was always taught to be polite and accept an offer of refreshments, and obviously Dell was too, for we both said yes to iced tea.

"You haven't been back here in a long time." Aaron took a large pitcher from the refrigerator and filled three pale blue glasses, first with ice, then tea. Sunlight slashed through the window and sparkled in the amber liquid.

"Yeah, well, you know how it is," Dell said. "I'll be selling the house as soon as I get Dad's affairs in order. Of course, there's the funeral to arrange."

"Can I do anything to help? Your dad was always friendly with me."

"I guess not. Thanks. There's not much to do really. There'll be a graveside service tomorrow out at the cemetery where we buried Mom. But we came here for something else, and I hope it's not going to upset you too much."

"Takes a lot to upset me these days," Aaron said, but his green eyes glittered at him over the rim of his glass.

Dell looked at me. "Go ahead, Anna. It's your story. Tell it."

"I . . . I don't know exactly where to begin."

"Just open your mouth and start. What's it about?" Aaron moved that penetrating gaze to me.

"This is going to sound crazy, but . . ."

Both men gazed at me, and I could've kicked Dell for getting me into this situation. What did I think I was going to solve coming here and reminding this poor man of what had happened so long ago? Surely he wanted to forget a tragedy that had killed the girl he loved and put him in that chair.

"It's about Mindy, Aaron," Dell supplied.

The man's jaws tightened and his eyes grew moist. In a ragged voice, he said, "It was last night, you know. Twenty years ago last night that she died, and I . . ." He pounded his useless legs, glanced back at me, and his tone hardened. "What are you, a reporter or something?"

"No, nothing like that. She . . . I mean, Mindy . . ." Dear God, how to say it. "Mindy came to my house last night—"

"Is this some kind of joke? You a psychic? This is rubbish." He pivoted the chair, knocked into a table, and something thumped to the floor.

Aghast, I saw the outline of a pistol, shifted my gaze to Aaron. He looked up and in that second our eyes met, and I knew what he'd been about to do. Knew because I understood his loss.

And now I also understood why Mindy had waited so long. She came back to save this man she loved. And because of my circumstances she'd chosen me as her messenger. So many things had to be right for this to have worked out. I marveled at the serendipity of it all.

Aaron still wasn't convinced, though. "Get out of here. Now," he said.

Dell bent down and picked up the gun. "I don't guess you were going hunting?" he asked, trying, I supposed, to lighten the moment.

"You have no business here, either of you. What are you trying to do to me?"

"Save your life, it looks like. Or rather, Mindy is trying to save your life."

"That's utter hogwash. I won't listen anymore." Again, he tried to get out of the room.

Dell's words stopped him. "It's not hogwash. Let me go get the sweater."

Aaron still wasn't buying it, but at least he'd stopped slamming the chair around the room like a madman.

"Please, hear me out." I was determined to convince him that what I was saying was true. He needed to know, to believe that Mindy didn't blame him for the accident. That she didn't want anyone else to either.

Dell slammed out the door on a run, leaving me behind to contend with Aaron's ranting. I wanted to touch him, to assure him that I was not some crazy lunatic.

"You've got to believe me, Aaron. I'm a normal, ordinary person trying to deal with something very extraordinary. This is not a joke or some cruel prank.

"My husband died in a car accident seven months ago, and I would never be so heartless as to do such a thing if I didn't believe I actually talked to Mindy. I live near where you had your accident . . . in Sycamore. She had a reason for coming back, Aaron, and it was for you." And me, I added silently, though I was only beginning to see that.

His hands shook so badly he clenched them together, flexing the strong muscles in his arms. "Are you asking me to believe in ghosts?"

"I don't know what I'm asking you to believe in. Maybe yourself. Maybe her lasting love for you. Maybe I need to believe in that kind of love as well. I don't know. All I know is she was frantic for me to tell you . . . and everyone else something."

Dell came back in carrying the sweater and held it out to Aaron, who'd been staring at me as if I'd lost my mind. For a moment, he didn't move or reach for the sweater, but his face blanched. Then, with trembling hands he took it and held it against his chest. The tears that had pooled in his eyes now trickled down his cheeks.

"She was wearing this that night. Tell me what she said." His voice had gone soft.

"She said, 'Tell everyone it wasn't his fault, it was mine.' She said, 'Tell him I'll always love him, and ask him to forgive me.'" I stared down at the floor and thought of Randy and how I'd blamed him for dying and leaving me to deal with the mess he'd made.

My voice would hardly choke out the rest. "'Forgive me so I can go home,' she said. Then she told me she needed to go home. I thought . . . I thought she meant . . . but now I see . . ." I couldn't finish, but joined Aaron's sobs with some of my own.

He buried his face in the sweater, shoulders heaving. I dropped to my knees beside him, felt the heat from his body go all over me as we cried together.

Minutes passed. Our crying softened. Outside a mockingbird began its joyful call, singing as if its heart might burst with happiness.

"Come on, let's go," I whispered to Dell. "I think I've done all the damage I can here." I rose, touched Aaron's arm. "I'm so sorry, I didn't mean to hurt you. But you see I had to come."

He lifted his head. "She was driving that night, but you couldn't have known that. Thank you for telling me. I don't think I understand how this happened or why she chose you to bring this message to me, but I'm grateful. Do you know what it's like to hate someone you love?"

"All too well," I said.

He didn't seem to have heard me. "That night, she was so full of fun. Teasing, laughing, flirting with everyone. We were having a great time." He wiped his eyes, then stared into the distance, reliving the past. "After the dance, we decided to drive to Huntsville just for the fun of it. Maybe get some ice cream or a coke and burger."

For a moment he paused and ran his fingers over the figure eight on the back of the sweater. "This was in the back seat, and the night was chilly. She had on that flimsy dress, so I helped her put on the sweater. Mindy always got what she wanted—I never could deny her anything—so when she started begging me to let her drive . . ." He shrugged, the tiniest of smiles curling his lips. ". . . I let her, but I'd give my life if I hadn't. The road is dangerous, narrow and full of S curves and she . . . she got to cutting up, not paying attention . . . she was so alive, so sure of herself. I guess we both were, like all kids. We felt invincible, you know? I guess I was having as good a time as her."

He covered my hand with his, and I felt a calming energy flow between us, like we shared a secret.

"I don't remember anything else till I woke up in the hospital. They said we were both thrown free of the car when it went airborne and slammed into a tree. Everyone assumed I was driving . . . she didn't have a license and they had seen me racing through those curves at breakneck speed too many times . . . and so her death was my fault. Her folks never got over it. They left soon after her funeral, but they never came to see me in the hospital. We were close, all of us, so I knew they couldn't forgive the boy who'd killed their only child, even if I had been like a son to them."

"She was driving," I said. "And that's what she wanted me to tell everyone, so they wouldn't blame you anymore."

All three of us were quiet for a long time. I don't know about them, but I was speechless, thinking about what Mindy's message meant, both to me and to Aaron.

Finally, I spoke. "Mostly, though, I think she wanted to ask your forgiveness so you wouldn't hate her anymore."

And she had a good reason for seeking me out to do the telling. So I wouldn't hate Randy anymore. I kept that to myself.

Dell reached for my hand and squeezed it, and I wondered if he knew what I was thinking. His hand on mine felt warm and reassuring. A glimmer of hope rested in my soul.

"Thank you," Aaron said, patting the sweater.

"And thank you too," I answered, then whispered it silently to Mindy, wherever she might be.

VELDA BROTHERTON BIOGRAPHY

Velda Brotherton writes historical fiction and non-fiction, short stories, and articles. Her weekly historical column, "Wandering the Ozarks" is published in the *White River Valley News*, Elkins, Arkansas. A native of Arkansas, she lives near Winslow with her husband, Don. They've been married fifty years. Her latest books are *Wandering in the Shadows of Time; An Ozarks Odyssey; Springdale: The Courage of Shiloh—a Making of America Series* from Arcadia Publishing; *Washington County—an Images of America Series* from Arcadia Publishing. In addition to three non-fiction books, she has a total of six historical romance novels published with Penguin (Topaz) under the pseudonym of Elizabeth Gregg and with Leisure under the name of Samantha Lee. Her writing has won many awards, the latest being the Crème de la Crème (best of all winners in over 30 categories) at the Oklahoma Writers Federation, Inc. conference for her unpublished novel, *Once There Were Sad Songs*. She is working on two historical novels.

Velda has two websites: www.writerspages.com/velda-brotherton and www.authorsden.com/veldabrotherton.

She also welcomes email at eldabro@valuelinx.net.

Her secret is out and Alice doesn't care. She loves Tom too much.

THE COLLEGE DORM SECRET

Carolyn Gray Thornton

Alice was visibly agitated when she saw that the large oak tree near the second story dorm window had been split by lightning during the midnight storm. The remains of the tree lay shattered on the soggy campus below.

"Oh, oh, I need to go downstairs. I have to get a better look at the tree," she told Vivian.

"You can't do that. It's still raining and it isn't time for the doors to be unlocked yet. It is only five-thirty. We can look at it better when we go to classes. Besides, why do you want to look at that tree? It will be a relief not to have it standing so close to our window."

Alice was near tears as she replied, "But I have to go down and see it. I can get out even if the doors are still locked."

Vivian countered with, "But you can't get back in again until seven. What's the big deal about the tree anyway?"

"I can't tell you. But I just have to go. And I have to go right away before it is too late."

"I think I know what your worry is. You don't think you have been sneaking Tom into your bed all these nights without me knowing what is going on. I never knew how you got him in here without anyone seeing him. Now I guess that he comes and goes by that tree. I guess he's athletic and strong enough to make that jump. How does he know when you will be here to open the window for him?"

Vivian paused for a moment then continued, "I also know that you have all sorts of treats for him in the bed. I think it is disgusting. You don't know anything about him. You don't even know where he comes from or his name. All of us just started calling him Tom when we saw him hanging around the door. He is awfully good-looking, but I don't think it is right for you to share your bed with him this way. I haven't said anything to anyone. I knew how homesick you were at first and after you met Tom you seemed to be happier."

"Oh," Alice sighed. "It is such a relief to know that you know about Tom. You're right, that is why I have to look at the tree more closely. You see, when the storm came up, I knew he'd better leave in case we had to go to a shelter. I didn't want him to get caught in my bed, and he sure couldn't go with us. So I made him leave while you were down the hall. He didn't want to go out in the storm but I insisted. Now I am afraid that maybe he didn't make it down the tree before the lightning struck. Remember that big flash of light and a boom that sounded like we had been hit? Tom had just left the window when it came."

"Why on earth did you make him leave when it was so bad?" Vivian was irritated with her roommate but shared her concern about Tom also. "You could have let him stay here until the storm was over."

"I know, I know. I was just so afraid that someone would find out that Tom had been spending most of his nights with me. It's against all rules and my parents would have been so ashamed of me. Something like that was never allowed in our home. They would think I was awful. But they couldn't know how much better I felt when Tom was with me at night. Just feeling his body by me was all I needed to be happy. I have to go see if he got away safely."

"Well, if you're going, let me go with you."

The two girls dressed quickly, putting on hooded rain gear, and went quietly down the steps to the outside door. Alice put a book in the exit door to keep it from closing on them as they slipped outside.

They ran to the splintered tree and began looking through the twisted branches.

"Oh, Tom, Tom, I hope you aren't caught in this mess somewhere," Alice cried.

As if in answer to her voice, they heard a low cry over the noise of the rain. Following that sound, they came to a portion of the trunk that lay away from the main part. There the girls found the pinned-down body of Alice's beloved Tom.

"Is he still alive?" Vivian called to Alice. "Shall I go for help?"

Alice was hysterical as she ran to Tom. "Oh, Tom, can you hear me?" He moved his head toward Alice and opened his eyes. "Vivian! He's alive. Come help me get this trunk off of his body."

The girls worked together to remove the smaller trunk and finally were able to release Tom.

"Don't lift him. He might have something broken," Vivian ordered. But before they could do more, Tom stood up shakily.

Alice gathered him in her arms. "I'm so sorry, Tom. You must be chilled to the bone being pinned under that tree all night in the rain. I'm going to take you to our room and dry you off. We'll just go through the door and not worry about this old tree anymore. I don't care what people say now. The important thing is that you are okay. I'm not going to sneak around anymore. I am so glad that you are alive."

Tom rubbed his head against Alice's shoulder and began to purr.

CAROLYN GRAY THORNTON BIOGRAPHY

Carolyn Gray Thornton, Nevada, Missouri, a retired social worker, has been a newspaper columnist and "Senior Page" editor for the *Nevada Daily Mail* since her United Methodist minister husband, Lester Thornton, retired. She has used her age in life, which she calls Middle Age Plus, as the subject for weekly columns and articles. These have been combined in two books, *A Funny Thing Happened on the Road to Senility* (Best Book award from the Missouri Writer's Guild in 2000) and *For Everything There Is A Season,* both published by Skyward Publishing, Inc. of Dallas. Also from Skyward, she has written with her sister, Ellen Gray Massey, *Family Fun and Games: A Hundred Year Tradition.* Her latest book is *Whither Thou Goest? You've Got to Be Kidding*, telling of her years as a wife of a minister, released in 2004.

In addition to her writing and work with the United Methodist Women, she teaches Elderhostels on humor and games and with her sister gives presentations entitled, "Siblings' Revelry," for clubs, retreats, and church groups. Active in civic affairs in her hometown, she also enjoys hosting her large family of four children, seven grandchildren and six great-grandchildren.

Her website is www.geocities.com/carolyngthornton.

*Can high school friends relive their football glory
days? Hank learned the answer on a float trip.*

TRUTH OR DARE

by J. Masterson

We were too young to die, but not old enough to
know that didn't matter. I had a long time to think about
this and other things I'd rather not have as I paddled
down the river with my dead friend in my canoe.

I hadn't been back to Lesterville much since I
graduated. My parents were dead and so was the person
I'd been in high school. It had been ten years, and ten
years can erase a lot of bad memories, though it didn't
take long for them all to come roaring back.

"Skank," Rick called across the yard as I arrived. I
hadn't heard that nickname since I left. Maybe it was
why I left.

"Is anybody else here yet?"

"Just Moose."

Dear God, why had I come? That's what I asked
myself as I was lying on the ground with 250 pounds of
Moose on top of me and my arms in his latest favorite
wrestling hold.

"Hi, Moose," I managed to gasp out beneath the
human vise.

"I thought you'd come with Nick," Moose said as he
released me.

"St. Louis is a big place. I haven't seen him in years.
He lives in fashionable West County. I just have my
little apartment in the city."

"I thought he'd be here by now. Remember Nick and Rick, they were like Siamese twins. Is he still with Laura? She was so hot."

"Still is," I said.

"How do you know? I thought you said you hadn't seen them in years."

"I haven't. They're here." They had pulled in across the yard, and Laura was already getting out of the car. The former head cheerleader hadn't lost a single, dark curve even after ten years and two kids. The tight white shorts brought back a host of adolescent fantasies. Moose was already making his way across the grass to give Nick his standard headlock greeting. I followed for the rescue.

I put out my hand to help Nick up and received the too-perfect, firm handshake of the former quarterback. "How's the stockbroker game?"

"The market's been hell the past few years, but I make the same commission whether they're selling or buying. How's the newspaper biz?" Nick asked, as he brushed his Ralph Lauren shorts ensemble. I didn't even hear my own lame answer as I watched Rick load the four canoes on the trailer, unaware as I was that one of the eight paddles would soon end the life of one of my friends. But that's not how the day started.

I had forgotten how beautiful the area was. The edge was taken off the summer heat by the green rolling hills. We wound through them on the long, bumpy ride in an old school bus. The canoe trailer rode behind on our way to the river landing. The Black River is little more than a creek really, but the shallow gravel bottom and overhanging trees made it seem remote and primeval. The river was faster than I remembered it. The water was clearer. Rick said it was because of rains upstream. He should know. This is what he did for a living every day–renting canoes out of the front yard we'd played in as kids. All we talked about in high school was that we couldn't wait to get out of this place. Rick got stuck.

Jimmy had chosen to stay. He'd done all right for himself. Jimmy had always been the ladies' man, a smooth talker that could talk any girl into anything. Which made it all the funnier that he'd been with the same girl since high school. I guess he'd turned his charms to other uses.

The river was cold that day. Nick and Laura set out first, naturally. Followed by Rick and his wife, Natalie. She had been a year behind in school, but she looked older than most of us, having dropped out her senior year to have Rick's first child. Jimmy and Darla had been the last to arrive. He lived a whole mile away. They weren't married but had dated for years. They took the third canoe, leaving the last one for me and Moose. Moose had already chosen the rear, leaving my end of the canoe sticking up in the air. We'd also been given the privilege of carrying the cooler with the Jell-O shots, since no one in his right mind would tip over Moose, if his temper were still half of what it used to be.

The three other canoes soon spaced themselves in a long single file ahead of us. I could see them all on the straightaways, but Laura was too far ahead for a good look when she removed her shirt in favor of the string bikini top underneath. I had to use my imagination. It wasn't hard. Laughs and shouts echoed ahead as we rounded several bends and the river picked up speed. I couldn't hear what Rick said as he turned around, motioning wildly to Jimmy and Darla behind him. Jimmy spun around in turn to warn us about the treacherous turn ahead.

I saw their canoe flip over, and before I could take another breath, it was wedged under a newly-fallen tree. Our canoe was headed straight for them with Moose's substantial girth giving us the steering response of the Titanic. We rammed the side of their canoe harder than Moose's best pile driver. I saw Darla's head pop up from behind the downed log as our canoe was deflected and hurdled downstream.

Rick and Nick had grounded their canoes and were walking back over a gravel bar to assist. As the river slowed, I turned back to check on Jimmy. Darla now stood in the water. The canoe was held securely in place by the rushing current—still no sign of Jimmy. That couldn't be good. How long could he hold his breath? I saw Rick break into a trot across the rocks.

When Jimmy's head finally popped up, we all heaved a sigh of relief. Relief turned to shock as I watched Darla raise the paddle above her head and bring it down on the water with a force that reverberated down the carved dirt banks. Jimmy's head disappeared behind the log again.

Rick had stopped running. Moose kept repeating, "What? What?"

"Just row toward the shore," I commanded.

When we finally reached Darla, she frantically explained that a water moccasin had been heading straight for Jimmy.

"I didn't see no snake," Moose blurted.

Jimmy was lying on the gravel bank, unconscious.

"I'm a nurse," Darla offered and waded over to attend her boyfriend. "No snakebite," she said.

No snake, I thought.

She bent him over and started beating on his back, as if she hadn't done enough. He spit up enough water to rival the gin he'd wasted in the same way on our senior prom. Soon he was coughing and joking and sitting back in the canoe that had nearly killed him minutes before.

"It's time for a drink," Nick called from his canoe, and Moose tossed him a rainbow of Jell-O shots, each one hitting its mark. Where else but a float trip can you have a drink at eleven in the morning without anyone looking at you funny. I reached in the cooler and grabbed a handful of yellow Jell-O.

"What the hell do you think you're doing?" Moose snapped.

I thought he was kidding till he started to move down the canoe toward me, shaking it like a California quake with each step.

"Okay. Okay." I relented, dumping the plastic cups back in the cooler before he dumped us. "Whatever you say."

"You're too much of a lightweight to handle them anyway," he said, attempting to laugh it off, though his red face betrayed his agitation. He tossed me a couple of green shots. Great, just like the lime glop they served us in high school. All I needed now was a pimple to make the memories complete.

Rick had set up a two-day float trip for us. He'd picked a slow time of the season, so we'd had the river almost to ourselves, passing only the occasional sunburned tuber. Rick and Natalie's canoe, which didn't tip the whole day, held the tents. Moose managed to tip us every half mile or so, usually during an attempt to tip one of the other canoes. I ended the day wet and tired and full of more green Jell-O than the average hospital cafeteria.

The sun dropped out of the sky while I was still trying to put the pop to a pop-up tent. Someone had built a bonfire, and Nick brought out enough beer to make all of us forget what happened the last time we drank that much beer. I don't even know who suggested we play truth or dare. I would have preferred a game of spin the bottle with Laura sitting at the low spot on the circle.

The game started off friendly. Of course, we started off sober. We'd developed our own rules back in high school, and these still held. Darla got the first question that raised the stakes.

Laura eagerly asked, "Truth or dare, why do you think Jimmy won't marry you?"

We all fell silent, especially Jimmy. I couldn't believe it when I heard Darla choose, "Truth."

Then Moose farted, and he wasn't the only one that was relieved.

Everyone had a good laugh, and I caught a glimpse of what had bound us together as friends all those years ago. We always managed to have a good time. When we lost the football semi-finals our senior year, Moose cracked us up by streaking through the winning team's locker room. We were there when Laura broke Jimmy's heart. We were there when Laura broke Nick's heart, and we were there again when she married him. Rick had painted "Send Help" on the bottom of the groom's shoes. I don't think his mother appreciated that joke.

We'd shared our dreams with each other. I would write the great American novel. Moose would play professional football. Jimmy would take over the Playboy mansion. Nick would marry Laura, well, we all wanted to marry Laura. Rick would be a pilot, and none of us would let life make us old.

Life had a way of changing one's dreams, and Darla always had a way of spoiling our fun. She did it again this night. "Tell 'em, Jimmy. Tell 'em why we're not married. I'll tell you then. It's because he's still in love with Laura."

Everyone looked shocked, except Jimmy. He looked drunk. I don't blame him. I'd drink too if Darla were my girlfriend.

Darla kept going, "Don't pretend you're surprised," she yelled at Laura. "You egged it on. You just had to buy your stereo equipment from Jimmy, like there isn't anyone who sells it in the city. Then you had to call him to 'adjust' it every time Nick was conveniently out of town."

So much for the laughs we used to have. Darla had turned things serious. We all would have taken her even more seriously if she hadn't picked that moment to stand to stress her point. She promptly stumbled backward and landed bottom side first in the water.

Moose snorted. We were all laughing again. Nobody moved to help. Half of us privately hoped she'd drown, but the water was only two feet deep. She splashed and flayed, adding a few more snorts for us.

"Where's Darla?" Jimmy asked. And we all roared again.

That could have ended the game of truth or dare, but Darla insisted she be given a chance to ask her own questions. Rick's wife first insisted on passing out another round of drinks. That was bound to help. To my surprise, when it came time for Darla to ask her question, she didn't ask it of Laura or Jimmy or even Nick. She instead turned her sights on Rick, our host.

"Who do you think is the real father of Rick Jr.?"

His wife, Natalie, dropped her beer, and the bottle shattered on the ground.

"I don't have to answer that," Rick protested.

"Then you'll have to take the dare," Darla persisted.

"What kind of dare?"

"I dare you to tell us the name of Rick's real father."

We all protested, never mind the insensitivity of her question, but we all knew the time-honored rules. You simply could not use the dare to ask the same question. This meant Darla forfeited her dare. Darla got up in a huff and walked away from the light of the campfire. Good riddance.

Next it was my turn to ask a question. I don't know if it was the liberal amounts of alcohol with which I'd besotted my brain or the return to the learned high school patterns of behavior. I chose to ask Laura a question. In front of God and her husband and the whole world, I asked her, "So why didn't you ever date me in high school?"

"Oh, Hank, that's what I always liked about you. You're so funny. I could have never dated you. I always thought of you as more of a brother." And she laughed. We all laughed. At least, she hadn't called me Skank.

The questions stayed light and funny for a while, until it was Darla's turn again. This time she picked on Moose.

"Moose, truth or dare, how did you graduate high school if you never learned to read?"

"How do you know about that? You guys swore you'd never tell."

"Laura told me," Darla explained.

"Nick, did you tell her?"

"Not me, man."

"Jimmy, did you?" Moose stood over Jimmy, fist cocked back. Jimmy didn't seem to notice. He just sat there in his own private recriminations, mumbling and crying about something. Nobody likes a sad drunk. Moose backed down.

I missed the next several questions as I took a trip to the facilities, which looked remarkably like a cottonwood tree. Had to make room for more beer. I had walked upstream beyond the reach of the flickering firelight. I heard a roar of laughter and a snort from Moose, but I couldn't make out any of the words as they bounced up the ever-flowing river toward me. When I returned to the circle, the question asking had moved to Nick.

"Darla, truth or dare, were you born mean or did you just pick it up along the way?"

"What kind of question is that?" Darla protested.

"Truth or dare?"

"You never did like me, none of you. You were always jealous 'cause I pushed Jimmy into making something of himself."

"Yeah, a bachelor," Rick added.

"That's a good one," Nick laughed.

"Just shut up, all of you." Jimmy roused from his near catatonic state and threw himself at Nick.

Nick wasn't expecting the attack and fell backward off the log he'd been sitting on. It was all curses and elbows from where I sat. Nick got out from under Jimmy with one good right cross and began to crawl away. Jimmy lunged at him again, and the two were again rolling on the ground. With Moose's help, Rick and I were able to finally separate them, dragging each to a neutral corner. I was appointed Nick's guardian, while the ladies huddled around the fire, used to letting us boys sort out our own problems. I took Nick down to the water to clean himself up. The moon and its reflection in the water provided our only light. It was enough to see that Nick would take home a nice swollen lip.

"He's crazy," Nick said, wiping the blood from his lip.

"He's just drunk."

"We're all drunk, but you don't see me jumping nobody for no reason."

"He's just jealous of you."

"That's a laugh. What's he got to be jealous of? The market's been horrible. I can't make any money. I'll be lucky if I can hold onto the house."

Amazing how alcohol can loosen a tongue. I didn't interrupt.

"It's no fantasy world living with Laura, either. Everyone thinks I lucked out, got the girl everyone wanted. Try living with her. 'I want this, buy me that.' They invented the words 'high maintenance' for her."

I refused to let his words ruin my own fantasy, but I made sympathetic noises nonetheless.

The brawl ended the game of truth or dare, but not the evening. Jimmy retired early out of embarrassment or something near alcohol poisoning. The rest of us sat around attempting to increase our own alcohol-to-blood ratio and to sort out the problems of the universe. I was especially profound.

"You know, our lives are like a truth or dare game," I began. "Some choose truth, and some choose dare." About as enlightening as a weatherman's fifty percent chance of rain so far, but the alcohol told me I was on a roll. "Choosing truth is like choosing to stay in town after high school. Choosing dare is like moving away to the city. If you choose the dare, you can either succeed at the dare or fail, living out your dream or failing. If you choose truth, you can either tell the truth or lie. Telling the truth would be coming to terms with who you are, having the town accept you for the person you see yourself as, like Jimmy and his stereo equipment business. Choosing to lie would be never overcoming your high school persona, like . . ." I didn't finish my thought but let it die there in the still night air. Why couldn't Moose fart now.

Rick stood up. "I'm going to call it a night. Last one up remember to douse the fire."

"Okay," we all mumbled.

Rick didn't go straight to his tent but took time to make sure the canoes were pulled up enough and to gather the oars and trash. Natalie followed him on his rounds, retiring to the tent just ahead of him.

My philosophizing had created a lull in the conversation. I guess they were still pondering the thoughts. Try saying "philosophizing" when you're drunk. Now, that's something to ponder.

Moose started reliving our senior year football season. Nick was all into it. I decided to call it a night, even though I'd had a firsthand view of all the action, spending most of the season sitting on the bench.

I awoke to the scream. At first I thought it was just part of a dream, but what would Pamela Anderson be screaming for? It was morning—or what passes for morning on a Lesterville farm. The sun was up, if just barely. I had a tent to myself and awoke disoriented. The screaming persisted. I crawled toward the light at the end of the tent. Natalie stood at the water's edge. She had stopped screaming but was still trembling uncontrollably. She watched as two of the others dragged a limp body to the shore. Rick started CPR, but I could tell from my distance and through the thickness of my early morning thoughts that CPR would be futile.

Laura was dead. Nick crumbled to the ground beside her body, apparently too stunned for words or tears.

Natalie made up for his inability to express his emotions in a torrent of her own tears. Rick and Moose had placed the body on a patch of sand.

"Somebody call for help," Moose shouted.

"We don't have our phone," Darla called back—then turned and gave Jimmy a whack, "I told you we should bring our phone."

"It's too late for that," Rick stated, "besides, none of us brought our phones."

"Because of Nick," Moose said before he'd thought better of it. Nick didn't appear to hear what he'd said, but we all knew it to be true. We'd all agreed not to bring cell phones in deference to Nick and his often intrusive work as a stockbroker. Not that anything could have been done at this point to save his wife.

Darla covered Laura's body. The first thoughtful thing she'd managed the whole trip. Jimmy and I managed to pull Rick away from Nick's hearing.

"What do we do now?" Jimmy asked.

"We don't have much choice," Rick answered more calmly than I felt. "We're nowhere near a road at this point. There aren't any other campgrounds or cabins near here. That's why I chose this spot in the first place. The river crosses under a bridge a few miles down, but our cars aren't much farther than that. I suggest we put the body in one of the canoes and head there."

"Won't the police get upset if we move the body from the crime scene?" I suggested.

"What crime scene? We were all drunk. Most likely, she slipped and hit her head. It doesn't take more than a couple of inches of water to drown. Besides, who would want to hurt Laura? You've been a big city reporter too long." With that he ended the discussion.

Who would want to hurt Laura? Darla, for one, I thought, but kept my mouth shut till Rick and Jimmy left and Moose joined me. "What do you think of all this?" I asked him.

"Pretty freaky. She was so pale."

"She probably lost a lot of blood when she hit her head."

"I didn't see no blood."

"It probably washed away in the water."

Rick rejoined us. "Whose canoe are we going to put the body in?" he asked. "Obviously, Nick can't be by himself, and my Natalie's pretty shook up."

"I'll ride with Nick," Moose volunteered.

"You can put Laura in my canoe," I heard myself saying.

"It's settled then," Rick concluded. "Let's get things packed up."

The tent collapsed with considerable more ease than it took to erect. It seems it's always easier to tear things down than it is to build them up. I traveled as light in leisure as I did in life. I was packed up long before the others, and so I found myself helping Rick ready the canoes.

I followed Rick's lead, him being the expert on all things floating. Not that I would have even been capable of lugging a canoe to the water myself. We dropped the first canoe and headed up for another. I almost ran into him as he stopped dead in his tracks and picked up one of the paddles.

"I think you might be right," he said.

I wasn't sure about what, because I hadn't said anything in a while.

"There's blood and hair on this paddle. Maybe it wasn't just an accident."

"And now your fingerprints are all over it." I pointed out.

"My fingerprints are all over all the paddles. I own the joint.

"That'll seem pretty convenient to the police."

"What? Do you think I killed her?"

"Keep your voice down. The others will hear you."

He lowered his voice, but not his anger.

"I can't believe you think I'd kill her," he said. "Jimmy's not the only one who was still in love with her."

I didn't know what to say. If Rick was living the life of a failed truth, I was living the life of a failed dare. We'd each had to see our dreams downsized into more practical terms. My great American novel took the form of articles about the local Parent Teacher Association bake sale. His entrepreneurial dreams were reduced to renting canoes out of his front yard. What could I say? "Let's get the rest of the canoes in the water. We have a long day ahead of us."

And so it was—Rick and Natalie took the point this time, followed by Nick and Moose, Darla and Jimmy, and me and my dead friend. We had decided it would be best to keep Laura from Nick's sight. I didn't mind. It gave me time to think. Maybe too much time.

I could hear Jimmy and Darla arguing, nothing new for them. Nick seemed subdued, but Moose, well, Moose was Moose. He tipped the canoe twice, once trying to grab a sandwich from Rick's canoe. The second time he had stood up, God only knows why, he dumped not only himself and Nick but also the entire contents of his cooler. Rick stopped to fish the floating rainbow of Jell-O shots out of the river. Moose was apologizing profusely to Nick, while Rick and Jimmy and Darla stood in the river playing fetch with the bobbing little plastic containers.

Eventually the canoe was righted, most of the Jell-O recovered, and Moose, well, Moose never was quite right to begin with. We'd lost most of the ice when Moose capsized, so we were forced to finish off the rescued shots. Everyone kept whatever they'd rescued and used them to numb the reality of what we'd found this morning.

"What's the deal with these yellow ones?" Jimmy called. "There's no alcohol in them." And Jimmy was an expert on alcohol content.

Rick tried one from his own canoe, "You're right. What gives, Moose? You sucked down a dozen of these last night. You seemed like you were drunk like the rest of us, but you couldn't possibly have been."

"None of your business," Moose hollered and reached for the yellow shots in the other canoes, dumping him and Nick in the water again.

Rick jumped in the water next to Moose and waited until the Goliath righted himself. "I think it is my business—when the rest of us were passed out or sleeping, someone killed one of our friends." Rick had lowered his voice, but not enough.

"What do you mean *killed*?" Nick asked. "I thought she drowned."

"She had help," Rick said.

"How do you know that?"

"I found the paddle they used."

Nick moaned.

"It wasn't me," Moose protested.

"Yeah," Jimmy answered, "then why pretend to be drunk?"

"None of your business," Moose yelled again.

"I think we've already covered that," Darla said in a tone patented by Darla.

Moose slapped the water in resignation. "I guess it doesn't matter anymore. You've already blabbed half my life to the whole world already." He took a deep breath. "I'm an alcoholic. That's why I didn't put any booze in my Jell-O."

"Then why did you volunteer to make the shots?" Natalie asked almost sympathetically.

"I didn't want anybody to know, and that way I could rig up some non-alcoholic ones for me. I just wanted it be like the old times. It's different for you guys. You've all got wives and great jobs, but I'm stuck in the factory every day. All I've got is the memories of our football days, when everyone was cheering for me, when we were all best friends. First I started drinking to remember, then I was drinking to forget. I just wanted it to be like it used to be. But I guess it can never be like that again."

"Get over it," Darla snapped. "There never were any old times. I knew this was a mistake. None of you ever liked me. You only accepted Natalie 'cause you thought Rick got her knocked up. And Laura used all of you by pretending you might have a shot at the brass ring. Well, I'm glad she's dead."

Nick didn't say a word, but the other half of Rick and Nick sprang to Laura's defense. "I knew you killed her, you witch. You were always jealous of her."

Jimmy's turn to defend. "You set this whole thing up. It's your fault she's dead. You probably killed her yourself, because she knew Natalie's secret."

"You take that back," Rick hollered.

"Guys, what are we doing here?" I cut in. Rick and Jimmy stopped where they were. Moose stood between them with a hand held out toward each. Okay, so Moose probably had more to do with stopping them than I did, but now I had their attention. "All this screaming at each other's getting us nowhere. Let's get back in the canoes and head for the cars. Remember when we were a team. We never cut each other down this way. We were unbeatable together." I didn't remind them that we'd lost the last game of our senior season. "Let's load up and agree to keep things quiet the rest of the trip."

Quiet was good. It gave me time to sort things out in my head. What would the police think of all this mess? Darla had been jealous of Laura. Rick had set up the whole float trip. Moose had pretended to be drunk when he really wasn't. Maybe he'd seen something that the rest missed? Probably not or he would have said something by now when all the accusations were flying. Nick could have done it. Maybe even quiet little Natalie. It could have been any of us. Would the police ever be able to unravel it?

It's a shame that Laura would be remembered only for the bad things people thought of her, for their possible motives. Maybe Moose was right. Maybe things would never again be like they had been for all of us. God forbid, maybe Darla was right. Maybe things had never been as good as we had remembered them. That was certainly true for me.

It was time for the ghosts of the past to be laid to rest. I spoke quietly enough for no one beyond my canoe to hear, "I can't believe you're gone. You were always so beautiful, not just your looks. You saw something special in each of us. Why was I just the funny friend? I wish it hadn't ended this way. I wish we could take back the things that were said. Why did you make me do this?"

J. MASTERSON BIOGRAPHY

J. Masterson is a tenth generation descendant of the founding family of Missouri's oldest town, Ste. Genevieve, where he writes murder mysteries for the Steiger Haus Bed and Breakfast. J. has written seventy mystery plots, which have been performed well over 2,000 times for tens of thousands of guests. Steiger Haus continues to host his murder mystery overnights every week.

Six of the Masterson mystery plots are available as mystery home games, enabling people to portray the suspects in the mystery at their own dinner parties, as they attempt to solve the crime. J. is currently working on a mystery novel and series of stories featuring a twelve-year-old sleuth, Mattie Brown.

During the guerrilla war he was waging in south-ern Missouri in 1864, Jim didn't know who was the traitor to his band—his brother-in-law, his best friend, or even his father-in-law who hated both sides. He never suspected the one it turned out to be.

DOUBLE CROSS MY HEART AND HOPE TO LIVE

by Larry Wood

My small guerrilla band and I were lying in ambush along the Neosho to Carthage Road at the crossing of Center Creek, waiting for the Union wagon train we expected to pass any minute. Hidden by the timber, we were mounted and ready to charge out of the woods as soon as the Yanks approached. Sitting astride his horse on one side of me was Isaac Munson, my first lieutenant and also my brother-in-law. I was married to Rebecca, Ike's only sister. On the other side of me was Billy Goforth, my childhood best friend and second lieu-tenant. We three officers and a couple of the other boys at the front had donned Federal uniforms to trick the enemy, while the rest of the band were dressed in every-day butternut.

"You reckon Charlie Peck will be among the guard?" asked Ike. Charlie and Ike, like Billy and me, had been best pals as kids, and all four of us had grown up together. Charlie, though, had enlisted in the Union Army at the start of the war, while the rest of us had joined up to fight for the South.

"Wouldn't be surprised," I allowed. "Weren't you the one told me he was stationed at Neosho now?"

Ike nodded. "I haven't seen him, but that's what I been told."

"There's a good chance he'll be along then."

"They should have been here by now," Billy complained.

Twenty minutes later, the Union wagon train still hadn't appeared. "They must have taken a different route," I speculated, "or decided to lay over somewhere."

"Or turned back for Neosho," Ike added. "Problem is this isn't the first time something like this has happened lately."

Ike was right. Several times in recent months we'd received what we thought was reliable intelligence about the movements of Federal troops and supply trains only to find they weren't at the designated location when we got there. It was starting to seem like more than coincidence.

"Well, we're not doing any good here," I decided. "Let's disband and get back together in a couple of days. I'll send word."

When I rode into the colonel's place on Shoal Creek that evening, Rebecca hurried from the house and met me in the front yard as I dismounted. She caught her breath and took my hands in hers as she greeted me with a smile. Her pretty face glowed with the flush of expectant motherhood.

"You mustn't exert yourself, Rebecca," I reminded her.

"I suppose you're right, but I can't help being glad to see you, Jim. Ike said you sent everyone home hours ago, and I was worried something might have happened to you."

"No, I been to Granby for ammo. I guess I should have sent word by Ike."

I kissed Rebecca on the cheek, and then we walked arm in arm toward the big house. Actually it was a mansion, but I still didn't like living in it. I'd left for the war right after Rebecca and I were married before we had a chance to get a place of our own. Wounded and captured at Vicksburg in the spring of '63, I was paroled the following fall after taking the oath. Since I'd been home, though, I hadn't had the opportunity or means to see about getting my own place. The first couple of months I was still convalescing, and after I got back my strength, I still had no way of buying any property of my own. That was partly why I'd taken to the bush in spite of having sworn allegiance to the Union. Bushwhacking beat lying around idle in somebody else's house. Besides, I had a kid brother who died at Corinth, and I hated the Yanks for it.

That evening Rebecca's father told me General Sterling Price's invasion of Missouri had begun. "A lot of good it's going to do," Colonel Munson added.

"I thought you'd be glad," I said.

"The thing that would have made me glad is if the Confederacy hadn't deserted the state two and a half years ago. It's a little late to be trying to take it back now."

Back in '62, the colonel was among those who'd held out for the Missouri State Guard. Ike and I had followed Price into the Confederacy and marched off to Mississippi, while Ike's pa had stayed to carry on what he called the "fight for Missouri."

The colonel resented Old Pap coming back to take up the fight after being away so long. I didn't share his bitterness, though, and I couldn't loll around while General Price was trying to regain Missouri for the South. So when Billy stopped by the next day, I proposed a surprise attack on the Federal installation at Neosho. He, Ike, and I began plotting the raid in the front room of the big house.

"Wouldn't Sarcoxie or some other Union post work just as well?" Ike asked.

"You need to start worrying about yourself," I advised, "and quit worrying so much about Charlie."

"I'd just hate to have to shoot him," Ike explained.

"Charlie made his choice a long time ago," I said sternly.

"Yeah," Billy offered, "wouldn't bother me and Jim to shoot him, would it, Jim?"

I turned to face Billy. "And just what do you mean by that?"

"Nothing." He shrugged as a flush crept into his face. He glanced around to make sure no one else was within earshot. "I guess I was just thinking of Rebecca."

"You leave Rebecca out of this."

I knew what Billy meant. I'd married Ike's sister at the beginning of the war, but Charlie had courted her before I had. Some people said she chose me over Charlie only because her pa was a colonel in the Missouri State Guard and she couldn't bring herself to betray her family, but I didn't believe it. I suppose Billy thought I was worried Charlie might try to take Rebecca away from me and that, if I could kill him during time of war, it would be a convenient way to eliminate the competition. But the only thing I had against Charlie was he was a Yankee.

"Yeah, Billy," Ike added, "maybe you're the one who's jealous. Maybe you'd like to see Charlie and Jim tangle and end up killing each other. Then they'd both be out of the way."

"That ain't true," Billy exploded as he jumped to his feet. "I reckon maybe you're the one needs killing."

Ike stood to face Billy, but I quickly intervened. "Hey, you two, settle down. We don't need to be fighting each other."

"Well, what he said is a dang lie," Billy insisted. "I ain't jealous of you, Jim. I always liked Rebecca but just as a friend."

"Only because she wouldn't have anything to do with you any other way," Ike accused.

"All right, that's enough!" I said. "Let's get back to planning this raid."

Afterwards, though, it was hard for me to keep my mind on military matters. I kept thinking about the accusation Ike had leveled against Billy. I wanted to believe Billy's denial, but his overreaction made me think Ike's words might have hit too close to the mark. Maybe Ike knew something I didn't.

Before we could get back to planning the attack on Neosho, though, Rebecca walked into the room, and all three of us greeted her with mute stares. She couldn't have picked a more awkward time to make an appearance. "What's wrong?" she asked. "Am I interrupting something?"

"We're just talking strategy, Becca," I said. "Is there something you need?"

"No, I just thought y'all might like something cool to drink."

"None for me, Sis," Ike said.

"Not now," I said, "but thanks anyway."

Billy shook his head without saying a word.

Rebecca's smile dissolved into an aggrieved look. "In that case, I'll leave you men with your military matters." She turned and swept out of the room.

The next morning the band mustered on a creek that ran through the colonel's farm, and then we rode south toward Neosho. It was almost noon when we reached the outskirts of town, where I called a halt to let the stragglers catch up.

All along the road leading into the heart of town I couldn't see any Union pickets. I figured the Yankees were getting complacent. Except for an occasional foray by my small band, there had been very little rebel activity in the area during the past year, and Price's army, far to the northeast, posed no immediate threat.

Well, the Feds are in for a surprise this time, I thought. Then I turned to give final instructions. "Half of you go with Ike and sneak around to the west side of the square. The rest of you stay with me, and we'll come in from the north. At the signal, both squads will charge onto the square. We should catch a bunch of the Yankees lazing on the courthouse grounds."

Ike's squad circled around toward the west, and I detailed a private to take up a position halfway between the two squads to act as a signalman. As soon as Ike's men were in position, I gave the word. The private waved to relay the order. Both squads dashed onto the square at the same time, shouting rebel yells and firing into the air. But there wasn't a person to be seen, neither soldier nor civilian.

Suddenly a regular fusillade erupted from the second floor of the courthouse. No one was hit, but the boys began to panic. I didn't blame them, because we couldn't even see who was shooting at us. We only knew it was coming from the courthouse. It would be suicide to assault an army fortified inside a brick building when all we had were handguns.

"Retreat!" I shouted. The band galloped pell-mell from the square in every direction amid a hail of bullets.

By the time we regrouped north of town, I'd had time to think about what had happened. "Somebody must have tipped 'em off," I decided aloud. "They were laying for us."

"Yeah," Ike agreed, "we were lucky nobody was hit."

"The Yanks never were very straight shooters," Billy said. "Who you think tipped 'em off, Jim?"

I shook my head to suggest I had no idea. Then I reined my horse toward home and shouted, "Giddup."

The truth was, though, I had plenty of ideas about who might have betrayed us. Mulling the possibilities over in my mind as we trotted north at a leisurely gait, I knew the best candidates were riding right along beside me. It could have been Ike because of the way he was so concerned about not wanting to shoot Charlie. Maybe that explained why none of us were hurt in the attack. Maybe Charlie had agreed not to shoot any of us in exchange for knowing we were coming.

Billy was another possibility. I didn't want to believe it, but, after the way he'd acted when Ike had accused him of jealousy, I couldn't rule him out, either. Remembering Colonel Munson's bitterness toward General Price and the regular Southern Army, I even entertained the idea that Rebecca's father might be the one who was betraying us, although I couldn't figure out why, since he still hated the Union at least as much as he hated the Confederacy. The fact was I was full of suspicions, but that's all they were. I didn't want to air my doubts in front of the whole band without more evidence to go on.

After we got back from Neosho, I told the boys to lay low for awhile and I'd be back in touch with them. In early November, though, I learned that, after a last stand at nearby Newtonia, Price had been driven from the state. His grand invasion and effort to regain Missouri for the South had failed. The whole war was dying down, and with cold weather coming on, I was less inclined to go chasing across the countryside sabotaging Union targets in what increasingly seemed like a futile and meaningless effort.

Then two days before Christmas, Rebecca gave birth to our first child, a baby girl we named Sarah after Rebecca's departed mother. Being a father seemed to change me more than being married ever had, and I spent the whole winter staying close to home. Finding the disloyal member of my guerrilla band seemed gradually less important, and the whole idea of waging war lost its appeal.

Early the next spring, Billy stopped by one day with the news that Quantrill's old guerrilla band was in Indian Territory on their way back to north Missouri after spending the winter in Texas. Quantrill himself wasn't with them, and some of the other leaders, like Bloody Bill Anderson, were dead, but the band still numbered over a hundred men. Billy had met an advance scout who told him the band would be crossing through our area the next day. "They're planning an attack on Carthage," Billy said, "and the scout asked if we wanted to help 'em out. Can you imagine that, Jim? Riding with Quantrill's men?"

"What'd you tell him?"

"I told him I was game but I'd have to check with you."

I nodded. "See about rounding up the rest of the boys."

When I told Ike about the plan, he agreed to ride along with Quantrill's veteran bushwhackers, but Rebecca started sobbing and trying to talk me out of the escapade when I broke the news to her that evening. "Think of Sarah," she pleaded. "What if you get yourself killed? Do you want her to grow up without a daddy? It's not worth it, Jim. The war's almost over. Besides, Quantrill's men are little more than a gang of outlaws."

I shared Rebecca's concerns, but I didn't see how I could back out now. I'd ridden with Billy and the rest of the boys too long. I couldn't let them think I was a traitor or a coward. "I'm sorry, Becca." I stepped over to where she stood beside Sarah's crib and started to take her in my arms, but she recoiled. "I'm sorry," I repeated as she ran from the room in tears. Taking a cue from her mother, Sarah started crying too. I picked the baby up and tried to comfort her, but she kept bawling for her mother.

At midmorning the next day, I was out in the barn getting ready to start for the rendezvous spot to meet Billy and the rest of the boys. I had my horse saddled and was waiting on Ike, but I hadn't seen him all morning. I was beginning to wonder if he'd backed out on me. Come to think of it, he hadn't been very enthusiastic about this mission even when I'd first mentioned it to him the day before.

I'd just about decided to ride to the rendezvous by myself when I heard the sound of hoof beats approaching. I stepped outside the barn and saw a whole squad of Federals riding toward me. There were too many of them to fight. My next impulse was to run, but that course seemed futile too because I'd left my horse in the barn. I couldn't outrun the Feds on foot. The only thing left to do was to try to pretend I was an innocent civilian.

My last hope died, though, as the Yankees drew near enough for me to see their faces.

I recognized Ike riding at the head of the squad dressed in a Federal uniform. Next to him was Charlie Peck, his good friend and first lieutenant in the Union Army. It all seemed clear now. My brother-in-law had betrayed me. He'd been the one who had been feeding secrets to the Feds all along. Apparently his friendship with Charlie was more important to him than the Southern cause.

I raised my hands in surrender as several members of the squad trained their weapons on me. "You're under arrest," said Charlie Peck, "on charges of disloyalty."

Maybe now wasn't the best time, but I let my anger get the best of me and flew into a rage. "From where I stand, I ain't the disloyal one," I shouted. "That double-crossing scoundrel sitting next to you is the treacherous one." I looked at Ike with a scowl and spat toward his horse's feet.

"Jim, you blamed fool!" Ike yelled. "Can't you see I'm their prisoner?"

For the first time I noticed that Ike didn't have a weapon. He'd been disarmed. "Well . . ." I stammered in confusion.

"I was trying to come to warn you," Ike explained, "but they caught me about a mile down the road."

I studied Ike with a curious stare. "If it wasn't you," I asked, "then who?"

Ike shot a glance toward the big house. "I think you'd better ask Rebecca. I hate to have to say it, because she's my sister as well as your wife."

"What are you talking about?" I demanded.

"I think she's the one been giving away our secrets, Jim. Charlie and I got to talking after he arrested me, and he asked about you and your family. Mentioned Sarah by name. How did he even know you and Becca had a baby, much less her name? He wouldn't tell me when I asked him."

As I looked up at Charlie Peck, I could hardly keep from charging wildly. "Is what Ike says true?" I demanded.

"Don't matter how I knew," Charlie said. "The thing is you're under arrest."

Charlie's refusal to answer was all the answer I needed. My own wife had betrayed me. I guess the people who had said she preferred Charlie over me were right after all.

The Feds followed me into the barn and watched me mount up. When I rode at the head of the squad past the big house as their prisoner, Rebecca came running outside with a look of fright. She rushed up to my horse and tried to grab hold of my leg, but I let the horse keep walking.

"I did it for you, Jim," she cried as she clung vainly to my pant leg. "I couldn't stand to see you get hurt."

"How could you?" I snarled.

Charlie Peck rode up beside me as Rebecca trudged back toward the house. "Ike was right, Jim. You are a dang fool, if you think Rebecca was untrue to you. The only reason she came to me is the reason she said. She was terrified something might happen to you. She always made me promise not to hurt you before she told me anything—like the time on the Neosho square when we shot above your heads on purpose. She must really love you to take the chances she did."

"You mean you and she . . ." I paused, unable to finish the thought.

He shook his head, anticipating my question. "Nope, never was. You're the only one she ever cared for."

I turned back toward the house and saw Rebecca still standing outside watching us. "Can you give me a minute?" I asked.

"Yeah, you can have a minute," Charlie agreed.

I rode back and dismounted beside Rebecca. "I reckon I was a little too hasty in my judgment. I don't know quite what else to say right now, but I'll try to make it up to you when I get back home."

"I'm just glad you'll be coming home." She sobbed. "That's the only reason I did what I did, Jim. I just wanted to make sure you came home."

"I know, Becca." I took her in my arms and gave her a long hug.

"I love you," she whispered.

"I love you too." I broke the embrace and turned to mount up. "I'll be seeing you soon. Give Sarah my love."

"I will and her love goes with you."

On the ride to Neosho, I mulled over in my mind all that had happened since the war began. Becca and I had gotten married in 1861, but it seemed our life together had been put on hold. Now that the fighting was finally almost over, maybe we could make a fresh start.

In my reverie, I kept gazing at the dogwood trees, flowering beneath a canopy of budding oaks, as I rode along. The world seemed suddenly alive with new life. I'd ridden this road for the last four years, but maybe I'd never crossed here in spring. Or maybe I just hadn't noticed.

LARRY WOOD BIOGRAPHY

Larry Wood, a retired public school teacher from Joplin, Missouri, currently teaches a course for Long Ridge Writers Group entitled "Breaking Into Print." As a free-lance writer, he specializes in historical topics with emphasis on the Ozark region. He has published about two hundred stories and articles in a variety of regional and national publications, winning numerous writing awards. He is a member of the Western Writers of America, the Missouri Writers Guild, and the Ozarks Writers League. His latest book is *The Civil War Story of Bloody Bill Anderson*, published by Eakin Press.

Young love, old love, and a love of gardening are intertwined with an unusual climax.

WHERE THE YELLOW FLOWERS GROW

by Frank Watson

The old man stood silently in the tomato patch with its brilliant red orbs of summer next to the square patch of yellow flowers that were showing the first signs of withering from the August heat. The tiny wheels of the green oxygen tank had started to bury themselves in the rich mulch–Uncle Ray's legacy of forty years of careful gardening in the same patch of Ozark soil. The tiny plastic lifeline led from the tank to the little Y that fit neatly into the nostrils. A sound like miniature air brakes joined the sounds of crickets and birds in and around the garden each time Ray took a breath.

He took a step, but the little piece of equipment keeping him alive didn't want to move from the rut in which it had gotten stuck. Uncle Ray pulled. The plastic tubing stretched, looked as if it were going to break, so fourteen-year-old Jeremy jumped into action from where he had been sitting on the grassy spot at the edge of the garden.

"Here, Uncle Ray, let me help you with that."

A look of vacant confusion spread across Ray's florid face. He had been on oxygen for almost a year, but he still was not used to his loss of mobility. It had been a tough year since he had gotten out of the hospital. He could no longer go coon hunting with his friends, drink beer and smoke down at the Paper Doll

Lounge on Saturdays, or even plow his own garden.
Jake Tinsley, who farmed a few acres down the road,
had plowed up the ground for him in the spring, and
young Alice Tinsley, who was just a year or two older
than Jeremy, had helped him plant. (In fact, she had
done all of the planting and weeding until Jeremy had
started his annual visit with Nora and Ray, who were
actually his great-aunt and uncle. But family is family.)
When the produce started getting ripe, Nora and
Jeremy—and sometimes Alice—had done almost all the
picking. And Ray didn't like it one bit.

So he was now outside, trying to reclaim his garden,
during one of the hottest August days of the year, when
the air wrapped itself around him like a blanket on a sick
bed, and he had to be rescued from such an insignificant
little walk that had effectively trapped him among the
eggplants, zucchini, and tomatoes.

No sooner had Jeremy spoken than he was by Ray's
side, reaching down to gently lift the wheels from the
dirt.

"Thank you, Jeremy," Ray growled. "But I would
have been fine."

The boy had gotten used to that tone of voice. Ray
had never been an easy person to get along with, though
he had always been nice to his grandnephew—nicer
than his feuding parents ever were. This summer,
however, Ray had been worse than usual, fussing at him
and especially at Nora. Jeremy figured that it had
something to do with the hospital stay and the oxygen.
Or he might just have been doing what old people do.
But Jeremy liked the old guy anyway and tried to help,
especially now that his uncle could barely walk from
one room to another without gasping for breath.

"I know," Jeremy answered. "But I was out here
waiting for Alice. It's no trouble."

Ray laughed and coughed, followed by louder air-
break sounds. He had forgotten his hat, and the un-
combed, wispy gray hairs circling his almost red scalp

waved wildly as he tried to regain control of his sickened body. When the coughing quieted down, Ray said, wheezing, "Alice. She's a nice one. Helped me with the garden this year. About your age too, I think."

He motioned for Jeremy to put down the oxygen canister, but Jeremy did not let go. He took a step toward the house, through the tall tomato plants, and Ray decided to follow rather than argue.

"Not really," Jeremy answered. "She's sixteen. Almost seventeen."

To Jeremy, Alice was an older woman, mysterious and as far from him as the pictures in the adult magazines from the used bookstore that he sneaked into his home in the city. This was in spite of the fact that they had known each other for years, since the first summer Jeremy had stayed with Ray and Nora, and had played the usual games of cowboys and Indians and pick-up softball in the big side yard. But the summer before she had changed into the woman of his dreams: long blonde hair framing a narrow face; slim, long legs stretching beneath her short cut-off jeans; the tops of tanned breasts and stomach providing inviting glimpses from above and below her halter top. To Jeremy those years between him and Alice could have been an eternity. Heck, back home, the girls in his own class— taller and more mature than he—wouldn't give him a second look, preferring to date the juniors, seniors, and, in at least one case, a college freshman. Alice might as well have been one of those *Playboy* centerfolds, for all the good it did him.

He hadn't quite figured out why she was still nice to him. Maybe helping him pick the beans for Ray had more to do with helping an old man than having a chance to talk to a boy? Or maybe she was just being nice because they had known each other so long? Was it possible that she actually liked him, at least a little? After all, she had touched his arm a time or two in the garden, and sometimes as they walked or sat and talked, she would move close enough that he could feel her warmth and smell the summer aroma of her hair.

Ray started to laugh again, then caught himself and chuckled.

Before the hospital stay, Ray had laughed often and loudly. This summer, he had barely smiled. Jeremy was glad to see Ray with a little life in him again, though he didn't understand the humor of the situation.

"What's so funny?" Jeremy asked.

"So you think Alice is too old for you?"

"We're not even in the same grade."

Ray reached into his shirt pocket for a cigarette in a move that had become familiar to Jeremy over the years. Finding the pocket empty, Ray scowled and roughly adjusted the plastic tubing leading from the oxygen canister.

"She likes you, son."

"Maybe a little. After all, we've known each other *forever*. But this is different." The talk made Jeremy a little uncomfortable. In the past, Ray had talked with him mainly about fishing, coon hunting, baseball, gardening. This summer he had started to talk with him more like an adult—about girls, jobs, and what to do with his life. It was unsettling. Nobody else had talked with him that way. Not his mother, who mainly just yelled at him. And certainly not his dad, who seldom talked about much at all.

Ray chuckled. "When you get to my age, you'll learn what's important in life. You'll learn."

Jeremy didn't want to wait *that* long. He was already fourteen—and felt that life was passing him by.

"What do you think, Uncle Ray? I do really like her, you know." He made the admission somewhat sheepishly. "But I don't know what to do about it. You think maybe I should save up my money and send flowers?"

"Why send flowers if you can grow them?" Ray asked. "I planted those black-eyed Susans for Nora a long time ago. I've never sent flowers to her. And look at us!"

Jeremy was confused. Maybe Ray didn't understand his question.

"So you think I should plant a patch of flowers for Alice?"

Uncle Ray tried to breathe normally. He said, "Life is like a garden, son. Everything grows at its own pace. And you have to take care of it. You just gotta be patient."

Jeremy wasn't sure how to respond to this bit of wisdom. In fact, it left him more confused than before. Ray was smiling, looking at the boy as if he were waiting for a response, but Jeremy was spared this by the sight of his aunt rushing from the enclosed porch, leading to the kitchen. Before either man or boy could say a word, Nora had grabbed the oxygen tank from Jeremy's hand.

"Ray! Just *what* do you think you're doing? Out here in the hot sun! You could get yourself killed!"

"Don't get yourself so worked up," Ray said. "I'm sick and tired of being cooped up in the house all the time. I feel like I'm going to croak if I can't get out of the house sometimes. The garden needs my attention."

"You're too sick to be out here. You know what the doctor said."

"To hell with the doctor." Ray hobbled behind his wife, Jeremy trailing along. "Hell, look at some of these plants. Even your yellow flowers are starting to wilt! Don't you remember anything about gardening that I've tried to teach you!"

Nora walked deliberately, her blue-veined legs pumping furiously beneath her dress, narrowly missing some of the neat plants in the rows. She led Ray by the tank toward the house. He was still grumbling about the sorry state of the garden as they disappeared into the enclosed porch. Jeremy could just see a glimpse of the backs of their heads through the porch window as they went into the kitchen.

Jeremy, apparently forgotten for the moment, paused in the sunshine. Yes, it was hot. But the sun beating down on him felt almost good, wrapping him in a throbbing heat. He closed his eyes and directed his face toward the blazing yellow in the sky.

"Don't you know you could go blind that way?"

Jeremy spun around, feeling as if he had been caught in the act of something not quite decent. He must have looked really stupid standing in the middle of the garden with his face to the sun.

Alice was standing on the patch of green at the end of the garden near the black-eyed Susans.

"Hi, Alice. I was waiting for you when Uncle Ray needed a little help."

"Maybe you need a little help. Why don't you come over here and join me? Or did you decide you didn't want to walk, after all?"

"No. I mean, yes." He hurried across the dirt, tried to step over an eggplant, almost tripped. Alice smiled, turned, and started down the barely-paved road. The asphalt and blackened gravel was hot, but Alice, in her bare feet, didn't seem to mind. Today she was wearing a pair of denim shorts that resembled overalls and a tie-dyed tube top. A piece of hay from when she had helped her dad with the cows earlier in the day was stuck in her hair. She seemed oblivious to the sun and presented a ghost-like image through the heat—shimmering from the road as Jeremy raced to catch up.

"I like summers," she said, finally. "I know it's hard on old people, like Ray and Nora. But I like it hot. Don't you?"

Her face was suntanned, as were her legs and shoulders.

"Me too," Jeremy said.

They walked awhile in silence, as they had always done since they were children. Sometimes they would run around and scream, climbing trees and jumping fences, and sometimes they would just sit around or walk, saying almost nothing, but still enjoying the time. Since he had gotten older, the silences had perplexed Jeremy, but sometimes in the summer, silence just seemed to be called for. Now that the summer was drawing to a close, Jeremy realized that he was going to miss these moments. So what if he never dated Alice? They had worked together in Ray's garden, they had enjoyed walks and talks, had even visited one of the small-town fairs that always indicated the end of summer and the start of fall. They had some good times.

Today, they walked a good two miles, through the sometimes shade and sometimes sunny patches of the tree-lined road, arriving at Miller's Pond. They skipped some rocks and hunted frogs in the mud, before turning back around as the sun started to slip toward the horizon.

When they again neared Ray's place, Jeremy wanted to ask about what would make Alice happy. What could he do to help her remember him and the summer, when he returned to the city and she started school? They both knew this would be his last full day of the summer, though neither commented on it. Instead, he blurted out, "I'm worried about Uncle Ray. He doesn't look too good."

"Yeah. That's why I've been helping him and Nora with the garden. I guessed that's why you've been too." They paused at the end of the yard. Alice walked over, pulled a ripe tomato from the vine, and sat on the grass near the yellow flowers. Jeremy joined her as she took a taste, daintily wiping her mouth with the back of her hand. "Here. Have a bite."

Jeremy took the fruit, took a bite. Juice dribbled down his chin as the sharp aroma filled the air. The two ate without words, when Jeremy decided to try again.

"I have a question for you."

"Shoot."

"What would you think if somebody sent you flowers?"

Alice laughed, shaking her blonde hair out behind her as she leaned backwards on the grass. "Why do you ask that?"

Jeremy shrugged. "I don't know. Ray and I were talking. He said that women don't care for that. He said he never sent Nora flowers. And she's happy."

Alice crossed her palms behind her head.

"I don't know. You think Nora's happy?"

"Why wouldn't she be?"

"Maybe Nora was right. Are you men all alike?" Alice spoke without rancor, as if she were puzzling over the words. "We were picking beans the other day, and she was grumbling something fierce. Talked about how this was the first summer that Ray hadn't spent in the garden instead of being inside with her, and now he was too sick to do anything but moan. She was almost talking to herself, saying if she had to do it over again, she'd be better off just keeping to herself. Then she said to me, 'Alice, you may think now that boys are important. But watch yourself. They're all alike. Don't let no boy take advantage of you. Once you're married, it's too late.' As if she thought I was interested in getting married! Old people say some of the strangest things."

Jeremy leaned forward, watching her. He couldn't remember Nora ever talking about such things to him. Maybe it was a girl thing? When Jeremy had once asked Ray about Nora's quiet nature, he had replied, "She's a good woman. Knows her place. Keeps her opinions to herself." Jeremy didn't know much about women, but he figured that was something he had best keep to himself. Alice might not understand—and think poorly of Ray. Instead, he said, "Maybe she was just tired. I guess him being in the hospital and all would be hard on her too."

"Maybe."

"He did plant the flowers for her."

Jeremy suddenly had an idea.

"He is a darned good gardener, isn't he?"

Jeremy stood. Alice lay back with eyes closed, the dappled shadows from the trees growing longer on her. Jeremy took the few paces to the flower bed, looked closely until he found what he was looking for, reached down and plucked what he thought was the perfect blossom, not yet fully opened and not yet withered.

Sheepishly, he walked quietly, sat down beside Alice, and said softly, "For you." She opened her eyes. He handed her the flower.

Her eyes grew large, and to Jeremy's surprise, she didn't kid him.

She sat up, stretched, her head upturned, touched his face with her free hand, and kissed him.

Jeremy, shocked, was suddenly lost in the moist lips against his, the warm breasts against his chest, and the warm, dry touch of a hand on his face. He wanted to return the kiss, but his head was spinning and he wasn't sure how to do it properly, when the magic was broken by a cough.

Nora was in the garden with a bucket half-filled with tomatoes. She pretended she hadn't seen, but she obviously wasn't happy at what she had seen. She kept her eyes straight ahead, grabbed the tomatoes with rough force and almost threw them into the bucket. Then, with the container only three-quarters full, she went back inside, slamming the porch door behind her. Jeremy could see her disappear into the house through the porch window.

Alice and Jeremy looked at each other, not knowing what to say.

"I'd better be going," Alice finally muttered, holding on to the flower. "You're a nice guy. I'll miss you."

"I'll remember this summer forever," Jeremy said. He watched Alice walk down the road, her long hair swinging behind her, until she was only a shadow and was then out of sight.

Jeremy was afraid that Ray and Nora would be angry with him and Alice, but that night they didn't say a word all during supper and before going to bed. The tension in the air was hard to take. Jeremy wished that they would just give him a talking to and be done with it.

But he figured the kiss was worth whatever was to come.

The next morning, Jeremy woke almost as the sun came up, though it was the loud voices from the kitchen that disturbed him rather than the sun streaming through the checkered curtains on the window. Jeremy got out of bed and quickly pulled on his jeans.

"What are you *doing*?" Nora asked.

"Going to work in the garden," Ray answered, just as loudly. "You know good and well that Jeremy is going home this afternoon. And with Alice starting school, that leaves only you. And you haven't been worth a damn all summer. Just look at the garden! Flowers are wilting. Tomatoes are already almost gone. I *have* to work it if it's going to do any good."

"You can't. You're too weak. You can't handle the sun."

"My garden has been the one bright spot in my life," Ray protested. "And the way you're blundering around out there is no good. My God, you even bruised the tomatoes last night! And some of them were even green! I know I don't have long to live. At least let me die happy."

"Listen to reason, Ray, I can't let you out there. I can't let you kill yourself."

"I'll die if I don't have the garden. At least this way I can die happy."

"You never did know what's best for you."

Jeremy walked into the room. Ray and Nora both glanced at him. Nora continued setting the table. Ray then said in a calmer tone of voice, "Maybe you're right." He was again wheezing through the oxygen tube in his nose. Jeremy thought he looked even grayer and weaker than he had the day before.

During breakfast—bacon, eggs, grits—Nora and Ray seemed more like themselves again. They chatted about the music on the radio, about going into town for groceries, about the late arrival of the newspaper that morning. Jeremy was relieved that they had gotten over their apparent anger at him and Alice. He went back to his room to finish packing. His parents were supposed to pick him up that afternoon.

It was after breakfast, while Nora was cleaning up the dishes, that she looked through the gingham-curtained window over the sink and saw her husband again in the garden with his oxygen canister. He was barely moving, and with blinking eyes, looked blankly around him.

"Jeremy!" The woman's voice was almost hysterical. "Come here, quick!"

At the sound of her voice, Jeremy rushed into the room and followed her from the kitchen onto the porch and into the yard. He wasn't sure who was more scared. His aunt grabbed at his uncle with her white arms and dishpan wet hands as if to keep him from falling. His uncle stood, dazed and confused, trying to catch his breath.

"Leave me alone!" His voice came in puffs. "I'm happy here! It's all I have left of my life! Just let me be. I'll be fine, if you both would stop bothering me."

Even so, he did not resist as the woman and boy led him back inside.

"Don't you worry," Nora said. "I'll take care of the garden for you."

As they neared the porch, painfully slowly, Jeremy noticed that Ray's eyes were becoming a little clearer again. His voice was slightly less wheezy. "Bless you." He looked over the generally healthy, growing plants with pride. "Guess maybe I'm in worse shape than I thought. I would appreciate it very much if you would take care of the garden."

"Don't you worry," Nora said firmly when they got to the relative cool of the enclosed porch. "Jeremy, you stay here with Ray. Make sure he stays put."

Jeremy remained standing while Ray sat heavily in the vinyl lawn chair on the porch. On the table next to the chair were some green tomatoes that Nora had left out to ripen. After a few minutes, the older man was breathing more easily again, though Jeremy wondered if he was yet in his right mind.

"Nora saw you and Alice last night," Ray said. Jeremy looked down at his feet. "But that's okay. Somehow I always see you as a boy, but I guess you're growing up. So let me give you some advice. The first kisses are always sweet. Nora and I had our share, back in the beginning. But it's been awhile. I think maybe Nora was more jealous of you and Alice than mad."

Jeremy fidgeted with the laces of his tennis shoes. He wasn't sure that he wanted to hear this—and was not sure that Ray would be talking this way if he had still been in his right mind.

"She's a good woman," Ray continued. "I know I haven't always treated her as well as I should. I've been cross with her, yelled at her too many times, maybe. And maybe I haven't loved her like I should. But I've always worked hard for her. Spent the best part of my life in the factory. Made her a good living. Wasn't able to give her a home right away, but I scrimped, worked hard, and finally bought her this house. Always put food on the table. Got her a new dress every spring. She's never complained. Don't you think that's love, son?"

He looked up at the boy, who concentrated on his shoe, trying to brush some dirt from the sole. The sunlight streaming through the window gave Ray's face an ashen look that was almost frightening. Jeremy could hear the faint chopping sounds of Nora in the garden.

Ray picked up one of the tomatoes from the table.

"I've never trusted her with my garden," he said. "Guess I've been kind of particular about it. But it made me happy during a lot of bad times. I love that old garden. It took awhile, but Nora finally learned how to handle a shovel and when to pick the tomatoes." He held up the brilliant red orb of summer. "At least most of the time." His laugh ended in another round of coughing and wheezing. "So I guess I shouldn't mind now if she wants to take care of it for me."

Ray leaned back weakly. Jeremy was afraid that his uncle might croak right there in the chair. But he said, "Don't you worry about me. Why don't you go on out and join her? I don't want the old woman to hurt herself by helping me. I'll be okay. I'll rest another minute, then I can watch you all from the window. Go on. Get."

Reluctantly, Jeremy did as he was told. As soon as he was outside the door, he knew something was horribly wrong.

Nora had an expression on her face he had never seen before in his young life. Her eyes were bulging, her face red, muscles bulged on her skinny arms with the blue veins as she yanked first one tomato plant and then another—all filled with lush, red fruit—and threw them on a growing heap. She had already cut down the beans with a hoe. She had tossed it to one side on the ground, sharp side up. Dangerous, like his uncle had taught him never to do.

Jeremy didn't know what to do. The garden had been around as long as he had known his aunt and uncle. Why was she doing this? He was frozen in place long enough for her to grab the last tomato plant, which she easily freed by the roots from the soft, moist soil.

"Why? Aunt Nora? Why?"

She moved to the eggplants, and at first the boy thought she wasn't going to answer. She kicked at the glossy purple ovals hanging from the stiff plants, and the boy winced, as if she were kicking at a man's balls, taking away his very manhood forever in a vicious moment of pain. The fruit splattered across the uprooted chaos.

She suddenly stood, placed the palms of her hands on her back, and stretched. She looked over the almost demolished garden with a look that seemed to the boy like the kind of look his uncle used to have when he had put in the last plant and plowed in the good manure he had bought from Jake Tinsley down the road.

Jeremy asked again, "Why are you doing this?"

"Why do you think?" she asked in a thin voice.

"I don't know."

"Why, I love the old coot, of course. I'm doing this for his own good. You saw how he was this morning? If I didn't do this, he would be out here again and again. I never could do anything with him when he gets so full of himself. He would kill himself. I'm doing this for his own good."

She then reached down, grabbed a handful of the yellow flowers.

"I never liked these blasted weeds, anyway," she muttered to herself.

The boy glanced over at the porch, as the old man slumped silently at the window, tomato falling from his hand.

FRANK WATSON BIOGRAPHY

Frank Watson has published novels with Fawcett under his own name (*A Cold, Dark Trail* and *The Homecoming of Billy Buchanan*) and under a pseudonym with Zebra. An article about creating believable fictional characters will be included in an e-book soon to be released by Authorsource. A previous version of "Where the Yellow Flowers Grow" received the 2001 Graduate Fiction Award from the University of Missouri-St. Louis. Frank is also an experienced journalist, business writer, and technical writer. He lives with his wife, Deborah, in St. Louis, where he teaches writing on the university level and also with Writers Digest Schools and Criticism Service. He has two sons, Jonathan and Matthew, and one daughter, Jennifer. He may be contacted at franknolenwatson@sbcglobal.net.

The police had good reason for deciding that Widow Dixon killed her three hired hands. She as much as said so.

THE SHAPE OF A HEART

by Donna Volkenaunnt

Inky crows shrieked in the treetops, and a mixture of frost and fallen leaves crunched beneath Claudia Blair's Nikes during her morning jog. After turning thirty the year before, she vowed to keep in shape, and running every day not only kept her slim and fit but also made her feel free.

With Godiva, her chocolate Lab, pulling hard on the leash, Claudia sprinted down the half-mile gravel road of her sprawling sixty-acre estate. Her husband, Matt, paid a premium price for this land in a far corner of Osage County, Missouri. A middle-aged lawyer with old money and a weak, but generous heart, he had an eighteen-room home built as a wedding gift for Claudia ten years before.

The first hint of autumn sunlight rose above the gentle slope of the Ozark hills, chasing away the mist that settled in the valley. When Claudia neared the end of the road, she stopped and tucked her wheat-colored hair under her St. Louis Cardinals ball cap while Godiva sniffed the ground.

When a rabbit bounded from beneath a woodpile, the dog bolted. Dragging her leash behind, Godiva raced past the witness tree marking the dividing line between the Blairs' estate and the Widow Dixon's farm.

Claudia ran deeper into the woods, following the dog's urgent bark. "Bad dog," she yelled. "Get back here." She wiped her hands on her sweat pants and bent over to take a few deep breaths before tramping onto the Widow Dixon's property.

Minutes later she found Godiva, tail wagging, nose buried in the ground, clawing at the base of an elder tree. When the Lab looked up, mud and oak leaves clung to her snout.

Claudia grabbed for the leash, but the dog evaded her, dropping the muddy, snake-skin cowboy boot she held in her jaw. Continuing to dig, the dog unearthed the skeletal remains of a foot.

Claudia couldn't squelch her piercing scream. The loud noise jarred turkey vultures from their roosts and her nearest neighbors from their breakfast table.

Across the ridge, Tina and Darwin Wilder heard the shriek while eating biscuits and gravy and listening to the weather forecast.

"What's that?" Tina asked, running to the window.

"I don't know, but it can't be good. Call Sheriff Wilson," Darwin shouted as he grabbed his Remington from the gun rack and jumped in his pickup.

Darwin spotted Claudia racing from the woods, a wide-eyed look of terror on her face. Her chocolate Lab followed close behind, carrying a long bone in her mouth.

Claudia kept glancing over her shoulder and shouting, "Drop it!" Her dog refused to obey.

Darwin watched her trip over a root hidden beneath the nest of leaves and fall, hitting her cheek on a rock. He pulled his truck next to her, jumped out of the cab, and extended a hand to help her to her feet. "You okay, Mrs. Blair?"

She refused his hand and stood, gasping for air. "I'm just tired from my run. I need to get home and rest."

Just then Godiva loped next to them and dropped the bone at their feet before trotting away.

Darwin examined the bone. "This didn't come from an animal. At least not a four-legged one."

Claudia leaned against a tree to keep from falling. "I need to find my dog and get home."

When Godiva returned a few minutes later with the muddy cowboy boot, Darwin said. "I'll be. That sure looks like one of Randy's boots."

At the mention of Randy's name, the color drained from Claudia's face as she collapsed into Darwin's arms.

Tina arrived several minutes later with a thermos of hot chocolate, a box of tissues, and a ton of questions. She asked Darwin, "You sure it's Randy's boot? And his leg bone? Where'd the dog dig it up?"

Darwin hitched his thumb towards the elder tree, standing a few yards from a hunting shack belonging to the late Mr. Dixon.

Tina picked up the boot and said, "Yes, that's Randy's boot all right. He was always saying how he had them made special somewhere in Texas. Damn, he was a looker."

Darwin held an open hand to his wife. "Keep your voice down. Can't you see Mrs. Blair's in a state? She don't need you reminding her about how good looking Randy was."

Tina stood with her feet planted on the dirt and put her hands on her hips. "Don't you tell me to keep quiet. Women know about these things. You go calm down that damned dog. That barking is what's upsetting Mrs. Blair."

While Darwin checked on the dog, Tina climbed into the pickup and poured Claudia a cup of hot chocolate.

"Here, hon. Drink this. It'll help calm you down."

After taking a few sips, Claudia stopped shaking.

"That's better," Tina said. Tina took her silence as an invitation to continue talking. "So, do you think the Widow Dixon killed Randy?"

Claudia opened her mouth to answer, but all that came out was a high-pitched mew. Her hands began to shake again.

"Don't worry," Tina said, patting a hand. "You're safe. She can't hurt you here."

Claudia didn't answer. She clutched the cup of chocolate and stared into it like it was a crystal ball holding the answers to a frightening future.

"Some say the Widow took out insurance policies on her handymen and then croaked them for the cash when they tried to quit. Randy was the only one that lasted two seasons."

The mention of Randy's name caused Claudia to sob. She tried to push the door open and leave, but Tina put a beefy arm around her neck.

"That's okay, honey. Go ahead and cry. You and Randy was friends, wasn't you?"

Calming down from her fright, Claudia remembered the first time she met Randy Chase. She was researching old newspaper articles one evening while Matt was out of town, which was usually two weeks a month. While scanning records on the microfiche, someone with long legs in faded denim jeans scooted a chair next to hers.

A deep, friendly voice asked, "This seat taken, neighbor?"

Claudia glanced from the screen into emerald eyes. She felt her cheeks redden and her breath quicken. It was Randy Chase.

"You're Claudia Blair, aren't you? Your place is right next to Widow Dixon's."

Claudia nodded and fiddled with a wisp of blond hair. "Have we met?"

"Not formally," he said. "But I've seen you plenty. Name's Randy Chase. I run the farm for the Widow."

"Glad to meet you." Claudia wiped a damp hand on her Levis, then stretched it out to Randy, although she didn't need an introduction. All the ladies in Osage

County between the ages of sixteen and sixty knew who he was.

Randy leaned closer, smelling of Aramis, draft beer, and Dentyne. "Sure is a beautiful sight."

"What?"

"You on your morning run. I watch from the Widow's window while I drink my coffee."

Claudia felt her heart flutter. She licked her lips, imagining him watching her.

"What you reading?" he asked.

"Nothing," she said, trying with no success to block Randy from reading what was on the screen.

"Death notices?"

Claudia twisted in her chair. "They're nothing. Just old newspaper records."

"Why you reading them?"

Claudia gave him a devilish smile. "Let's just say I've got a lot of time on my hands."

Randy rubbed a knee against hers. "I can think of lots of better ways to spend your time. How about I take you away from this morgue, and we go over to Bo's tavern for a drink."

Every instinct told her to turn away from him and keep studying the humming machine and the tiny printing on the screen, but an even stronger urge caused her to say, "Sounds like fun."

That night Randy taught Claudia the Texas two-step and reminded her how much fun it was to feel alive.

"Nice boots," she said when they took a break from the dance floor and sat down to finish their second pitcher of beer.

"Snakeskin. Got them made special in El Paso, Texas. I was stationed at Fort Bliss for three years."

"I love the southwest," she said, relaxing after drinking more beer than she had since before she was married. "Never been to El Paso, but my husband took me to Santa Fe when he was on a business trip. It's so exotic and full of mystery. And I love all that silver jewelry."

Randy smiled. "How about this? You like it?" He fingered the bolo tie at the neck of his chambray shirt. The tie had two black strings with silver tips that ran through a silver heart-shaped center. "Bought it in Texas too—just before I got out of the Army."

"So, what brings you to Missouri?"

"Grew up here. My folks passed on while I was in the service. Left me forty acres the other side of Jeff City. Soon as I pay off my Harley and scrape together enough cash to buy a new tractor, I'm gonna farm for myself."

"Bet Widow Dixon won't be too happy about that. And I wouldn't want to have her mad at me."

"She's harmless," Randy said. "Kinda like an old dog. All bark and no bite."

Claudia leaned across the table and said, "I'm not too sure about that. One day I got her mail by mistake. When I walked over to return it, she told me to keep my 'whoring-Jezebel ass' off her property."

"She's a colorful one all right. Since old man Dixon died, her farm's all she's got. Nobody believes a word she says, anyway."

His last statement caused Claudia to smile, something she hadn't done in a while.

Randy took her hands in his and said, "If you don't mind my asking, why would a pretty young thing like you marry an old man like Mr. Blair?"

In the hours that followed, she told Randy about how she met Matt, her biggest tipper, when she was a nineteen-year-old waitress in Jefferson City. After showing up at work with a black eye, she told him about her abusive boyfriend. That same day, Matt paid rent for an apartment and helped her move out of her boyfriend's mobile home. Shortly afterwards, Claudia's boyfriend was found dead, the victim of a hit and run.

"Matt's not much to look at, but he gives me everything I want."

"Everything?" Randy winked.

Claudia raised an eyebrow and tapped a finger on her lips. "Well, almost everything."

"Bet he can't give you what I got, darling."

"That's not what I meant."

"What else is there that a beautiful woman like you would want?"

Swallowing hard to keep from crying, she said, "Kids. I've always wanted to be a mother."

Randy draped his arm around her shoulder and squeezed. "With that house of yours and your husband being a lawyer and all, you damned sure can afford a house full of kids."

Claudia nodded and turned to look Randy in the eyes. "Matt told me he doesn't want to share me with anyone else—not even kids."

"I hate to break it to you, darling, but that ain't love. That's possession."

Claudia started to reply but was interrupted when Bo shouted, "Last call."

With a look of horror, she stared at her watch. It was almost midnight.

"I gotta go. Thanks for the beer and the dance lessons."

"My pleasure." Randy whispered something in her ear, then winked. "See you later?"

Claudia rushed outside, hopped in her Mustang, and raced home. She practiced several excuses to tell Matt why she was late, but she didn't need to use any of them. There was no message on the machine. Matt didn't call until the next morning.

The week Matt was in Washington was the most exciting in Claudia's life. It was also the last time anyone remembered seeing Randy Chase.

Most of the men figured Randy took off on his motorcycle, until it was found at the end of a deserted road near the Dixon farm. Others reasoned Randy got tired of making bike payments and took off with some sweet young thing.

The women just hoped he would turn up again someday.

And he did, the day Godiva found his boot in a shallow grave on Widow Dixon's farm.

The squeal of sirens echoed through the woods when Sheriff Brandon and his deputies blasted onto the scene. Brandon escorted Claudia to his cruiser and began his interrogation. "Mrs. Blair, I know you've had an awful morning, but I need to ask you a few questions."

In a flat, even voice, Claudia recounted how Godiva found the boot. The sheriff arched his eyebrows and signaled to his deputies.

"Get out your shovels and start digging, boys. I'm gonna go talk to the Widow."

Hazel Dixon saw the flashing lights, grabbed her shotgun, and greeted the sheriff with a blast across his cruiser.

"Get off my property."

"Now, Hazel, put the gun down. We gotta talk."

"I didn't break no laws. You're the one breaking the law trespassing on my land, just like all them others."

"What you talking about, Hazel? What others?"

"Them thieving bastards."

While Brandon tried to reason with Hazel, his deputies were unearthing the remains of Randall Chase, along with former handymen Willie Mason and Ben Richards. All three were found buried in shallow graves near the old hunting shack.

After one of the deputies radioed the sheriff of their grisly discovery, Brandon told them to hurry on over for backup. He was going to disarm the Widow.

One of the deputies hid behind a barren lilac bush. As a warning to her to drop her gun, he shot out a window in her living room. In her hurry to reach her basement, she tumbled down the thin wooden stairs.

The sheriff rushed downstairs to find she had split her head on the concrete floor. He tried to stop the blood that oozed from Hazel's scalp. Despite her injury, she was still able to speak.

"Why'd you do it, Hazel?" Brandon asked. He cradled her head in his arms while his deputy called for an ambulance.

"They found my secret hiding spot and stole my morels. Gave them a roof over their heads and a decent wage. And they still stole my mushrooms. Told them all to go to hell before . . ." Hazel gasped for breath.

"Before what? Did you say you sent them all to hell?"

"Them was my mushrooms" were the last words Hazel Dixon ever muttered.

In his report, the sheriff wrote that Mrs. Dixon admitted to the murders. The results of autopsies showed all the victims had traces of alcohol and tranquilizers in their blood. Fingerprints from all of the victims were found on a shovel inside the hunting shack.

The report speculated she must have lured them to the shack, asked them to dig a hole, then shot them. Each victim had been shot in the heart with a small caliber revolver. Despite searching Hazel Dixon's home and grounds, the murder weapon was never discovered.

The following spring Claudia was checking on boxes for the movers. Matt had accepted a transfer to Washington after telling her a fresh start would help her get over her shock and depression.

Moving day was hectic, but after what had happened last fall, Claudia had learned to cope. Weekly, rather than monthly, visits to her psychiatrist after Randy's body was discovered helped a great deal. Increasing her medication, along with intensive counseling, erased almost all memories of the day Godiva found the cowboy boot.

A wisp of hair kept falling in her face every time she bent over, but she couldn't remember where she had packed her hair ties. She pushed aside a heavy crate and found a shoelace wedged beneath a floorboard in her bedroom closet. When she tugged on the lace, she dislodged it from the silver, heart-shaped center that remained buried beneath the floor. The heart landed beside the now empty box that had held bullets for the pearl-handled revolver Matt gave her for protection while he was out of town.

"Just what I need!" She picked up the black lace with the silver tips and tied her hair up into a ponytail.

Matt strolled into the room and embraced the only woman who had ever given him a second look. Even before she knew how much money he had, she always smiled and flirted with him when she waited on him at the restaurant near his office. After seeing the black eye her boyfriend gave her, he knew he had to rescue her from the abuse. It was the wisest decision he had ever made.

The couple began to slow dance to "The Shape of a Heart," a Jackson Browne tune playing on the radio. It was one of Claudia's favorites.

As she swayed to the music, Claudia sighed. One last time she let the sequence of events run through her mind. Then she would leave those unhappy memories behind. After Widow Dixon's handymen, Willy and Ben, threatened to blackmail Claudia about their affairs with her, what choice did she have but to silence them? Permanently. She was proud of how she lured them out to the Widow's hunting shack while Matt was out of town. She told them she had buried a cash box with their blackmail money. While they dug she fed them beer laced with her sleeping pills. As soon as they passed out, she shot them in the heart and covered their bodies with dirt and leaves.

She murdered them all, just like she had her abusive boyfriend after he beat her up and Matt moved her into an apartment. Luckily, the news of her boyfriend's death never made it to the local papers, so no one would be likely to connect her to his murder, once the handymen started to disappear.

The only one she felt bad about was Randy, the Texas Two-Stepper. He didn't once threaten to blackmail her. And every time they made love in the hunting cabin, she felt like a woman from head to toe. He told her that the week they spent together was the best in his life. He asked her to run off with him and promised to give her as many kids as she wanted. But she knew that wouldn't work, especially if Randy found out about her past. And giving up her fancy house and all that money was out of the question.

What choice did she have except to kill him too? Her mistake was not digging the grave deep enough. She'd have to remember that.

The only other person with an inkling of what Claudia had done was that nosey Widow Dixon, who caught her sneaking away from the hunting shack more than one night. She must've thought Claudia was looking for those damn mushrooms. Oh, well, guess that crazy old woman took more to her grave than the secret hiding place of her mushrooms.

When the dance music ended, Claudia closed her eyes and kissed her husband, long and hard. She prayed with all her heart that he would never find out. She knew if he ever learned the truth, it would be the death of him.

DONNA VOLKENANNT BIOGRAPHY

Donna Duly Volkenannt is a native of St. Louis who divides her time between her home in St. Peters and her country getaway in Osage County, Missouri. In September 2003 she retired as a management analyst for the Department of Defense to devote more time to her family and her writing. She and her husband, Walter, have been married for thirty-five years and have two children and two grandchildren. She serves as second vice-president and membership chair of the Missouri Writers Guild (MWG), president of Saturday Writers chapter of the MWG, and secretary of the Ozarks Writers League (OWL). Her fiction, non-fiction, essays, and poetry have received first-place awards from MWG, OWL, Ozark Creative Writers (OCW), Springfield Writers Guild, and the Oklahoma Writers Federation, Inc. In 2001 one of her short stories received honorable mention in the national Steinbeck competition. Her work has appeared in *St. Louis Events and Storyteller* magazines. Recent publication credits in-clude contributions to *Murder, Mystery, Madness, Magic, and Mayhem* published by Cave Hollow Press (www.rmkinder.com), and *A Cup of Comfort for Women* and *A Cup of Comfort for Christmas* published by Adams Media (www.cupofcomfort.com).

When Elizabeth's husband showed her how to oper-
ate his pepperbox pistol, he didn't know how she
would have to use it.

THE LAST BULLET

by Vicki Cox

"Mama! Mama!" Eight-year-old Isabel McKinley skipped towards her mother, her pink sunbonnet flopping behind her. "Look what I found!"

Elizabeth McKinley straightened up from the bean row and rubbed the small of her back.

Even if she weren't mine, I do believe that child is lit with joy, she thought, watching her young daughter approach from the spring, twirling a mysterious object in her hands. The sun caught in her hair, burnishing her blonde hair. I swear, she is the prettiest, sweetest thing west of the Mississippi.

"What is it, child?" Elizabeth asked, wiping her hands on her apron. "What treasure have you found today?"

"Look, Mama," said Isabel, proudly holding out a long, white feather, tipped in black. "This is a new kind of feather. What does it come from?"

Elizabeth's stomach turned into a knot. There was no doubt the feather wasn't from any bird she or Isabel had seen circling in the sky. That was an eagle feather. And eagle feathers meant Indians.

"Where did you find this, sweetie?" Elizabeth asked as casually as she could.

"Down at the spring," Isabel responded. "It was on the ground just under the big cedar tree. Can I have it,

Mama? It's so pretty. Could Papa make a pen from it? Could he?"

Elizabeth said. "We'll show Pa when he and Dancy come up for dinner. I'm sure he'll want to see it. Then we'll see about a new pen for you." She reached out and drew Isabel to her in a gentle hug.

"Where, young lady, is the bucket of water I sent you for?"

"I drew it, Mama. I just set it down when I found the feather. I'll go right back and get it."

"You best do that right now," Elizabeth said, smiling indulgently. "Your Pa and Dancy will need it shortly. Put the feather next to Pa's wash basin."

Isabel pulled away from her mother's arm, hurrying towards the cabin.

"And put your sunbonnet back on."

"Yes, Mama," Isabel said, over her shoulder. She walked towards the cabin, the feather in her hand. She emerged a few seconds later, her bonnet properly covering her face.

"I'll be right back, Mama."

Elizabeth hardly noticed as Isabel headed back to the spring or her return with the water bucket full.

Indians? Elizabeth thought. So close to the cabin? Why would the Osage venture so far into the farm? She had once glimpsed the mighty warriors in the fall, when small bands had passed over the ridge for their last hunt of the season. But they'd never been more than silent shadows, passing through the pin oak forest. What does this feather mean?

Isabel came out of the cabin and to the garden.

"Mama, I put the plates on the table and filled the water glasses. Can I ring for Papa and Dancy? Please?"

"Yes, sweetie," replied Elizabeth. "I guess it is time."

Elizabeth picked up her basket full of beans as Isabel disappeared into the cabin and returned with the dinner bell.

Clang! Clang! Clang! Clang! She briskly shook the bell four times.

"That'll bring them running, for sure," she said to her mother.

"We'll have tomato sandwiches and cold apple pie. That way we won't have to heat up the stove before supper," Elizabeth said. "You wash your hands and wet down your hair part. I swear your hair has a mind of its own."

Elizabeth and Isabel busied themselves in the lean-to kitchen. Isabel placed the butter and apple pie on the table while Elizabeth cut thick slices of her homemade bread. The clink and creak of the wagon and the murmur of voices brought Isabel to the door.

"Dancy, give Pat and Mike plenty of water," Stephen McKinley was telling his young son. "Let's see what these fine ladies have fixed us for dinner. We'll unload the wood after we've eaten."

"Papa! Papa!" Isabel cried. "I found a 'play pretty' today. Come see," she said, grabbing his big hand and pulling him towards the wash basin. "What bird does it come from, Papa? Can I keep it? Can I keep it? Will you make me a pen from it? Will you?"

"What is this, Miss Pris?" he said, hanging his hat on the peg and rolling up his sleeve. "What has my sweet Isabel found today?"

Stephen's smile faded as he picked up the eagle feather and glanced quickly at Elizabeth.

"Where did you get this, Isabel?" he asked, squatting on his knees and putting his hand around his daughter. "Could you show Papa where you found this?"

"Oh, yes," Isabel said, taking her father's hand. "It was by the cedar tree. Shall I show you now?"

"We'll be back soon," Stephen told his wife. "Nothing like a treasure hunt before eating to whet the appetite. "Dancy, you want to come too?" he asked as his teenaged son walked in from the porch.

"Naw," Dancy said, with a grin. "I'm no pirate. I'll just lay me down under the hickory until you get back."

"Hurry back, you two," Elizabeth said. "I don't want the butter to melt in this heat."

The two walked down the hill past the lean-to barn, slowly disappearing from sight. Their voices blurred to undistinguishable sounds. A few minutes later, they returned. Isabel was jostling on her father's shoulders.

"Did I miss anything?" Dancy teased, as he sat up under the tree. "Or did Isabel find another trinket for her cedar box?"

Stephen swung his daughter down from his shoulders.

"At least, I found the feather! Papa says it's an Indian's coup feather," Isabel retorted. "What did you find today?"

Stephen and his children walked to the cabin. Stephen washed his hands in the basin, followed by Dancy and Isabel.

"Well, Mama," Stephen said to his wife, "looks like we've got us a real expert feather collector."

"That's me, Mama," Isabel piped in.

"Did you find anything else?" Elizabeth asked, her eyes searching her husband's face.

"No more feathers," said Stephen, "but there were a fair number of horse prints along the creek edge. Unshod hooves."

"Let's eat, shall we?" Elizabeth said, abruptly.

"Isabel, will you say grace for us today?" Stephen asked.

"Yes, Papa," said Isabel, folding her hands. "Dear Lord, we thank you for your care, the food we eat, the clothes we wear. Be present with us everywhere. Amen."

"Amen," the others responded.

"Ma, you make the best bread and butter in the county," Dancy said, lathering his bread with creamy, new butter.

"Isabel churned the butter this morning," Elizabeth said, turning to her daughter. "She's a big help around the house."

After the apple pie with the lattice top crust, the men stretched out to rest and let their dinner settle. Elizabeth and Isabel straightened the table and laid a clean tablecloth over the food. By the time they had finished, the men stirred to empty the wagon and return for another load of wood.

"You can start unloading without me, can't you, Dancy?" Stephen asked. "I want to talk to your mother for a minute."

"Sure, Pa. Just as long as 'squirt' here doesn't bother me," he said, tugging Isabel's curls.

"I'm coming, and you can't stop me," Isabel retorted and ran out before him.

They all laughed. "Oh, yes, I can," Darcy called out and loped after her.

"Elizabeth, let's walk," Stephen said. Elizabeth tied her bonnet on and put her hand in his as they strolled towards their small vineyard.

"What do the feather and hoof prints mean?" Elizabeth asked as soon as they were away from the children.

"It means trouble," Stephen said. "The Osages have left us alone up to this point. But someone, quite a few someones, by the looks of those horse prints, have been watering at our spring and probably looking us over. I looked for signs closer to the cabin. I think I saw some behind the barn, but the leaves make it pretty hard to see—if they are there."

"Stephen, the Osages know we were harmless."

"It might not be the Osages. Old Pawhuska wouldn't war with the whites. That would shut down trade with the government. But the Cherokee have been seen in these parts, up from the south. And the Kickapoo are living on land the Osages think is theirs. If either attacks the Osages, we'll be caught in the middle.

"We need to be cautious. I'll leave my pepperbox pistol on the mantle, loaded. It's got six barrels and six bullets. You just shoot, turn the barrel to the next cylinder, recock and fire again. If there's anything suspicious at all, you ring the alarm. Dancy and I'll take our rifles with us. We'll work closer to the cabin. Keep Isabel close by. No more wandering about looking for play pretties for her."

"I'll tie her to my apron strings if I have to," Elizabeth said with a small smile. Then it faded. "I'm scared, Stephen."

"No need to be scared yet," Stephen reassured her. "Just be careful. Let's get back." He put his arm around her.

"There's work to be done."

Stephen and Dancy headed the team back to the woods.

"Time to practice your cross-stitch," Elizabeth announced, pulling her rocker on to the porch, "while I mend this tear in your father's shirt."

"Can I use red thread?" Isabel asked. "I love red."

"Yes, Miss Pris, you can use red," Elizabeth answered. "Can you thread the needle by yourself?"

"Yes," Isabel said adamantly. "I can do it myself."

For three days the August heat bore down. The sun parched the grass to whiskers. The leaves on the oaks clacked in the hot winds. Even the soil seemed bleached to a chalky white. The milk cow huddled under the shade, swishing flies from its back. Even working in the shade of the trees, the brutal heat battered Stephen and Dancy as they chopped and sawed wood. Their faded blue work shirts were dark with sweat as they walked wearily to the house for noon and supper meals.

Elizabeth and Isabel worked in the garden behind the cabin, weeding and hoeing. They walked together to the spring for water. Elizabeth always carried the dinner bell with her. Despite her protest, Isabel could no longer play in the barn alone.

"If I dig up one more rock, I'm going back to Kentucky," Elizabeth muttered as she struck the hard ground with her hoe.

"Oh, Mama," said Isabel, "rocks can be good too. You can do lots with rocks. You can make a fence. You can make a campfire. You can make a castle and a moat to protect us from Indians."

Elizabeth laughed despite herself. "You are right, Miss Pris, we should look on the bright side of things. We have a new life, a new house, and a forest full of firewood. We'll eat good this winter too if this heat doesn't pop the corn on the stalk before we can pick it."

"Someone's coming up the road," Isabel exclaimed, shading her face with her hand. "Company's coming to our house!"

"It looks like Mr. Atkins' horse," said her mother.

Abraham Atkins rode slowly up to the cabin on a draft horse. His face was streaked with dust and sweat; even his hat seemed wilted over his face. He cradled his rifle in his arms. He reined in the horse at the hitching post.

"Afternoon, ma'am," he said, tipping his hat. "Hello, Miss Isabel," he said. "You are looking prettier every day."

"Oh, Mr. Atkins!" said Isabel, blushing with pleasure. She turned, running into the cabin.

"Menfolk around?" Atkins asked Elizabeth.

"Stephen and Dancy will be coming up shortly," Elizabeth replied. "They're cutting wood along the north field. They shouldn't be too long. Won't you set with us a spell and stay for supper?"

"Look, Mr. Atkins, I found an eagle feather!" said Isabel, coming out the door with her recent find.

Abraham Atkins looked quickly at Elizabeth and frowned.

"Really? Can I see it, missy?"

"Oh, yes," Isabel said. "It's real pretty. I want Papa to make a pen out of it for me."

"That's a mighty fine looking feather," Atkins said, taking it from Isabel's hand. "Where did you find it?"

"Down by the spring," she answered.

"We don't know why she should have found such a thing so close to the house," Elizabeth said, guardedly. "We've never seen anything like it before."

"I may have the answer to that," said Abraham. "You'll have a fine pen," he told Isabel, handing the feather back to her.

"Where are our manners?" said Elizabeth. "Isabel, will you bring Mr. Atkins a cool drink?"

"Yes, Mama," she said.

With Isabel in the house, Abraham spoke openly. "We've had some news from near White Hair's village on the Neosho. It's not good."

"Here's your drink," Isabel said, coming through the door.

"There's Pa and Dancy. They must have a winter's worth of wood in the wagon."

Stephen and Dancy slowly moved the wagon through the wispy stalks of hay and down the slope of the small sinkhole. The horses labored as they pulled the wagon up the other side.

"Good day, Abraham," Steven said as he swung down off the wagon.

"Stephen," Abraham replied, extending his hand as the McKinley men strode up the porch. "Hot, ain't it?"

"Dancy." He gravely shook hands with the young man. "You've become a man since I last seen you. Need a hand unloading your wood?"

"Much obliged," Stephen said. "We can talk at the same time."

"Come, Isabel," said Elizabeth, "we'd better get to fixing dinner for our company."

"All right, Mama," said Isabel. "Can I set the table? With the blue napkins?"

"Yes, sweetie, we'll make the table look pretty."

With his mother and sister inside, Dancy turned the wagon. Stephen and Abraham walked beside it towards the woodpile.

"What brings you all the way over here, Abraham?" Stephen asked. "We haven't seen you since early spring."

"Things are bad up north," Abraham replied. "All hell's broke loose. It's not the Osage. No, that's not exactly true. It is the Osage. But they didn't start it this time. The Cherokee did that. They attacked a group of new settlers along the Neosho."

"Good god almighty!" said Stephen, rubbing the back of his neck.

"That's not the worst of it," Abraham said. "Seems a goldurn posse of vigilantes couldn't tell the difference from an Osage and a Cherokee. Lord knows how they could make that mistake. They attacked a small Osage camp. The braves were gone, hunting. So they shot the old men, scalped the women and children, and left their bodies to rot."

"No!" said Stephen. "That's the dumbest thing I ever heard of. The Osage revere their children as much as we do our own."

"Two Feathers' family was killed in the raid. He's gone crazy with grief. Not even Pawhuska can control him now."

"Who could blame him?" said Dancy. "If anyone tried to hurt Ma or Isabel, I'd hunt them down and skin them alive."

"Two Feathers and a few hot bloods have broke from the tribe," said Abraham. "They're bent on avenging what the settlers did. They strike isolated farms. They capture men and then torture their women and children in front of them. They've been seen all over the old Osage lands. If that eagle feather means what I think it does, you'd best pack up until Pawhuska gets control of his braves or the government sends in troops.

"No," Stephen said. "We will not run. This is our home. We have treated the Osage fairly. Pawhuska has treated us fairly in the past. He will again."

"I'm telling you, Stephen," said Atkins roughly, "Elizabeth and Isabel are their targets. They'll be raped and then scalped and who knows what else."

"That won't happen while I'm here," Dancy said, grimly.

"Thank you for helping rick the wood," Stephen said, his mouth a tight line. "You're welcome to stay for supper."

"No, I've said my piece." Abraham replied. "I hoped you'd come back and stay with us. I best get back before nightfall. Won't you reconsider?"

"Thanks for dropping by," Stephen replied. "We'd better tell Elizabeth you aren't staying. Dancy, will you see to Pat and Mike?"

The men walked back to the house with Dancy leading the horses to the barn.

"I'm sorry, Elizabeth," Abraham said, as he stepped inside the cabin. "It's getting late. I should get back to my own place."

Elizabeth turned from her frying pan. "But Mr. Atkins, I'm frying pork chops for us. Please stay."

"I best not tarry," Abraham answered. "But I thank you kindly for your invitation."

"Mr. Atkins, can't you stay, please?" Isabel asked.

"No, missy, but if I could, I'd be sitting right next to you at supper," he said.

"Will you take a piece of my apple pie?" the youngest McKinley asked. "I helped Mama make the crust."

"I would like that very much, Miss Isabel." Abraham said.

"God bless."

Taking the napkin Isabel had placed around the pie, he mounted his horse and turned towards the road.

"Elizabeth, we'll be late for supper," Stephen said, "Dancy and I need to do a little work around the house."

"What did Mr. Atkins tell you?" Elizabeth asked.

"Two Feathers and some renegades are raiding neighboring farms," Stephen said. "Dancy and I will lay some surprises about—if they visit us. We'll bring extra water from the spring. You take blankets to the root cellar and get my pepperbox pistol too."

Dancy and Stephen worked until dark, laying beaver and wolf traps along the blackjacks and in the bean rows in the garden. They ran a line of gunpowder in front of the porch and ran a second line up the stairs and into the cabin. They loaded their pistols and guns, laid the powder and patches on the table.

"Now Elizabeth, remember when I showed you how to load the rifle? If an attack comes, Dancy and I'll make every bullet count. Every time we fire, you take our gun and reload it for us."

"What can I do, Papa?" said Isabel.

"Your job will be to keep watch over the garden. If you see anything move, you must yell quick and loud. Right now, you soak these flour sacks in water real good for us."

They hurried about fortifying their cabin. Their traps were set outside. Their ammunition was ready. Without lighting the candles, they sat at the table to eat.

"I'm scared, Papa," said Isabel. "I can't eat a thing."

No one else could eat either. Their attention was riveted to each snapping twig, each cooing dove outside, each whinny of the animals in the barn. Night fell like silt over the cabin.

Finally, Stephen spoke. "Isabel, you can go to bed now. Your eyes need to be rested when we need a lookout."

"Yes, Papa," Isabel said.

"I love you, Papa. I love you, Mama. I love you, Dancy," she said as she started up the ladder to her bed in the loft. Halfway up she turned, "Papa, if I gave my eagle feather back to the Osages, would they go away?"

"No, Miss Pris," her father responded, surprised. "I don't think so. These Osages are really mad at other people, but not at us."

Quickly Elizabeth came to the ladder.

"Isabel, sweetheart, come here," she said softly. Taking her daughter in her arms, she kissed the top of her head and stroked her hair.

"Look at me, sweetie. You didn't do anything wrong by finding the feather. Not one thing. And these Indians are not going to hurt you. I would never, ever, let anyone hurt you. I promise you that. And your Papa promises you that, and Dancy promises you that. Do you understand?"

"Yes, Mama," she said, clutching her mother tight.

"Love you, Isabel," said her mother, softly.

"Love you, Miss Pris," said her father.

"Love you too, squirt," said Dancy with his hand on the door latch. Elizabeth released her daughter. Isabel climbed up the ladder into her loft. The adults then settled in to wait. Dancy slipped out to hide in the chicken house. Stephen took his post at the back. Elizabeth watched the front.

Then, just at daybreak, came the unmistakable sound of horses' hooves. A lot of them.

"At last," Stephen whispered. "Wake Isabel, Elizabeth. Remember, we've got to make every bullet count. We've got a few tricks for Two Feathers, but we've got to make every bullet count."

The ponies galloped up to the rock fence, encircling the house, their riders whooping and yelping.

"There must be a dozen of them," Elizabeth whispered.

"Mama, they don't have any hair," said Isabel, her voice full of fear.

Slick of head and eyebrows, the Osages had stuck their feathers in a roach of thick hair that ran in a line down to their necks. They carried spears, bows and arrows, war clubs, and tomahawks. Their chests and faces were heavily tattooed. They seemed too big for their horses. They rode up under the big blackjack tree, their horses prancing in place.

"Now!" yelled Stephen. Dancy, hidden behind the chicken house, jerked the rope. The huge tarp they had used to cover the haystack fell from the tree branches. The twine tangled in the horses' hooves of three warriors and trapped their war bonnets, weapons, and arms like huge tentacles.

While the Indians fought to control their horses, Dancy sprinted towards the cabin. Stephen stepped out of the cabin and fired his Kentucky rifle. An Osage fell from his horse.

Dancy darted inside the door, and Stephen stepped inside immediately after him. Elizabeth grasped the gun and quickly began the reloading. Stephen grasped the flintlock and, taking aim out the window, fired. Another warrior grabbed his shoulder and fell backwards off his horse.

The Indians wheeled their horses to the rise behind the barn, regrouped, and charged again. As they approached the rock fence, they slid off their horses and began running towards the cabin. Suddenly another Indian screamed and went down, grabbing his leg. Another followed, writhing and rolling on the ground. A third and fourth felt the sting of Dancy's and Stephen's bullets.

"Papa, they're coming out of the garden," Isabel yelled. Her warning was followed by more screams as more Osages stepped into the beaver traps that had been hidden in the corn and beans.

Again, the Osages fell back to reorganize. Six Indians down, but at least six more were upright, readying to attack again.

"They'll come at us without stopping this time," Stephen said, checking his ammunition. "Elizabeth, you and Isabel get to the root cellar and close the door. Don't open it for anything. Dancy and I will take care of the rest of them. Don't open the door until I come for you. Remember what I told you about the pistol. You have six shots. Shoot. Turn the barrel. Recock. Then shoot."

"No, Stephen! I won't leave you," cried Elizabeth. Isabel began to whimper.

"Do it," he yelled back. "Save Isabel."

Quickly, Elizabeth and Isabel crawled through the kitchen's trap door and scrambled into the root cellar. Elizabeth slammed the door behind them and threw the iron rod through the latch. She grabbed Isabel, holding her close with one hand. Her other hand closed over the pistol. Isabel sobbed.

More shots were fired. Yelps of the savages came nearer. Two loud explosions followed.

"Dancy! Behind you!" Elizabeth heard Stephen yell. "Pa!"

Then there was a shrill cry. The shooting stopped.

With a loud crash, a war club splintered the door. An Indian loomed above them, knife in hand. Elizabeth took aim and pulled the trigger. With a yelp, he fell backward. Isabel screamed.

Another savage swung at the door. The wood splintered again, his tomahawk and arm came through the hole.

Turn the barrel. Recock. Shoot, she told herself, her hands trembling. She fired again. Missed. The Osage lunged at her. *Turn the barrel. Recock. Fire.* Her next shot hit him in the chest.

A third Indian charged the door before Elizabeth could fire again. *Turn the barrel. Recock. Fire.* That stopped him.

"Mama! Look!" Isabel yelled. "The window!"

Elizabeth half turned just as another Osage thrust himself halfway through the window above her summer beans. *Turn the barrel. Recock. Fire.* He was crashing over the shelves before she shot him in the face. Blood splattered over her face and Isabel's back.

Above her, another yelping warrior broke the last cross board of the door. In a second terrible motion he flung his hatchet at her.

Pain slammed through her chest. She looked down to see the blade buried in her shoulder. Slowly she sank to the floor. The air dimmed. Isabel screamed as the blood spread down her mother's dress.

"Mama!" Isabel flung herself protectively over her mother. "Oh, Mama! Mama!" she cried.

The warrior whooped again as he threw off the last boards. *Turn the barrel. Recock. Fire.* Elizabeth fired again. The shot grazed the Indian's arm. He howled but continued coming. Stepping over the ruined door with one foot, he grabbed Isabel's blonde curls and pulled her head back. Isabel flailed about. She screamed.

Turn the barrel.

The Osage's mouth was twisted with hate and rage. His war cry was gutted in grief, protesting the injustices played upon him and his people for decades.

Recock. Elizabeth's hands fumbled over the hammer.

Dragging Isabel backwards off Elizabeth, the Osage raised a knife to swipe it across her scalp. Isabel was struggling, screaming. Her eyes were wide in terror.

With tremendous effort, Elizabeth raised the gun. Only one bullet left. Even as the darkness overtook her, she knew what she had to do.

Shoot.

With her last strength, she squeezed the trigger. And shot her lovely Isabel in the heart.

VICKI COX BIOGRAPHY

Vicki Cox is the author of *Rising Stars and Ozark Constellations* (Skyward Publishing). A collection of profiles and features about contemporary people and places in the Ozarks, in 2002 the book was the Missouri Writers Guild Best Book about Missouri. She has published four biographies for middle and high school readers: *Diana, Princess of Wales* (2001), *Marion Jones* (2002), *Hosni Mubarak* (2003), and *Fidel Castro* (2004), all for Chelsea House Publishers. Her award-winning column, "Ozark Soul," appears monthly in *The Ozarks Mountaineer*. Her 500 features have appeared in the *St. Louis Post Dispatch*, *Christian Science Monitor*, *Western Horseman*, *American Profile Magazine*, *Today's Christian Women*, as well as other magazines and newspapers in fifteen states. Retiring from public school education after twenty-five years and fifteen seconds, she teaches culture of the Ozark classes for Drury University (Springfield, Missouri). She has been active in Western Writers of America, Ozark Writers League, and in 2003 was president of Missouri Writers Guild. She speaks frequently about her two passions: writing and the Ozark culture. Though her clothes hang in Lebanon, Missouri, she resides mostly in her car. www.geocities.com/vicki-cox001.

Every area has its tales of strange and arcane happenings, including the Ozarks. Are these tales merely legends? Are they true? No one knows. Perhaps only you can decide for sure.

THE MONSTER AT PETER BOTTOM CAVE

by Shirleen Sando

The air was so still it felt like a heavy blanket was smothering the earth. There was no moon, no noise, nothing but darkness and the night sky. Rob noticed the unnerving quiet, and he sensed the way it changed the moment he and his older brother Ted slid from their Hondas, their dusty tennis shoes hitting the hard, hot earth. "Listen," Rob said. "Someone's there!"

When the bushes on the far side of the woods rustled, Rob sent a flash of light toward a clump of trees as he stood, statue like, imagining strange, shadowy creatures lurking beneath the twisted leaves.

Ted put a muscled hand to one ear. "Just crows."

Uncertain if Ted was right, Rob moved cautiously. The noises grew more intense. Almost instantly another deafening silence controlled the woods. With frayed nerves, Rob pushed in closer to Ted. Rubbing the sides of his temples to ease the growing pain in his head, Rob felt his body weaken under the heat. As he wiped sweaty hands on his jeans, he wished he could stop the profuse sweating. Knowing he couldn't, he tightened moist fingers around his flashlight as if the grip could give him renewed strength.

As a child, he often dreamed of entering Peter Bottom Cave, the place of evil omens and curses. Every dream held a new layer of reality and though dripped with death and destruction, each held a sinister charm. It was his fascination with the macabre that appalled him the most. Even though he awoke from those hellish visions, his clammy, cold body violently shaking, he was exhilarated. Not even the throbbing headaches that sometimes stayed for days could detour him. The nightmares continually reminded him that an evil spirit controlled part of him, and while he found it loathsome, it provided a strange tension that kept him alive.

Though Rob remained uncertain as to when he became aware of his evil spirit, if it were real or some invention of his mind, he was certain it had something to do with the myths and legends he had grown up hearing. Old-timers told mesmerizing tales of an evil creature living at Peter Bottom Cave. Rob clearly visualized the beast. From his mental image, he pictured it as a giant, a strange, hairy fiend.

When he was younger, he was chilled and fascinated by the tales of the curse that legend said would follow those who encountered the monster. Now those stories were repulsive. But he had to make this journey, if only to prove or disprove the monster's existence, to find a way to rid himself of this evil spirit.

Sucking in a deep breath, Rob warned Ted, "Something's there! And it's headed this way." As he spoke, he squeezed the flashlight so hard he thought it would crush in his hands.

"Get over it," Ted said, his voice agitated, his leg rubbing a blackberry vine. "You've heard too many ghost stories."

"What if they are true?" Rob asked, again reminding himself that the tales were unscientific half-truths. His reasoning had never made the knots in his stomach go away nor made his dreams subside.

Without an answer from Ted, Rob avoided asking further questions. He just adjusted his nylon sack over his back and headed slowly toward the narrow dirt path that Ted turned onto.

Sauntering behind, Rob looked more intently at Ted. It was strange being with his brother now. They hadn't seen each other for seven months—and that a brief three-hour visit on Christmas Day. Rob marveled at the way Ted had grown so tall and blond over the summer. Working in the fields had left him burnt by sun and wind. In comparison, Rob looked at his own pale arms. He was so unlike Ted. As if to block out the pain of their differences, Rob pointed his flashlight to search the area, the yellow beam penetrating the region. He saw nothing, except the blackness and an expanding fog.

As silence squeezed the air, Rob knew he could never block all of his childhood memories, and since so many were good, he desperately wanted to cling to them, despite the wounds he carried of unshared memories created by his parent's divorce. As children, the brothers spent endless hours on the front porch of the old farmhouse in the rickety wooden swing or playing a favorite game of pick up sticks or checkers. Or, they passed away many a hot afternoon under massive oaks at the edge of the front yard, digging their knees into the dirt in fierce competition for the steelie, the prize marble.

Those days held good memories, but there were hard days as well. Rob grew up dreading field work every fall and having to get up very early to work.

Those and other memories filled his head as he searched the surrounding area. There was an irony in the way the two brothers, who now lived such diverse lives, were tramping through the woods as if they had one heart, one mind. Each surely had the same gnawing fear of this taboo place, though Ted would never admit it.

Pushing wet hair from his forehead, Rob re-membered when he would have shared every single fear with Ted, every nightmare, every awful dream. Ted was easier to get along with then. It wasn't until after their parents' separation that Ted blocked out the world, and that meant blocking out his brother along with the rest of what he considered outside annoyances. Rob had thought that perhaps a trip together, just the two of them, might bring them closer, allow them to reconnect, yet he feared the evil intent of the trip as well. He tried telling himself that the vile dreams were just dreams— nothing more. He would be safe in the woods with Ted. They would return tomorrow to the farm with a dozen made-up ghost stories. Everyone would laugh. The boys would tell the truth, and folks would finally realize that Peter Bottom Cave had no real monster—no real evil or curse.

Convincing himself again that the trip was harmless, Rob kept his thoughts on Ted. He wished he could break through the mental wall that separated them. He wondered what words would open them up to each other, take them back to youthful days of fun and laughter.

Since Rob could formulate no such words, he remained quiet and followed Ted. To peel away the darkness, he kept a steady stream of light before him as his feet continually stepped around junipers. He watched with some interest as the flicker of his flashlight hit splotches of dried, flaky manure.

As Ted moved faster along the path, Rob quickened his pace to keep up. Sweat accumulated in the waistband of his jeans. His forehead popped with wet beads as the dull ache intensified in his temple.

Stepping around a rock, his stomach tightened. Something was scurrying through the woods. Flashing his light, seeing it was merely a scampering red squirrel and wasn't a monster or a ghost, he smiled and let the knot in his stomach collapse.

Since Ted took the darkness and fog in stride, Rob wondered if Ted had been to Peter Bottom Cave. As far as he knew, Ted, nor anyone, had ever been this close in. But it was strange the way Ted seemed to be familiar with the area, knew which way to turn and knew what to expect. As boys, they never ventured into the valley surrounding the cave. Their mother repeatedly warned them to stay away, and she often told of the curse. Yet, it was the mysterious, wicked curse that made Peter Bottom Cave all the more appealing, much like death can be repulsive and fascinating to a boy's mind.

Rob turned his attention to something he knew was a fact. He was certainly going to be the first person to photograph the evil creature, if it did, indeed, live in the area. Yet tonight, nearing the valley's edge that pointed to the cave, he felt a renewed tremor in his belly, a feeling of doom. He was afraid.

Rob shook the evil force so he could concentrate on the trip. He listened to a branch breaking in the distance followed by a shushing, swishing from the edge of the valley. A faint hoot disturbed the air. "What's that?" Rob asked, slowing his pace.

Ted turned quickly, his jaw muscles tight as steel, his face directly in front of Rob's. Ted threw a light in Rob's eyes. "It's an owl. A stupid old owl. You baby. I can't believe how city living has taken a toll on you." Ted jerked his body around, his back to Rob as he added, "Camp's just ahead."

Rob looked hard at the sweat spot growing on the back of Ted's red T-shirt. "I'm not a baby. I'm almost sixteen." He gulped air as he put more force in his words. "I forgot what a stupid old owl sounds like . . . that's all."

"You've been at Fayetteville two years with Dad, and you don't remember what an owl sounds like?"

"I forgot, okay?" Rob said with venom. As his voice trailed off, another noise emitted from the valley ahead. Rob imagined he saw the figure of a monster dimly visible in the distance. The cave was out there, somewhere, but he saw nothing of it.

Suddenly, without warning, a yellow glow gushed into the night sky. Rob froze.

"Holy cow. Did you see that?" Rob whispered as he gazed his eyes steadily into the distance.

"Yeah, the monster," Ted said, laughing and turning to hit his brother's brown curly hair. "Swamp gas, stupid."

Rob had forgotten about the gas. He had heard it threw off light. He had seen it from a distance as a child, but from this close the light took on a peculiar appearance.

He admitted that maybe Ted was right about him being a scary cat who needed to grow up.

A soft moan came from the valley. The muffled noise grew louder and scarier. "That's not gas," Rob said, "and I saw something earlier . . . something big and ghostlike." Ignoring the foul smell, he took an extra-deep breath to gather his nerve. "Maybe we should go back. I mean . . . what if those stories are true? What if whoever finds the monster really is cursed?" He wanted to mention the nightmares that had warned him, but since Ted had little patience these days with the ghost story idea, he said nothing more.

"A curse . . . yeah, right." Ted stopped and turned sharply toward Rob. "You're really pathetic." Poking a finger hard at Rob's chest, Ted added, "Now that we've come this far, we're staying. Got it?"

Ted reached into his backpack and pulled out a can of beer. Flipping the tab with his thumb, he pushed the cold can to his forehead before leaning his head back to wolf down a long drink. He shoved the can at Rob.

Staring at the can, Rob said, "What would Dad say?"

"Don't see dear ole Dad around here anywhere," Ted said, glancing from side to side, laughing. "When on earth will you grow up?"

"Guzzling booze don't mean you're grown," Rob said, pulling out a soda. Opening the top, his fingers cradled the can as the cold liquid cooled his burning throat. He continued, "Tom Parker at school doesn't drink, and he's seventeen."

"Who cares about dumb Tom Parker? You idiot," Ted said, swigging down his beer. "This fog is disgusting," he said as he started down the path.

"Why did you come, anyway?" Rob yelled, pushing a hickory limb from his face as he moved forward, his shoulders hunched, his head down.

"'Because it suited me."

Rob wanted to spew, but knowing his brother was trying to ratchet up the unpleasantness a notch, he thought it best to avoid further words. He knew from the way the evening was going that any thought he had of getting closer to his brother was over.

Listening to Ted breath deeply, Rob thought hard of something meaningful to say. "You know, Ted, if we capture this monster on film, we'll be rich. Everyone will want to know about this." Rob extended his index finger and thumb in the air to form the side of an imaginary frame. "I can just see our pictures now right on the front of *National Geographic*."

"I thought this was to get a better grade."

"Yeah, I thought it would assure me an A in Mrs. Wilson's history class, but now it's something bigger."

"From what Mom says you better get those grades up. She's promised to make you live on the farm if you don't, and the last thing I need is a nosey little brother poking around."

"I won't," Rob said defiantly. He waved his light sideways as he stomped hard on the path, his feet stepping over decaying logs and around sticks and through brush. "I told the judge I'm living with Dad, and I'm gonna."

"Works for me," Ted said, bending his broad shoulders to duck under a scruffy pine.

As they neared the valley, Rob beamed his light upward and saw how huge the trees rimming the valley were. He listened as a soft wind gusted across the area to make the trees whisper. The only other sound was

Ted popping another can. Ted used his free hand to push a wandering trumpet vine from his path.

After taking another drink and wiping a hand across his mouth, Ted said, "We're here." He pointed his flashlight downward to a spot under a fanning oak and tossed his backpack to the ground.

With a sour face, Rob pulled his shirt away from his skin. He scanned the area, wondering again what strange force lured them. Maybe their journey into this brutal world was exhilarating, terrifying, and thus satisfying in an abnormal sort of way to both of them.

Rob noticed the foliage from the oaks along the edge of the woods where the trees made an opening to the valley. Flashing his light ahead, hoping to get a better look at Peter Bottom Cave, he felt evil forces pushing in on him, controlling him, taking him to a third dimension. Surrounding him were eerie, shadowy images moving in shapeless fashion. Thinking he was peering through the window of a bizarre world, he lowered his light. Was he ready to enter and uncover the truth? His headache pushed heavy on him as he rubbed his pounding temples. His body dripped with sweat. This surrealistic world was the same one of his nightmares, yet it was no dream. But in spite of his extreme fear, he did not turn back.

"You think the monster's real?" Rob asked.

The brightness from Ted's flashlight hit Rob's face. "Why in thunder are we out here wading around in the dark if you don't think it's real?"

"How come folks don't look for it then?" Rob asked, his mind gaining more control. Rob rubbed his eyes when Ted moved the light away.

"Don't ask me why they do what they do. The world's full of idiots and weirdos," Ted's eyes fixed tensely on the dark valley. "People want to believe what they see. Don't see it, they call it a lie, but it ain't no lie."

"I heard two guys looked for it once," Rob said, shining light around the campground, flashing it over the ground, through limbs, and to the ground again.

"It was in 1966," Ted said, his eyes peering into the darkness. "These two guys were riding horses. Something spooked them . . . threw them off. They claim they saw a creature walking upright–said it ran toward them."

"Do you think it happened?"

"Don't know," Ted said, his voice taking a lighter tone. "Don't know why they'd make it up either."

"What would you do if you saw it?"

"Snap this," Ted said, holding up a camera. "That's what we came for, isn't it? Then they will believe."

"Brave Teddy," Rob said, feigning a laugh. "But, I'll bet if you saw it right now, you'd run like the dickens, and I'd be hitting fast behind."

"We'll find out soon enough," Ted said, shining his light toward the valley. "That thing's out there."

Rob wondered if his brother were telling the truth. He had a gut feeling that Ted not only wanted to film the monster but had the same desire to face it head on. For the first time, Rob realized that he and Ted perhaps shared the same reason to see if the monster were real.

Rob chided himself for letting his imagination run so wild. There could be no truth to such thoughts. "It's so foggy. How we gonna film anything? Or see anything?"

"We'll worry about that when we have something to film."

"It's creepy," Rob said, despite himself.

"You're just too citified," Ted said, pulling out another beer and grabbing a ham sandwich. Opening the can, he took a long drink. Rob wasn't happy. Ted was hard enough to get along with when he wasn't drinking, and this was only going to make matters worse. Taking a sandwich from his backpack, Rob unwrapped it and sat cross-legged to eat, his flashlight the only source of light.

When they finished eating, Ted stood and stretched his five-foot-ten frame. Bending, he pulled the lantern from his backpack, set it on the ground, and lit it. "The light will draw mosquitoes. Hope you have plenty of bug spray," Ted said.

"Great. Now we gotta worry about West Nile virus too," Rob said, trying to lighten up the situation. "I have a new can," he added, holding it up before spraying a fine mist over his arms. "Geeze, why did I come on this stupid trip in the first place?" Rob muttered under his breath.

Startled that Ted had heard him, Rob wished he had said nothing when Ted came back with, "'Because you wanted to film the stupid o-l-e monster." Ted shoved his brother. "Now just get over it, sissy."

Having enough of Ted's verbal lashes, Rob yelled, "Who you calling sissy?" Standing, Rob grabbed Ted's shirt and pushed his brother back against a tree. Rob didn't know what power possessed him to suddenly act out in anger, but he didn't care either. He had taken all the abuse he was going to take. It was time to stand up to Ted. "You always think you're so smart, don't you? Sacrificing to stay with Mom and all. Well, you ain't half as smart as you think."

"Back off, bud, before I smash in your head," Ted said, getting a firm grip on his brother's blue shirt. "And, don't you ever shove me again, hear?"

Ted let go of Rob's shirt. He pushed his brother hard to the ground. Rob slumped against an oak tree. Ted popped the lid on another beer.

Through the fog, Rob watched the light of the lantern as it cast a small glow in the dark woods. Eyeing Ted, Rob was fully aware of how little he knew of the strange, perverse face that sat across from him. He had somehow been severed by life from his brother, and the separation seemed complete. Rob feared nothing could pull them together again.

Rob had a morbid thought. What if Ted were playing some kind of sick game? Rob had never known Ted to actually believe in monsters. Even as children when Rob told about his horrid nightmares, Ted always cast them off as childish dreams. Brewing on this new idea, Rob felt a burning rage crawl in him. Without thinking, he spouted out, "You know there ain't no monster here . . . you're just playing some sick-o game." Rob rose, his body tense. "Is this your latest way to make me look stupid?"

"I don't have to make you look stupid. You do a good job of that all by yourself." Ted laughed. "I admit that I thought this might be a good chance to get you in the woods. You need to learn a man's ways." Ted guzzled more beer.

"Mom'll be upset when she finds out."

"Well, she ain't gonna find out, now is she?" Ted stood, staring his brother straight in the eye.

Rob at first met his gaze without flinching. Seeing the angry red in Ted's eyes, Rob lowered his head. "Don't suppose."

Frowning, Rob watched Ted toss his empty can into the woods. He opened another.

"Sure you d-o-n't want a guzzle?" Ted's tone was sarcastic; his hand held an open can. His mouth was curled in a malicious grin.

Grabbing the can, Rob smelled it, then took a sip. He immediately spit it on the ground and threw the can. "It's nasty."

"It's a man's drink."

Defeated, Rob slumped against a tree, his spine hitting the hard bark. Rob let his anger subside as he chewed hard on a twig and threw a shaft of light around the area.

"Jeepers, what's that?" Rob suddenly whispered, struggling to stand. He crept forward, shoulders slumped, with his flashlight fanning over a large footprint.

Ted moved in, saying, "Some very large creature's been here." Rob looked at Ted before searching the thick darkness, his ears picking up a scraping sound in the bush. Rob's neck prickled with fear as the noise ceased and a death-like silence swallowed the valley.

With head tossed back, Ted took a long drink, saying, "Birds," but Rob noticed the tense jaw and tight, grim face.

Rob promised himself to stay alert for strange and unusual sounds or images. Putting a hand on his camera, he realized he couldn't film anything on such a dark, foggy night, even if he had something to film.

Deciding the mystery of Peter Bottom Cave probably couldn't be resolved in one night, Rob unrolled his sleeping bag. He picked up the knife he had packed and ran a forefinger over the sharp, shiny blade. He heard more muffled noises in the woods, so he slipped the knife next to his pillow. He quietly kicked off his shoes before knocking off a mosquito and crawled into his bed.

"You know, bro," Ted said in a teasing voice, "if there's a monster, and we run into it, things could get pretty ugly around here. Why, I bet the very minute we kick out this lantern that fiend will come inching in here . . . and I heard it has these big jaws that can swallow up the whole of darkness . . . gobble, gobble, gobble." Ted showed his teeth as he rolled over on all fours and crawled slowly toward the sleeping bag, a deep growl coming from his throat.

"Stop it." Rob's chest tightened.

Ted rolled over and laughed. Standing, he stumbled toward the lantern. "Just a flicker of this knob and, and it's all dark."

Angered at the antics of his brother, Rob pretended to be asleep.

Ted laughed. "Wonder which one he'll eat first?" He moved closer to Rob and stuck his fingers in his brother's ribs. Unlike the time when this childish gesture would have made Rob laugh, this time he had the urge to smack Ted's face. Instead he rolled the other way.

In the quiet of the night, Rob listened as Ted tossed another can into the woods before dropping off to sleep. Restless, Rob listened to the creatures, the owl, crickets, and squirrels. A small breeze stirred hot air as the foul smell from the valley intensified.

To ease his fear, Rob swept his flashlight around the woods one more time. Then, he saw what he had feared seeing all along. He was sure he hadn't imagined it. There was a flicker. Something passed through the trees. He listened to the mosquitoes buzzing in the air. His mind all but collapsed in fear. The sound of feet scraping the ground told him that whatever was in the woods was moving.

Rob slowly rolled on his arm, and with a shaky hand, he played the light around the camp again, his eye catching the shadow of something moving through the trees. His hand shook more as the wind blew stronger. The foul smell increased. Slowly standing, he moved quietly toward the trees and listened as a strange groaning sound grew louder. He heard muffled breathing, like that of an injured animal, yet it was different and was the strangest noise he had ever heard. He held his breath.

Forcing himself to peer into the woods, he saw a shadowy figure standing near the edge of the campsite, a figure so dimly in view that he wasn't sure if it were real. Keeping his eyes fixed on the shape, his heart raced as it crept forward. It soon entered the beam of light. Rob was horrified. The creature was white and hairy. It had the face of a man with a flat head and feet the size of a bear. When he looked up, he saw evil in the hideous dark, red-rimmed eyes that gazed back at him.

Scarcely breathing, Rob held the flashlight motionless. The figure in front of him made a groan. It moved toward the campsite to where Ted was sleeping out cold.

"Ted," Rob screamed, running in a rage toward the creature. A gust of hot wind blasted against his body—wind that came from nowhere and stung him to the bone. Rob whirled in midair. An unearthly shriek split the night sky as Rob's body whizzed past the apparition. Falling hard on his face, Rob collapsed in a heap. The hairy monster staggered closer to Ted. Rob panicked as a hazy, yellowish silhouette formed in the background.

Long shadows streamed across the earth and through the valley as Rob stared at the monster, watching it edge closer to Ted. Panic assailed Rob all over again. He didn't know what to do, but he had to save his brother. Seized with fear, Rob watched as the loathsome fiend reached a long clawed hand toward Ted.

Scrambling to his feet, Rob ran toward Ted, screaming, "We have to get outta here! Wake up! We gotta run!"

Ted rolled over and groaned. Rob turned to face the creature. He could smell the fiend's sweat, feel the anger. Rob grabbed the creature by the throat. The monster did not buckle under. It threw its full weight at Rob. Rob lost his footing and tumbled to the ground. The monster kicked him in the ribs. With the wind knocked out of him, Rob pulled in a deep breath.

Rob caught a glimpse of the creature as it moved again closer to Ted. Rob grabbed his knife and squeezed the handle tightly with both hands. Darkness thickened. The fog whirled in sheets, making it difficult for Rob to make out more than a distorted image of the shadowy phantom. With full force, Rob stood on feeble legs and swung the knife hard. His eyes strained to pierce the darkness. He saw only matted hair. Gruesome red eyes. Tightening his hold on the knife, he swung more wildly than before, yelling, "Who are you? What do you want here?"

With the knife clasped tightly in hand, with the fog fanning in enormous sweeps, Rob crept closer and jabbed the knife with a mighty force into the fiend's body. Rob heard Ted's blood-curdling scream and then more and more screams—from the monster, from Ted, the sounds all ringing in Rob's ears.

Squinting with a mighty force, Rob watched the shape before him grow more visible. To his horror, the beast had Ted's neck in an arm lock. A giant hairy fist was smashing Ted's face. Rivulets of blood streamed from Ted's forehead, his eyes, his chest. Rob felt weak. Gasping, he thought he would throw up. His chest knotted fiercely. He had to do something. Barely able to breathe, he tried screaming. Only rasping noises came from his throat.

The shrill sounds of "Do something! Rob! Do something!" as the monster pulled Ted into the valley were deafening. Falling backward, Rob covered his ears. The screams continued in the distance. Holding his pounding head, he could not move. "Ted . . . Ted!" he feebly yelled. His face was wet with tears, with sweat. He was nauseated, dizzy. He called again and again. There was nothing. Filled with terror, Rob looked hard into the darkness. He heard a groan. He felt his head spinning, aching in a tormenting pain as sweat continued to pour from his face. He called again. He stood, listening, but heard nothing but the blood rushing in his ears. No birds or squirrels. It was as if all of nature waited, lifeless, motionless, and still.

Knowing he could do nothing to save his brother, still holding his knife, Rob started to run, his burning tears hitting the dirt path. On wobbly legs, he somehow found the path that led to the farm. His mind raced with confusion as he saw again and again the ghostly face of his brother, the oozing blood. Closing his eyes, Rob knew the memory would live with him forever. The demon from the cave had engulfed his very being. He would never be free from its grip.

Weary and full of pain, Rob saw the sun's morning glow rising behind the farmhouse. Like death walking, he moved slowly forward, his shoulders slumped, his lungs ready to burst. Though exhausted, he held firmly to the knife as he dragged his body onward. Suddenly, the beast was again before him, laughing. There were no cuts on its body, no bloodstains on its matted white hair. Rob let out a violent scream as he clutched the knife and waved it madly at the beast. There was nothing there. The monster had disappeared.

As if to ward off the evil the monster held over him, Rob squeezed his right wrist with his left hand to force his fingers from the knife's handle. His hands shook violently. He could not budge his fingers. "The curse," he said, forcing the muscles in his hand to move. Through garbled speech, he mumbled over and over, "The curse . . . the awful curse."

As his eyes saw the gory, blood-spattered blade, he fell in horror to the ground. His fingers one by one slowly loosened from the knife. Pulling his knees to his chest, he rocked back and forth, his brain feverish, his thoughts jumbled and confused as he tried to recall the scene. All he saw was the blood streaming on Ted's face, the bloodstains on the knife's blade. His heart raced. He looked at the sun as it stretched lazily upward in the eastern sky. He screamed.

"He's out," Rob's mother said to the doctor as she settled in her chair beside her son's bed and folded her hands across her stomach.

Dr. Smith was leaning forward now, listening to the boy's chest with his stethoscope. He pulled his eyebrows together in a frown. "Has there been any change?" he asked.

She shook her head. "I can't forget the way he looked . . . his arms wrapped around his drawn up legs, his head lowered. His body shook with force as he rocked back and forth," she said, chewing her lower lip. "He was terrified, and he pointed at Peter Bottom Cave. Just pointed. That's all. And it's been six days." Her voice was full of worry and helplessness. "Look at him. He isn't going to pull through, is he?"

"Can't say for sure," Dr. Smith, pushing his glasses to his wrinkled forehead. "I've seen cases like this before. Sometimes they get okay. Sometimes . . ."

Mrs. Callahan let the tears run down her cheeks. "First Ted and now Rob. How can I lose both my boys in one week?"

Dr. Smith clapped her shoulder. "I'm so very sorry," he said, shaking his head.

"It was a knife wound," Mrs. Callahan said between sobs, "and . . . Rob had that bloody . . ." She covered her face with both hands, her fingers digging at her forehead.

"I'm sure there's a good explanation," Dr. Smith said, "if only Rob could talk."

Mrs. Callahan nodded her head before raising it and wiping her swollen, red eyes. "If only they hadn't gone after that thing," she said, her voice bitter. Taking a deep breath to try to maintain some semblance of control, she continued. "Why, everyone knows about the curse. I warned them a dozen times. I should have said more."

"Don't blame yourself," Dr. Smith said. He peered at her over the rim of his glasses. "Some people just can't resist looking for strange things. Personally, I've always thought that thing was evil. Never wanted to know much about it, but young boys, well, they're more curious, I suppose."

"It's the curse," Mrs. Callahan said. "My boys were cursed." Her face turned ashen white when she glanced again at her youngest son, his body twitching as his fingers clung to the edge of the iron bed.

SHIRLEEN SANDO BIOGRAPHY

Serving six years as president of Skyward Publishing, Shirleen Sando handled and supervised a variety of jobs, including marketing, editing, and book production as well as writing articles, press releases, and other marketing materials.She currently serves as a publishing consultant for this company. For three years, she served as managing editor for the *Arkansas State Literary Magazine*.

Her first publication, *Beyond Low Fat Baking*, was a labor of love to encourage healthier eating in America. She serves as a director for Ozark Writers, Inc.; she is newsletter editor for Authorsource.biz; and she has two new online businesses with BestSoy.com being the first. Most recently she is working on a documentary, *The Enemy Within: Bipolar Disorders*; writing a book series with two authors, tentatively titled, *The Secret Lives of Young Detectives*; and co-authoring two children's television scripts that await production.

She has taught English and literature at Arkansas State University and the University of Memphis. She has previously worked with highly gifted children and has an interest in writing teen and preteen stories and television scripts. She is working with a team to develop a kid-friendly, interactive, educational website for junior high age kids.

Someone at the writers' retreat believed that the manuscript of a potential best-selling novel was worth killing for. But she made a crucial mistake.

SOLITUDE

by Stephen D. Rogers

Page carefully walked through the snow towards Helen's cabin. Upon arriving, she knocked, pushed open the door, and then screamed.

Marilyn, the first to arrive, had the presence of mind to keep the other women of the writers' retreat away from the cabin. "We need to preserve the scene," she said, switching from her present role as writer to detective. "Bring Page to the community room and fix her some strong tea. I'll be there shortly."

As soon as she saw the others heading for the community room, Marilyn stepped back into the cabin.

Helen was lying in the middle of the floor. Her body was still warm and there was no sign of rigor mortis.

White sediment lay at the bottom of the glass on the desk. Next to the glass was an empty plastic bag. Front and center was a strip of paper. "I'll never be a writer."

Marilyn sniffed. She could smell smoke.

In the bathroom, Marilyn discovered the toilet was filled with ash and burned bits of paper. She touched several pieces and stuck her finger in the thickest pockets of ash.

Then she went back outside and took a moment to survey the area before joining the rest of the group.

For the first time this month, the women were silent, scattered about the community room wearing pajamas under their coats. Only Page, the early bird, was dressed.

They turned almost in unison as Marilyn entered the room. "I'm sorry, but Helen is dead."

Marilyn raised her hands to quiet the sudden uproar and was glad to see it worked. While she'd taken charge of the situation out of uniform before, she'd never done it in her bunny slippers. "It appears Helen might have overdosed. She left a note."

Josie, the Ozark Writers Retreat director, took her arm from around Page's shoulder and stood. "What should we do?"

"I'll head down the mountain until I get reception on my phone. While I'm gone, you should all stay away from Helen's cabin. In fact, you should remain here."

The attendees nodded, faces white and eyes wide.

Marilyn walked over to Page. "How are you feeling?"

"I still can't believe it."

Marilyn knelt down beside her. "What made you go to Helen's cabin this morning?"

"Yesterday after dinner she asked me to stop over as soon as I woke up. She was hoping to have her final chapter ready and she wanted me to read it as soon as possible."

"How did she act?"

Page shrugged. "You know Helen."

Marilyn nodded. Helen had been the resident tortured artist. While the rest of the women here were professionals or full-time mothers, Helen had been sole beneficiary of her parents' insurance policy. Four hours into the retreat, Marilyn decided Helen would have been wise to sink the money into therapy.

"Did you touch anything?"

Page shook her head.

"Was the door open?"

"No, but I knocked first."

"So you did touch the door."

"I guess I did."

"Anything else?"

"Once I saw her laying there, I froze."

"You're doing just fine." Marilyn patted Page's knee. "Did you notice any footprints?"

"No. I was surprised to see it snowed overnight and I was thinking how beautiful the unbroken snow seemed."

Josie interrupted. "Why are you asking about footprints?"

"I'm trying to determine if Helen was alone when she died. It started snowing at midnight and Helen hasn't been dead more than three hours."

"I thought you said there was a note."

"All deaths outside of a hospital are treated as suspicious deaths and need to be investigated as such."

"Are you suggesting someone might have killed Helen?"

"I'm saying that we can't jump to conclusions. Given the state of the body and the temperature of the ashes I found, I'd guess Helen died between two and three hours ago. If there was someone in her cabin at the time, the person would have left footprints."

Josie licked her lips. "What ashes?"

Marilyn knew she shouldn't be discussing these details with the group but after living with the women for almost two weeks now, she had trouble resisting their questions. "There's burned paper in Helen's toilet."

"You don't think she burned her book, do you?" Terri, the professor from Southwest Missouri State University, appeared as disturbed by that thought as she was by Helen's death.

"I don't know what she burned."

"Perhaps it was the chore schedule." Doreen's joke brought a welcome round of chuckles and Marilyn could feel the tension in the room lift a little.

She stood. "I have to go make that call. Remember, nobody leave the community room. We don't want to be accused of tampering with evidence."

Outside, Marilyn confirmed that only two sets of tracks led to Helen's cabin, one from Page's and one from Marilyn's. Another set of tracks showed their separate trips to the community room. Marilyn returned to her cabin to dress.

The brochure for the Ozark Writers Retreat promised two weeks of solitude to write within a community of support.

Marilyn, her romance novel firmly under way, had only recently begun to think of herself as a writer instead of a Springfield police officer who dabbled with words. And now here she was playing cop again.

She slipped her handcuffs into her back pocket.

Someone knocked at the door.

"Come in."

Terri entered. "I know you said we should stay in the community room, but there's something I think you should know."

"Is it about Helen?"

Terri nodded. "Helen never showed me what she was writing, probably believing it too fine for my fantasy tastes. She did talk to me quite a bit though. She was one of those people who expected to be recognized only after her death, and she thought I could give her insights on how education decided what works to canonize."

"Did she suggest that her own death was on the horizon?"

"Not in so many words but then I don't think she really cared. The important thing, however, is that Helen would never have burned her manuscript. Her whole self-image was based on the idea that her work would outlive her."

"Perhaps her latest project convinced her that it wouldn't happen. Maybe she decided she didn't have what it took."

Terri shook her head. "There's something my mother says: a dead skunk still stinks. Helen may have been capable of taking her own life, but she would never have destroyed her own writing."

"Thanks for telling me."

"I better get back to the community room. I told the others I was getting a blanket for Page."

Marilyn raised a hand in farewell and turned to the notebooks on her desk. As much as she wanted to finish and publish her romance, Marilyn thought of writing as a hobby. She certainly didn't value what she wrote above her own life.

Never mind believing mere words justified murder.

Marilyn went back outside in time to see Terri return to the community room carrying a blanket. Then she knelt down to examine each set of footprints more closely.

The path from Page's cabin to Helen's was different from the rest, the prints less distinct as though she'd carefully stepped in the same places more than once.

After taking several deep breaths, Marilyn walked back to the community room. She had something to do before she called the authorities.

Page was wrapped in Terri's blanket, crouched over a steaming cup of tea.

Marilyn ignored Josie's questioning look and stopped in front of Page. "Why did you do it?"

"What do you mean?"

"I figured out your trick with the snow. That's the real reason you went to Helen's cabin before the rest of us were awake. You had to make sure nobody saw your tracks before you traveled the path for the third time."

"My one original thought and it's probably been in the police textbooks for a hundred years. I couldn't sleep and it started to snow. That's what gave me the idea."

Marilyn repeated her question. "Why?"

"Helen was the most beautiful writer I'd ever read, but she didn't appreciate her gift, know how to run with it. She wasn't interested in landing an agent, meeting with editors. She just wanted to write. Helen told me she had closets full of manuscripts that just sat there gathering dust."

"So you thought you'd take one."

"Wouldn't you? If you knew you'd never write a perfect book so effortlessly, wouldn't you have done the same thing?"

"No. And if you ask the other writers here, you'd receive the same answer." The other women were too visibly shocked to say anything.

Page sighed before straightening. "I told Helen to write out that she'd never be a writer to get it out of her system. She was weak. She didn't deserve her skill." Page shrugged off the blanket. "I think she might even have suspected what I was doing when I brought her the glass of water and suggested she drink."

"It's still murder." Marilyn took the handcuffs from her pocket. "You're under arrest."

STEPHEN D. ROGERS BIOGRAPHY

Over two hundred and fifty of Stephen's stories and poems have been selected to appear in over a hundred publications including the mystery anthologies, *Hardboiled*, Betancourt & Company (www.wildside-press.com) and *Down These Dark Streets*, Cyber-Pulp (www.come.to/cyberpulp). He writes the bi-monthly column "Murder Ink" at Writing-World.com and teaches Mystery Short Stories for WritersCollege.com. When not setting down words, he is busy keeping www.stephen-drogers.com safe for visitors.

*Professor Collier gave the folks of Beulah more
than the ability to sing in harmony. Even his disappearance helped.*

SONG OF THE DEVIL

by Kay Hively

Three long thin fingers pinched the chalk and
scratched it up and down the dusty blackboard. Every
eye in the small room watched in wonder as the bony
fingers moved methodically across the board, drawing
odd shapes.

It was warm, but the sun was hanging low and
would soon drop behind the far mountain. At dusk, the
air would always refresh. But even a cooling mountain
breeze would not keep away the heat that was soon to
build up inside the old Beulah schoolhouse.

The hand dropped from the blackboard and
Professor Wilfred Collier turned to face the crowd that
filled every seat in the schoolroom.

"These seven symbols—or shapes—are all you will
ever need to know," said Wilfred Collier in a high and
squeaky voice. "If you can learn these seven shapes,
you can sing in the best choir in heaven. It's this simple—do, re, mi, fa, so, la, ti, do."

Picking up a pointed stick, Professor Collier tapped
on the first odd-shaped symbol on the blackboard.
"Repeat after me," he commanded of his audience,
which in unison snapped to attention.

"Do," the man piped.

No one responded.

The professor rapped the blackboard again and shouted, "Repeat after me."

Once again, the crowd straightened in their seats and many pushed their tongues around their hot dry lips.

"Do!" Mr. Collier repeated again, and a loud response came back, "Do!"

The stage was set and the lesson began. In a very short time, the frail young singing school teacher in the rumpled black suit had everyone in the hot room going up and down the musical scale—singing, "Do, re, mi, fa, so, la, ti, do."

Under the persistent tutelage of Mr. Collier, the crowd was soon in near perfect harmony, and they raised the temperature of the small room with their rendition of "What a Friend We Have in Jesus."

Although many of the singers could not read one word from the books in their hands, they never missed a word on the page. Long ago they had memorized the old gospel songs. Even the smallest children could sing them as easily as their parents. But in what seemed like only a short moment, especially among the illiterate, there was a different feeling as they sang the old songs from a book.

Now, by actually using a hymnal, they could read the shape notes as they sang. Those who never went to school suddenly had a feeling of power and accomplishment—just from holding and using the songbook.

Mr. Wilfred Collier was a godsend to those who could not read.

He put the power of the book in their hands.

As the music rose to the open beams of the little schoolhouse, one distinct voice near the front of the room had a bird-like quality. The voice of sixteen-year-old Mary Ellen Hunt was a familiar sound at the schoolhouse, which on Sunday also served as the Beulah Community Church. Mary Ellen was the songbird of the congregation.

But three rows behind the sixteen-year-old songbird was another voice that also stood out from the crowd. That lovely tenor voice that overshadowed even the songbird belonged to Young Bill Todd.

Every girl in the building cast a secretive eye in the direction of the handsome lad everyone called "Young Bill." Even the old matrons smiled as his voice rolled around the walls of the schoolhouse.

But Young Bill's beautiful voice was seldom heard in polite company. He did not attend church each Sunday. On any Sabbath morning, he could usually be found in some haystack or barnyard, sleeping off the Saturday night fun he had enjoyed with his friends. So, when he did attend any public gathering where singing was encouraged, it was a musical treat for everyone in the neighborhood.

"Let's try another song, folks," Mr. Collier suggested. He called out a page number and for those who could not read, he announced the song title, "Nothing but the Blood."

With their new feelings of power, the illiterates fumbled to find the right pages by stealing glances at the books of their neighbors. Just a quick look at the correct page in their neighbors' books allowed them to find a duplicate page in their own hymnal.

Then, once again, using the power of the shape note, the singing surged into high gear. The new "sight readers" pushed their fingers over the strange shapes, reading every note and adding gusto to their voices.

Young Bill opened his book to the appropriate page, but his eyes were not on the song—they were focused on the blonde head of hair that sat three rows in front of him. Even as he sang, it was her voice that he heard, and his mind struggled with the idea of a duet. What music they could make together.

But the strong broad back that sat beside the blonde head would never allow a drunk to call on his sweet daughter songbird. Young Bill knew the penalty for any attempt to approach the cabin where the Hunt family lived on Devil's Ridge.

Over the course of five nights, the thin pale-skinned singing teacher became endeared to the entire community. With his modest but strict demeanor, Wilfred Collier gave an entire community confidence and taught them to sing on key. Furthermore, like the expectation of Santa's visit on Christmas Eve, Wilfred Collier had promised a great finale. It was a sure bet that no one would miss the last night at the singing school. Seats would be hard to find for those who didn't arrive at least a half-hour before the appointed starting time on Saturday night.

Saturday morning was cool. Fog gathered in the low spots and along the creeks. Everyone in the Beulah community started the day early. Mary Ellen, pleased at the progress her voice had made in the singing school, sang as she gathered two baskets of tomatoes from the garden. Water in the old black kettle came to a full boil just as she brought the fruit to the yard. Stooped over to place each tomato in the kettle, she sang again, and wondered what it would be like to stand next to Young Bill for a duet.

She was surprised to see Young Bill coming each night to the singing school. The only music Professor Collier presented was church music, and Mary Ellen didn't think Young Bill had much interest in that. He always seemed more interested in the "fiddle and jug" music that was heard back in the woods around the moonshine stills.

Even more surprising than seeing Young Bill at the singing school was seeing her own father finally speak to the boy with the fine tenor voice. As each session of the school passed, more and more church members welcomed Young Bill into the fold.

But it was Saturday and Mary Ellen wondered if she would hear that voice behind her come sunset. Or would it be singing to the fiddle and jug?

She added two more sticks of wood to the fire. Then squatting beside the kettle, she watched as the tomatoes bobbled in the hot water. Already, many were starting to peel as the water bubbled around the bright red tomatoes. She had her glass jars sitting nearby in a tub of hot water. Since she was just a child, she had watched her mother can tomatoes each summer. Now that her mother lay in the old cemetery, she was determined to carry on in her mother's place around the house.

East of Devil's Ridge where the Hunt cabin stood, Young Bill was fixing a fence along a lonely stretch of meadow that people had always called "Hell's Gate." The sinister names in the area were not weighed heavily upon by the people around Beulah. Such names were very common. The devil must have been on their minds when the first settlers came to these hills, for they had a habit of naming places after him and his fiery hell. Within a two-hour walk, Young Bill could find Devil's Washtub, Hell Cave, and Devil's Back Porch.

While Young Bill worked on the fence, traffic passed by the meadow as people made their way to town for shopping. Young people on horseback and families in wagons waved to the fence mender as they rode into Beulah. Among those who passed were the Kimbel brothers, Ben and Harvey. They stopped to talk about a new source of refreshment the gang planned to test that night. A new still, they said, had been set up on Haskill Ridge.

Laughingly, they told him to get his work done early. They said he would need to collect his wages from Tom Thaxton and be there in time for the first jar out of the copper tubes.

But Young Bill had second thoughts about this particular Saturday night. He wanted one more chance to sit behind that beautiful blonde hair. And he wanted one more chance to shake the hand of Sam Hunt.

Ben and Harvey could not believe Young Bill's admission that he was going to singing school on

Saturday night. They could not imagine him waiting a whole week before visiting the new still on Haskill Ridge.

"You'll never do it." Ben laughed. "You'll never spoil your reputation. You are the one man who can hold his liquor better than anyone on the mountain."

Young Bill just shook his head and repeated that he wouldn't be with the boys that night. He even confessed that the singing school teacher had asked him to sing a solo. He was going to do it.

"Just wait until the boys hear this," Ben Kimbel laughed. "Hard drinking Young Bill Todd would rather go sing in church than party on Saturday night. No one will believe that."

Though Young Bill felt the red creeping up his neck, he said nothing.

"Don't worry, by eight o'clock tonight he'll come to his senses," Harvey sputtered. "No snooty girl ever tasted as sweet as liquor fresh from the still. Just you wait and see."

Ben and Harvey mounted their horses and rode away, yelling and laughing at Young Bill as he returned to his fence mending.

All week, as he worked to fix Tom Thaxton's fence, he had time to think. Mostly he thought of Mary Ellen and imagined a future with her at his side. That would never be as long as her father disapproved of him and his drinking. Not only that, he knew he needed money to have a life that any woman would accept. That thought kept him working each time Tom had a job for him to do.

Late that afternoon, with the sun searching for the horizon, people gathered at the Beulah schoolhouse. Everyone was eager for a long night of singing and for whatever special event the singing school teacher had planned. Hurrying to get out of the wagons and buggies, ladies made their way into the building, vying for the same seats they had occupied for five nights.

Young Bill made his way into the crowded room. Everyone made room for the best voice in the building.

By seven o'clock, the schoolhouse was so full it didn't seem that another soul could be squeezed inside. Everyone was ready—everyone except Professor Collier.

The singing school teacher was missing—nowhere to be found.

Patience not being a common characteristic of Ozark hill people, folks soon became restless. Restlessness quickly turned to concern for the stranger who had come into their midst. Finally, concern melted into action.

Sam Hunt left his seat by his daughter and stepped to the front of the room. He called on three men to go with him, supposing the professor had somehow gotten lost or had become confused walking through the woods to the schoolhouse. He said they should search for him before darkness fell.

As the men turned to leave, Sam Hunt pointed at Young Bill and asked him to go with the search party. Mary Ellen blushed to see her father's sudden attachment to Bill.

Through the schoolhouse windows, the jilted singers watched the five men mount horses and ride to the west. Everyone knew that Professor Collier was staying in a small abandoned house on Tom Thaxton's farm. The Thaxton family weren't church-going people, but for a few coins, the old farm house was made available to the wandering music teacher.

While they waited, the women in the schoolhouse passed time with neighborhood gossip. Most of the men drifted outside to smoke their pipes and whittle tree limbs. Children begged to go outside and play.

At a gallop, the five searchers made their way over wagon roads and horse trails looking for the lost professor. Within fifteen minutes the search party had made its way to the cabin where the singing teacher was housed.

Dismounting, Sam Hunt walked up on the small front porch. Carefully he pushed the door open.

Inside the dark room, everything was in place. A few items of clothing hung from a peg and an empty suitcase sat on a broken down chair. A pallet on the floor was undisturbed.

"He's not here," Sam Hunt said as he emerged from the cabin.

The other men merely shook their heads as they sat on their mounts and pondered the fate of the singing school teacher.

"Let's get back to the school and keep our eyes and ears open as we go," Sam Hunt said. "It'll be dark soon and we'll have to give it up. We might as well go back. Our families are waiting."

Soon the five men returned to the Beulah school. Though everyone was eager for news, the men had nothing to offer.

Inside the schoolhouse, Sam Hunt took the floor and asked what people wanted to do.

Matthew Murphy, elder in the church, called for a prayer that the lost professor would be safe. Then most people agreed that the best thing to do was to spend the evening singing, just as Professor Collier would have wanted. They could start a new search at daybreak.

Elder Murphy, still in control of the meeting, raised his hand for quiet and then recommended that Young Bill take the professor's place and lead the singing.

This suggestion was met with wide approval from everyone, except Young Bill.

"Folks," he said, "I don't know how to lead a singing. I'm not a teacher."

"But you have the finest voice," a female at the back of the room called out.

"You can do it, Bill," came another voice from the back row.

"But, I'm too nervous to stand up here and lead you folks," Young Bill protested.

Suddenly a voice, coming from three rows in front of Young Bill, spoke up, "I'll stand with you. We'll do it together."

A great round of applause broke out. With an approving nod from Sam Hunt, the two young people left their seats and moved to the front of the room.

Performing as if they had done this all their lives, the young couple soon had the rafters ringing with the joyous sounds of the gospel. The music continued long into the night, interrupted only by an occasional pause for prayer as everyone thought about the little man who had come to Beulah and made them singers.

As the night deepened, small sleepy children were laid on blankets and shawls along the floor while their parents remained swept up in the power of the music. Influenced by the youths in charge of the night, most of the music was happy and upbeat, but an occasional somber number stretched the vocal abilities of the happy singers.

Professor Collier would have been proud—had he been able to attend.

Even though Young Bill and Mary Ellen could not get thoughts of the professor out of their minds, it became a night they would always remember. The mixing of their voices was music unlike any that had ever been heard in Beulah. Often, the beauty of their harmony so intrigued the other singers that everyone hushed and let the two voices blend into one. The angels themselves would have been jealous.

Late in the night, when most of the voices were exhausted and the moon was high in the sky, sleepy-headed children were bedded down in wagons and laid across mothers' laps. The singing school was closed. Patient horses and mules started on their way home.

Too awed by their experience, Mary Ellen and Young Bill could not even speak to each other. It was a time not for talk, but for thoughts that could not be publicly expressed.

When Young Bill finally lay down in his bunk that night, he mulled over the fate of Professor Collier. He knew the woods at night could be dangerous for a stranger. With all that had occurred this week, he became almost sick to think that something had happened to the professor. Only because of the singing school had he been able to win some respect from the community—and from Sam Hunt—and from Mary Ellen.

As Young Bill wrestled in his mind the disappearance of Professor Collier, his thoughts turned to the Kimbel brothers and the other Saturday night rowdies. More than bears or mountain lions, a stranger should fear young drunks who have too much liquor and like to have fun at the expense of others.

The mere thoughts of the Kimbels and their drunken friends meeting up with Professor Collier sent chills through Young Bill. He covered his face with his hands to stave off the dark thoughts that went through his mind.

Sleep would not come. All night long he had visions of the singing school teacher. None of the visions were pleasant. In the dark, he rose out of bed, dressed, and moved out onto the porch to sit in his father's chair. Just as Big Bill Todd had learned to do, his son rocked slowly. The chair's gentle sway had a calming affect on Big Bill, and in recent days, Young Bill had learned the power of the rocking chair.

He had promised to meet some of the men in the schoolyard at daybreak to begin the search again.

As he sat waiting, Young Bill longed to hear the first song of the birds that flittered each morning around the cabin. Many mornings the birds that seemed to be proclaiming that the sun was on its way had awakened him. But the longer he sat, the more he fought the ugly visions that paraded through his mind. He had seen only one man dead, but he had a strong feeling that death was waiting today.

At the first sound of a cardinal singing in the grapevines, Young Bill left the porch and went to the small barn across the yard. He led his horse outside where there was enough light to throw the saddle on his horse's back and cinch the strap. Then down the trail he rode, covering the two miles to the schoolhouse in five minutes.

No one was there. The sun was only halfway above the horizon. But, he decided, waiting in the schoolyard was easier than sitting at home on the porch.

Waiting for the other men, Young Bill played over in his mind where his old drinking friends might have gone on Haskill Ridge. Following the map in his mind, he imagined riding down the hill to the west and then turning to go past Hell's Gate where he fixed fence all week. From the meadow it would be up a small trail and over Black Bear Hump to the foot of Haskill Ridge. It wouldn't take long to find a still up there. Actually, Young Bill thought, the trail would probably be littered with sleeping bodies of those men who couldn't make it all the way home. Had it not been for the singing school, his own body might be littering the path.

But, Young Bill feared, that path also might contain another body—a body that probably never experienced the excitement of the fiddle and the jug.

One by one, five other men rode into the schoolyard to form the search party. Sam Hunt took the lead. He split them into two groups, sending Young Bill and two others over the same trail they had ridden the day before. Sam and two men headed farther south over a trail that eventually makes its way to the empty farmhouse.

Young Bill fell in behind the two older men. Silently they rode, occasionally casting their route in an arc to search in brush or over the side of an overlook. But Young Bill, believing the search was fruitless, fell farther and farther behind. In a short time, he was back far enough to change his direction. Quickly he took up the trail he had envisioned the night before. He had to find the location of the new moonshine still on Haskill Ridge.

Once away from his companions, Young Bill headed for Hell's Gate. Slowly he walked his horse along the fence he had worked on all week. Becoming completely familiar with all the area along the fence, he watched for any sign of change or disturbance in the bushes and grass. He found nothing at Hell's Gate.

At the end of the meadow, Young Bill located the trail that led up to Black Bear Hump. Along the route he saw fresh prints and broken twigs. It was obvious that the Saturday night rowdies had been that way. But had they gone up to the still and all come back? And what about Professor Collier? Could he have mistaken this trail as the route to the schoolhouse? Or, he hated to think it, could the singing school teacher have been forced up this trail?

Young Bill continued pushing his horse up the steep bank until the slope became too severe. Dismounting, he moved his horse a few feet off the trail and securely tied him to a small tree.

On foot, he worked his way to the top of the hump and, as he expected, he soon came upon a snoring body. Harvey Kimbel lay on his back, his mouth wide open. Even from a good distance, Young Bill could smell the liquor and hear the snoring.

Pushing further on, Bill once more heard the unmistakable sound of drunken sleep. "I guess this will be Ben Kimbel or some of the other boys," Young Bill muttered as he moved closer to the sound.

In an almost humorous mound of bodies, Young Bill found his Saturday night buddies piled on top of each other where they had fallen in their intoxicated stupor. In great heaving breaths, the men slept off their Saturday night's adventure. Albert Dunn, the biggest of the lot, lay sprawled out on top of the entire pile of bodies.

"It must have been some kind of liquor that still put out," Young Bill said as he looked in disgust at the tangled pile of humanity.

Knowing there was nothing he could do for the sleeping men, he turned to make his way back to the base of Black Bear Hump. That's when he noticed a shoe he did not recognize—a dress shoe, not like the rough leather boots his friends wore.

Quickly he pushed the big body of Albert Dunn aside and there, as hung over as all the rest, was Professor Wilfred Collier. Young Bill could hardly believe what he was seeing. The singing school teacher was as drunk as any man lying along the trail. And, for such a frail little man, he was snoring louder than anyone else.

Young Bill bent over and raised the professor's head. "Wake up, Professor," he said as he gently shook the little man. "Wake up."

Slowly, two dark eyes came open. The professor blinked several times and then smiled a silly grin. "Is that you, Young Bill?" the singing teacher asked in a slurred voice.

"Yes, it's me," Young Bill answered. "What in the world are you doing here?"

Once again, a silly grin slide across the man's face. "Well, you know Young Bill, I'm not really sure. I think I am on my way home from a party. Did you go to the party?"

"No, I didn't go to the party," Young Bill answered. "I went to the singing school."

"The singing school?" Professor Collier asked.

"Was I at the singing school?"

"No, you weren't there," Young Bill said. "You went to a party. I had to lead the singing school."

Professor Collier slowly raised his hand, smiled another grin, and slapped Young Bill on the chest. "And I'll bet you did a darn good job too," he sputtered. "Do you ever go to parties?"

"I used to," Young Bill said. "I used to."

"You know, Young Bill," the singing teacher said, "I bet you sang like an angel last night. And you know what else, I sang like the devil."

Convinced that the professor was probably not in any danger, Young Bill lowered him back onto the pile of snoring drunks and returned to the search party, which had returned to the schoolhouse.

Once he told the story, the men had a good laugh. They all agreed that the singing teacher could find his own way home just like all the others who had inaugurated the new still on Haskill Ridge.

Young Bill was glad he was not sleeping in that groggy pile on Black Bear Hump. He smiled to think of how last night he and the singing school teacher had traded places—and, for once, how he had gotten the best of a swap.

Folks around Beulah never saw Professor Wilfred Collier again. He carried on, going from town to town teaching music and selling songbooks. He soon forgot about Beulah, but the folks there never forgot him because music was not all he brought to them. He brought love, hope, friendship, and a feeling of confidence that had long been missing in Beulah.

KAY HIVELY BIOGRAPHY

Kay Hively, Neosho, Missouri, is a free-lance writer. She has been a feature writer and columnist for the *Neosho Daily News* for twenty-five years. She has written or co-written several local history books, including the highly successful *Red, Hot and Dusty: Tales of Camp Crowder*. She is also the co-author, with Albert E. Brumley Jr., of *I'll Fly Away*, the biography of Albert E. Brumley, a gospel songwriter who lived and worked in the Missouri Ozarks. Recently she has begun writing gospel songs. Three songs appeared on a Grammy-nominated duet album featuring Albert E. Brumley Jr. and Merle Haggard. She is the author of fourteen historical children's serial stories published by the Missouri Press Association. These stories are running in newspapers all over the United States. One of these stories, "Hannah's Diary," was published in book form in 2003.

A new book (tentatively entitled *Ozark Inventors*) will be published by the University of Missouri Press.

Is any act justified to keep the cups of coffee coming? Even murder?

MORNING COFFEE

by Betty Craker Henderson

Slapping a hefty tip onto the tabletop, I called out to Hannah and headed for the register. " I'm awake now, 'Mother.'" She laughed and rang up my breakfast tab. She likes it when I'm happy.

I watched a pair of customers exchange patronizing smiles. The regulars expect the daily routine, but strangers have no clue to the necessity behind the levity.

If I don't get my morning coffee, I'm a total wreck. Believe me. Nobody can live with me. My head hurts like fury, and my brain does strange things.

Hannah is the rope connecting me to my life preserver.

Today would be a good one, I hoped, though most are not. Hannah had tanked me up nicely before turning in my unchanging order—a soft egg, orange juice, dry toast. And then of course, more coffee. Always. More coffee. She fussed around for a bit because there was no grape jelly and scurried off to the kitchen to bring back a fork with sharp tines. I get cross when I'm handed a dull fork.

Yes, yes. I'll admit it. I suppose she spoils me. Well, I'm not the only one. Sometimes I watch her when she's busy with other customers. It really irks me to see her making those same nice gestures to others. But

I guess I have to go along with it. After all, I don't own her.

When I was young I didn't eat breakfast. And was I cranky! Ask anyone who knew me. Cranky probably isn't strong enough. Crabby. Cross. Irritable. Words don't do justice to the foul mood I'm in without food . . . soaked, you know, with potent black coffee.

Here in Scud, Arkansas, I'm known as that grumpy old broad with a book. My temper is notorious. Old geezers, little children, and dogs avoid me like the plague. Each day I sit in my booth (you notice I say *my* booth) and read. And slug away at my hot strong coffee.

Mornings are an abomination. I'm a night person. I'm a writer too, but that comes second. Reading at breakfast helps me through the day and into the evening. In fact, I read all morning. That's how I get a focus on things. It helps the bad times pass more quickly. Then, on the good days, when my head isn't pounding with wicked thoughts, and when I'm really wide awake, alive once more, I apply backside to chair and my brain begins, at last, to function. Mornings, it doesn't work at all.

After years of suffering and making others pay for it, I've found a good breakfast with a quart of hot black coffee works wonders.

As I said earlier, Hannah is the one who keeps things moving along. She pets me and soothes me and nearly drowns me with coffee. I couldn't get along without her. She is an absolute essential in my life.

That's why, when she mentioned something about a trip to Kansas City, my ears quivered. I pick up on bad news really fast.

It's surprising how much stuff you overhear, even while reading. Usually good stuff, but not always. Like today.

I stewed all day and into the nighttime hours, becoming angrier and angrier. Writing was impossible and production came to a screeching halt. By late evening, my head was pounding. Hannah's short comment was already ruining my life.

Early the next morning, lost sleep and ongoing anger had combined to make me a jittering wreck.

Right away Hannah knew something was wrong. "Here you go," she said, putting the cup gently before me. "Coffee time."

A short surge of gratitude flooded my body. It smelled wonderful. I took the first welcome swig, but I refused to meet her eyes.

"Got a problem this morning, hon?" she asked, as she hit the cup a second time a few minutes later. She straightened my juice glass and added several fresh napkins. She knows I need lots of napkins.

"Hey, hang on for a minute," I said, attempting to be civil, but seething inside. "What's this I hear about a vacation? Why would anyone with a spark of intelligence want to leave the Ozarks and go to a place like Kansas City?"

"Oh, is that what it is? You don't need to worry." She smiled. "You'll be taken care of, dearie. I know you need your coffee." Her short blond hair fell down over her eyes as she filled the cup to the brim again. "I haven't had any time off for over a year. These new waitresses never seem to work out for early morning." She sighed. "I'm about worn out, but there's a new girl starting tomorrow. This time I think we've got it licked. Once she learns the routine, I'm going to take off for a fun-filled week playing the slot machines in the riverside casinos. Hey, Kansas City, look out for me! Here I come!" She danced a quick little jig of delight as she moved on to the next booth.

I managed a weak smile. After all, I thought, Hannah does look after my needs. She deserves a little time to herself. Surely I can get along for a few days.

But by the second morning I was totally stressed. Worry and no sleep had about finished me off. That old familiar headache hammered nonstop within my temples and around the base of my skull. My eyes felt as if they would pop out at any minute. It was really bothering me that Hannah might be gone—for any reason. Nasty black thoughts swirled around in the thick muck of brain resting on my pillow. Shoving them away, I pulled on wrinkled khakis and an old sweatshirt.

"Patience," I told myself aloud. "Let's give the new waitress a chance to work out." There was a remote possibility things would be all right. Far be it from me to put my needs before those of someone nice like my Hannah.

Somehow I made it to the diner. Sliding into my booth, I blindly waited for my first cup of hot, black, satisfying caffeine.

Oh, my God! My fears were coming true. The Nightmare on Elm Street was trailing after my personal waitress. Blowsy, with frizzy purple hair—its black roots standing an inch off her scalp, loaded down with cheap jewelry, her legs rattling with gaudy ankle bracelets, she was chomping on a jawful of gum. She reeked of nicotine.

"Mornin'." Her tone was dull, monotone, and uninteresting. Hannah watched, apprehensive, as coffee splashed into my cup and across the tabletop.

"This is Gilda." Her voice sounded nervous but sort of proud at the same time. "You'll like her. She's a real sweetheart." She quickly wiped up the spill.

I took a tentative sip. Shit. Decaf. I sputtered, trying to keep my temper from flaring, and slammed the cup hard against the tabletop.

"What's the matter?" Hannah's voice was anxious.

"You know I need caffeine." Accusation dripped, like thick molasses, from my tongue. Hannah should have checked for herself. This was her fault.

She petted and soothed and brought me a fresh cup, but I knew it was all an act. I waited, suspicious, as she reassured me that everything would be fine. Gilda would shape up, things were dandy. All the stuff she thought I wanted to hear. Gilda hovered above me, offering her own weak attempts at conversation. As I listened, I downed my coffee. My hot black coffee.

I've been around. I know when I'm being conned.

Someone was going to be in trouble.

The mystery-slash-horror-slash-suspense genre has profited nicely over the years from the stories I write. I pride myself on producing the best of mean and nasty.

Ergo: what is put onto paper can also be used in real-life situations.

Sometimes the headaches I suffer from only serve to enrich the tale. Such was the case this time. Through the evening I plotted and wrote and wove words, until, at last, I came up with a workable story line.

Then I began to assemble the necessities.

When I was young (god-a-mighty, how long ago was that?) my job required me to travel. Actually, it seemed like I was never able to stay long in my Ozark home before I was required to ship out again. Seldom did I get to see the trees bud out or the dogwoods bloom. All my time, as well as any cash, had to be invested in fancy clothes, clattering jewelry, and running around all over the world. By the time I allowed myself to stay at home, I simply didn't care anymore. What a waste!

Sorry. I digress.

Although I've been on numerous cruises, I never got past a certain amount of seasickness. I always had to wear a patch. The patch was lightly coated with a prescribed solution, Scopolamine. A handy dandy little medication that, when used properly, could work wonders. Just between you and me, there are also a number of other ways it can be used. I kept the solution in a bottle, along with a box of costume jewelry, in an old black travel bag. The travel bag was on the top shelf of my closet—which had not been cleaned for fifteen years. Ever since I spit in the eye of my former boss and told him he could stuff it.

Perfect.

Assembling the things I needed was simple enough. I dug through the jewelry until I found the ideal piece, an ankle bracelet I'd picked up in Tijuana. Made of twisted copper and denim strips, it filled the bill wonderfully. Placing it in a small bowl, I poured Scopolamine until it covered the bracelet completely. Then I left it to soak overnight and dug out a pretty little pair of earrings for Hannah. If she wasn't going to get to take her trip, she deserved some little reward, right?

On Wednesday morning, I arose, clearheaded for once, filled with intent and purpose. It was strange. I actually walked into the restaurant instead of staggering.

"What in the world is with you today?" Hannah could hardly believe her eyes. For once I was in a good mood. She watched, goggle-eyed, as I tossed down my first cup and held it out for a refill. "I've never seen you in a better mood."

"Just a good day, I guess."

Across the room, I could see Gilda heaving herself around tables and bouncing off customers' ankles. It was as if a noisy mountain were attempting to move between tables. Jewelry clanked and clattered. Her flat nasal whine sliced the morning air like the sound of a tugboat siren.

"How's your waitress working out?" I asked. "Are you still taking a trip?"

"Leaving next Monday. Five glorious days." She crowed. "I can't wait." She watched the heaving bulk with pride. "She's doing fine. Not as used to it as she should be, but she's getting there."

"True," I agreed. "Look. I know I behaved badly the other day. Now I'd like to make amends. I was really rude to Gilda. And to you. I apologize."

"Oh, no problem." Hannah was always so sweet. Too bad she wasn't going to get that holiday. She really did deserve it. It was only that I needed her too much to let her go.

"I brought a little gift for each of you," I said, handing her the two boxes. They were plainly marked with the names of the women. I didn't want them to get mixed up. "Would you see Gilda gets it? Tell her I'd like her to wear it every day. That way I'll know she's forgiven me. Think she would?"

"I imagine I can talk her into it." Hannah smiled. "Thank you." I felt just a twinge of guilt. Hastily, I squashed it.

"I'll make it up to her someday," I promised myself.

On Thursday morning, the first thing I noticed was that Gilda was proudly decked out with her new ankle bracelet. She lunged my way as soon as I entered the door, and I knew I'd have to fend off suffocating hugs. I avoided her and tried to smile as she spurted thanks and blessings and slushy gratitude as she sloshed hot coffee in my direction. I couldn't wait 'til this thing was over.

By Friday morning, it was working. Anyone in the know could tell. Gilda may have been a dizzy-headed dame, but this dizziness was unnatural. She reeled like a drunken sailor. It's a wonder she didn't clobber a customer in the head with a plate.

Now and then she would pause and clutch her head. Anxious, Hannah hovered around her. "What's the matter?" she asked.

"I don't know." The flat monotone sounded sick. "I'm dizzy."

"Better sit down for a bit." Hannah reached for Gilda's coffeepot. "I'll take care of the customers."

Gilda staggered off toward the back. I smiled. It was just a matter of time. Slugging away at my wonderfully satisfying cup of black coffee, I wondered how much longer she would last. I'd done good. The Scopolamine wouldn't leave a residue. I'd looked it up in one of my mystery reference books to be sure.

On Saturday, Gilda was nowhere to be found. A subdued Hannah filled my cup.

"What's happened to your friend?" I asked, hiding a slightly satanic smile. "She run out on you?"

"She didn't show up this morning," Hannah explained. I'm going to check in on her later."

"Better let your boss take care of it. Too bad. Looks like your holiday is off." My voice was properly sympathetic. "I'm sorry."

"Me too. But what I'm really worried about is Gilda. You wouldn't believe how sick she was yesterday."

"Oh, she'll be okay. It's probably just one of those bugs that's going around." I held out my cup. "I wouldn't let myself stew too much about somebody like that."

My tone must have been wrong. Suspicious, Hannah glared at me. "What do you mean, somebody like that?"

I was immediately apologetic. "Nothing, nothing. Don't get me wrong. I think Gilda's the salt of the earth."

She flapped around a bit as she topped my coffee cup. I'd have to be more careful with my choice of words.

On Monday there she was. My dear Hannah. My rope. My anchor. The only trouble was, she looked terrible. Her eyes were red and swollen and her hands were shaking.

"Something wrong?"

"It's Gilda." She choked on the words and almost spilled my precious coffee.

"Careful! You're spilling it!"

Hannah ignored me as she continued, "She's dead."

"Oooohhh . . . My goodness. What happened?"

"When I went looking for her, she had collapsed in her apartment. She's dead. I don't know what was wrong." She sobbed and swabbed at her eyes.

"Well, don't worry about it," I scolded her. "It's nothing for you to put yourself out over. You didn't even know her very well, did you?"

"Know her? Of course I know her!" Hannah was horrified. "She was my sister! My older sister. Know her? I loved her." With a shaking hand she filled my cup until it overflowed onto the table. "And guess what else? The police said she might even have been murdered. Once they do an autopsy, we'll know for sure. Oh!" she wailed. "Who could do such a terrible thing? And why?"

My heart pounded. I thought I'd choke. What had I forgotten? I forced my voice to be casual. "What makes the police think it's murder?"

"I don't know."

My mind went over and over the whole procedure. Suddenly it came to me. I should have gone to the apartment and taken the bracelet back. I'd failed to remove the murder weapon. Stupid, stupid, stupid!

She hiccupped, fighting for emotional control. "I'll tell you one thing. I'll work 'til my last breath to figure out who killed her. If it's the final thing I do on this earth, I'll make that person sorry he . . . or she . . . was ever born."

A flare of hatred pulsed, circled, and hovered like a funnel cloud in the air above. The smell of hot biscuits and congealed eggs drifted through the room as I lifted my cup for what could very well be the last time.

"I don't blame you," I said. My head was beginning to pound again. "Hannah, do you think you could spare just one more cup of this wonderful morning coffee? Hot, black, and strong? I really think I'm going to need it. Please?"

BETTY CRAKER HENDERSON BIOGRAPHY

Betty Craker Henderson, Monett, Missouri, is a retired children's librarian and a former newspaper editor. For twenty-five years she has written feature articles and weekly columns for newspapers and magazines, focusing on her Ozark homeland, the subject dearest to her heart. Her novel, *Child Support*, published by Hard Shell Word Factory, was named Best Romance Novel of 2002 by the Missouri Writers Guild and she is in the early stages of several book projects. A speaker and entertainer, she sings in a country band and presents original programs featuring her alter ego, Granny Dingle. She is currently acting as hostess for Elderhostels in the Branson area that focus on the culture of the Ozarks (where Granny appears regularly). She is married, has three grown children, five grandchildren, and a great-granddaughter, which makes her a grandmother 98% of the time. Her website is www.grannydingle.com

Integrated pest management seems to be an alibi for murder in Edward Downie's first published detective story.

BOBBING FOR DEATH

by Edward Downie

"Wha . . ." began Henrietta.

"I Feng Shui-ed your office!" said Priscilla Oglethorpe, dancing with delight at Henrietta's surprise. "Don't you just love it!"

"Actually . . ." Henrietta tried again.

"I moved your desk to face west to attract the positive life energy 'chi.' In autumn the energy flows out of the west." Priscilla beamed with enthusiasm. "And the desk move necessitated a filing cabinet move, and a rearrangement of your pictures. I hope you like it!"

Truth be told, Henrietta was not keen about modifications in the layout of her little office at the *Scull Creek Weekly Register*, nor was she keen about Feng Shui, nor was she keen—for that matter—about Priscilla Oglethorpe.

"Thanks for volunteering your expertise," she said in a flat voice, as she shooed Priscilla out of the office.

Henrietta sat at her faux Formica desk and gazed past the computer monitor and out the window—now inconveniently on her left—to where a large yellow garden spider was weaving its multi-spoked web between two dogwood trees.

Despite the rustic ambiance, journalistic standards were high at the *Register*. The enclave of Scull Creek nestled in the shadow of a great university, and consequently the inhabitants tended to be over-educated, underemployed, and prone to use language that caused kindred folk in neighboring communities to say, "Huh?" or "What say?"

This week had been uneventful and Henrietta wondered idly what she could write to fill the four pages of the little paper. There was the Halloween party, presently in progress at the community center, but that was about all.

Suddenly the door burst open.

"Henrietta! Wow! Do we ever need you!" said a worried-looking man in a beret and checkered scarf. "There's been an incident." The speaker was Thadeus Grimp, who had spent the past week pouting because Sheriff Goodlow appointed Henrietta and not him substitute when the sheriff had gone to Branson on vacation. "You need to get over to the community center right away."

Henrietta regarded Grimp with the strained forbearance of one beset by a plague of locusts. Although Thadeus was not a large man, his capacity to irritate her was vast. He spoke in exclamation marks—"Wow!" and "No fooling!" and "That's incredible!"—while bouncing around and waving his arms. His voice rose and fell randomly like a rabbit crossing a cornfield. She fanaticized throttling him with his scarf or bashing him with a chair, but instead dutifully followed him to the community center.

Henrietta pushed through the pumpkins to a crowd of citizens standing around a galvanized iron washtub on a table. On the ground beside the tub lay the soggy figure of a man. She recognized the man as Homer Tackett, village misanthrope. Tackett was not moving.

"He doesn't look so good," said Henrietta. "Did anyone try CPR?"

"It's too late now," said Grimp. "We spent quite a bit of time discussing what to do. Some allowed as how if

God had chosen to take Homer, who were we to countermand the judgment of the Almighty?"

"Humph!" said Henrietta. "If Homer had won the Missouri Lottery, there'd have been plenty of people to question the Lord's judgment."

"Anyhow, CPR would have made no difference," said Grimp. "Homer never moved after we pulled him out of the apple-bobbing tub."

"Better fill me in on the details," Henrietta said. "Homer was bobbing for apples? And then what?"

"He went under, and he just never came up again. We all stood around for a while impressed with Homer's ability to hold his breath. Finally we got bored and wandered off to carve pumpkins. When we returned about twenty minutes later, Homer was still head down in the tub. It was then we suspected that something had gone wrong, and we pulled him out. And sent for you, Henrietta. So what do you think? Death due to natural causes?" suggested Grimp.

"I'm not so sure," said Henrietta. "This all seems not a little suspicious. And convenient. Homer didn't have any friends around here, and he had lots of enemies. Now he's dead. Makes one wonder."

"Even people with lots of enemies have to die sometime. What's suspicious about that?"

"We'll see." Henrietta was noncommittal.

"Let me have a look," said Doc Burton, the naturopath, as he navigated through the crowd. The doc had a salt-and-pepper beard and a salt-and-pepper ponytail, and from any little distance it was not easy to tell if he was coming or going. "I'd say Homer died of the West Nile virus. If he'd have taken the Echinacea like I recommended, he'd be alive still."

"That's a possibility," said Henrietta, "and yet I know of no other cases in which an attack of the West Nile virus caused anyone to keel over like that."

"Maybe Lyme disease, then." The doc amended his diagnosis. The prophylaxis that would have saved Homer stayed the same.

Holly Green spoke up. She was a recent graduate of the university with a degree in forestry, and awesomely fetching in tube top and low-slung jeans—between which articles of apparel a band of navel-punctuated tummy composed a scenic vista. She said she thought the red oak borer killed Homer.

"I bet if you open him up, you'll find him riddled with worm holes," she speculated.

A half dozen men nodded their heads thoughtfully, while a half dozen women shook theirs vehemently.

"Could be," said Henrietta. "Microbes and infestations have a way of jumping from one host to another, I've heard. Hey, what are those two little marks on Homer's neck?" she continued, making a more detailed examination of the victim. She shifted the bolo tie in order to see better.

"What do you figure? Vampires?" asked Grimp. "You watch too much television."

"Let's not rush to judgment. Haul that washtub outside, dump it, and see if there are any clues as to how Homer met his fate."

Several stalwart youths were persuaded to lift the washtub off the table and drag it outside to the banks of the creek.

"Okay," said Henrietta, "now, tip it over carefully, and let's see if there's anything in it besides water and apples."

Sundry citizens of the hamlet crowded close. There'd been a dearth of excitement in the last few years, in fact nothing spectacular since Sheriff Goodlow's epileptic cat Mervyn had been placed on anti-seizure medication.

Over the tub went, and as the apples spilled onto the ground, a small water moccasin emerged and slithered—without haste—down the bank and into the creek.

"Yow! Yow!! Yow!!!" the common scream went up. A dozen people danced backward, tripped over one another, slipped on the muddy bank, and thrashed about in a wriggling heap.

"Well, I guess that answers the question of what got Homer," said Grimp. He endeavored to regain his composure after joining the hasty retreat from the wash-tub.

"But why was no one else bitten?" a voice wondered. The voice belonged to Unsuitable, who had arrived somewhat late at the party—but was not hesitant to put his oar in.

"That's easy," said Grimp, "because Homer pushed to the front of the apple-bobbing line."

"But how did the snake get into the apple-bobbing tub?" Unsuitable persisted.

"I think we can conclude the snake didn't decide on his own to take a swim in the tub," said Henrietta. "Snakes don't eat apples. It's likely that someone put him in there. With murderous intent." She gazed levelly at her fellow citizens. They in turn gazed at the rocks in the creek, the branches in the trees, or at their nervously shuffling feet.

"Well, I don't like to say anything," prefaced Thadeus Grimp, who relished saying things that got people into trouble, "but the last person I saw in the vicinity of the tub before Homer went bobbing was Sister Perkins."

Everyone turned and looked at the woman.

Sister Perkins was a tall, rangy gal with green eyes and shoulder-length hair in which the hues of an Ozark sunset glowed. She presently enjoyed the brief period of freedom that came between the discarding of a prior husband and the acquisition of his successor. She was tough and resilient, but even she had been tested by the late Mr. Tackett, who had moved into her rent house, and neither would he pay the rent nor would he move out.

"You had some trouble with Tackett, didn't you, Sister Perkins?" asked Grimp.

"He was a sorry excuse for a man," she replied. "There was no meanness or underhandedness to which he would not stoop. He was lower than an earthworm's bellybutton."

"And isn't it true that you attend a church where snakes are handled in the service?" Grimp smiled unpleasantly.

"Rattlesnakes, not water moccasins."

"Lay off Sister Perkins, Thadeus. I don't think we have any reason to believe she put the snake in the tub." Henrietta crossed her arms.

"So who do you think you are? Miss Marple?"

"Cool it. I'm acting sheriff, and if you interfere with my investigation, I'm putting you in the hoosegow."

As Grimp slunk away, Unsuitable stepped forward to take his place.

"Sister Perkins is far from the only person with a motive to do in Homer," he said. "Consider that Homer pursued Ollie Henderson's wife, Mona, and wouldn't leave off. Isn't it true, Ollie, that Homer had the hots for Mona and wouldn't take no for an answer?"

"I dunno," said Ollie. "She never tried saying no."

"That's neither here nor there. You're a suspect just the same," said Henrietta.

"And yet if we're to get to the bottom of this mystery," said Priscilla Oglethorpe, "we must arrange the investigation taking into account the Feng Shui of our environment. For instance, that bois d'arc tree by the creek blocks the life energy flow."

"Blocked life energy not withstanding," said Henrietta, "I don't want to see any more Feng Shui-ing done without my prior permission."

She turned then to a tall, powerfully-built man who stood on the periphery of the group. "If I might have a word with you, Stephen Honey . . ."

"I don't think terms of endearment are appropriate in a quasi-legal proceeding," opined Thadeus Grimp.

"'Honey' is his surname!" Henrietta was indignant.

"Take it easy, Henrietta," said Unsuitable. "We're all under some strain. Let's try and keep calm, the better to solve this mystery."

Henrietta growled some—then allowed herself to be placated.

"Stephen Honey, I seem to recall you organized some protests against SUVs."

"Yes, that's correct. My friends and I are convinced that SUVs are the bane of not only Northwest Arkansas civilization, but also the balance of earthly civilization."

"You feel strongly about this, don't you?" Henrietta observed.

"Yes, of course."

"And since Homer Tackett drove the super-SUV, the Hummer, and since he liked to park it by the site of your rallies—upwind—and leave the motor idling, generating copious, toxic fumes to taunt you and your friends, you decided to kill him."

Stephen smiled. "Heh, heh, no such thing, Sheriff Henrietta. Homer's Hummer was a mere nuisance, nothing more."

"Perhaps," said Henrietta.

"You don't look guilty to me, Mr. Honey," said Sister Perkins.

Stephen showed mild surprise, as though noticing Sister Perkins for the first time. Sidling a little closer, he asked, "Would you like to go bicycling?"

Henrietta grew impatient. "Can we defer the woo pitching until after we've solved the murder?"

"And who are these people?" she asked as three gargoyle-visaged ladies marched up.

"We're the rapid-response team of the state chapter of PETA . . ." began the first visitor.

"Let's see," said Unsuitable. "That'd be . . ."

"People for the Ethical Treatment of Animals," amplified the second visitor, with a toss of her head and a curl of her lip.

"And we've received report of a snake-human interaction hereabouts," resumed the first visitor.

"We were dispatched to investigate and ensure that no animal abuse occurred, such as rough or callous treatment of the snake," said the second visitor.

Unsuitable, an expression of alarm spreading across his face, shifted his gaze back and forth from the PETA representatives to Henrietta. "It's true that we had a snake at the Halloween party, but he was treated very well. Indeed he was given every consideration. All provisions for his comfort were made, even though he behaved badly by some lights."

"May I see the snake?" asked the third member of the triumvirate.

"He's not available at this time," Unsuitable replied. "In fact we returned him to the creek in conformance with his wishes."

"Without checking to see if he were injured? Or traumatized?"

"He appeared to be in fine fettle when he left," said Unsuitable.

"Of course you had him examined by a competent herpetologist. Didn't you?"

"I've put up with about as much of this foolishness as I am able," roared Henrietta, pushed beyond—far beyond—human endurance. "I have a murder to investigate! Get these idiots out of here!"

"Who are you calling idiots!!! Animal abuser!"

Unsuitable guided the animal-rights activists away, but not before the first visitor could fire the parting shot at Henrietta: "You viper!" she shouted.

"Glory be, I don't see how Sheriff Goodlow got anything done," said Henrietta. "This place is a madhouse."

"Hey, what's Mervyn got?" asked Unsuitable.

The cat, which had been pawing through the apple debris dumped from the tub, had something in his mouth.

"I liked Mervyn better when he had periodic fits," said Henrietta. "Now he goes around acting weird all the time.

"Come here, Mervyn, and give me whatever it is you have," she requested of the animal.

The cat, reluctant to relinquish his treasure, skittered between her and Unsuitable and commenced a broken-field run for the end zone.

But he was brought up short.

"I got him!" announced Holly Green, who had experience outmaneuvering males of several species. "But I don't know what it is he had," she said, holding up a disk about four inches in diameter.

"Let's have a look," said Henrietta. "Why, it's a small compass surrounded by a series of rings inscribed with strange symbols."

"Can I see?" asked Sister Perkins. "I've seen one of these before. It's a Feng Shui compass."

"How on earth did Mervyn come by a Feng Shui compass?" Henrietta wondered out loud.

"It was among the apples dumped from the tub," said Unsuitable.

A pregnant silence followed.

"Priscilla Oglethorpe, may I have a word with you?" asked Henrietta.

"I . . . I have no idea how my compass—I think it's mine—it looks like mine—got among the apples. Surely you can't suspect me . . . of . . . of . . ."

But a circle of Scull Creek residents formed around Priscilla. They shook their heads, and their usually whimsical expressions were serious.

"Priscilla Oglethorpe, you have the right to remain silent," intoned Henrietta. "Anything you say may be taken down and used . . ."

"All right, all right, I did it," said Priscilla. "Clearly, someone had to. No one else would . . . would show the initiative, and the dirty deed fell to me. All of you should be grateful."

"I knew all along it was Priscilla," said Thadeus Grimp.

"Homer was surely a pill," began Henrietta, "however . . ."

"He was much more than a pill," said Priscilla. "He threatened us all. Homer generated negative 'sha' energy that sucked the balance out of the community. His removal was essential. The final straw was when he contributed onion and Tabasco on pumpernickel sandwiches to the potluck supper."

"Yeah, I remember," said Henrietta. "I had one, and they were pretty vile."

"He was a source of geotactic stress, a vortex of dark energy, and brought massive yin-yang inharmoniousness. I had no choice but to arrange for the snake's path to enlightenment to intersect Homer's," concluded Priscilla.

"Your argument is persuasive," said Henrietta. "I hope you'll be able to convince the jury to consider these extenuating circumstances. I wouldn't like to see you spend a long time as a guest of the Department of Corrections in Pine Bluff—or worse!"

Later in Henrietta's office, Unsuitable asked, "Well, what do you think? Will she get a lethal injection like she arranged for Homer?"

"Naw, not a chance. A good lawyer—Irene Carmichael comes to mind—will get her a short sentence or even off entirely. It's not like she chilled Homer by chemical or artificial means. A gun, for instance. No, she used environmentally-friendly, all-natural biological control, an example of integrated pest management, which is widely endorsed these days. That should affect a local jury favorably.

"And while you're here," Henrietta continued, "how about helping me move this desk back to where I had it."

EDWARD DOWNIE BIOGRAPHY

At age twelve, impressed by the work of A. Conan Doyle, Edward (Ned) Downie decided to write detective stories. He knew this undertaking would require preparation, but underestimated the fifty years before he realized his ambition. Meanwhile, he supported himself by other endeavors. Among the side excursions was a stint at the University of Arkansas at Fayetteville, where he began his association with the Ozarks. He left with a master's degree in psychology to work on radios for NASA in Iowa, and then to Georgia, where he taught psychology for two years before completing a Ph.D. For five years he taught psychology in Texas and Arkansas and even managed to do part-time engineering at a radio station and brain research at a medical school. In Illinois he was an engineer for a dozen years and clinical psychologist for a half dozen. At that point the pull of the Ozarks was irresistible, and he returned to Fayetteville, where he considers himself at "happily ever after," and glad to be writing detective stories at last!

Can evil enter nightmares to kill if you don't wake up? She couldn't believe that superstitious nonsense coming from her university professor sister.

LIFE-GIVING OXYGEN

Ellen Gray Massey

"I murdered a woman once."

My ninety-year-old sister didn't move from her reclined position in the lounge chair as she said these words. Her head rested wearily against a pillow and her stocking feet on the footrest pointed toward the ceiling. Though her keen eyes opened slightly from her brief nap, the expression on her face did not change.

Audrey had just returned from three weeks in the hospital, but her problem was a congestive heart, not her mind. When I didn't answer immediately, she turned her head toward me. She studied me for my reaction. Breathing naturally, she said in the same calm, matter-of-fact tone. "I have never told this to anyone before. Not even Mama. Especially not to Mama."

Moments before her wheezing had abated. Her exertion of walking across the room and getting settled into the chair had caused her to struggle for breath. Comfortable now, she fingered the plastic tubing running across the floor from the oxygen machine humming away against the opposite wall. She ran her hand up the tubing to her neck where it split into two lines that looped over her ears and came together again where the cannula fit into her nostrils.

Fearing that her mind was beginning to fade as a result of her ordeal at the hospital and thinking to humor her, I asked as if she had confessed to something as innocuous as hitting one of her younger brothers, "When was this?"

Audrey must have decided that I was taking her seriously, for she fixed her eyes on a stained glass hummingbird figurine in the window and lowered her eyebrows in thought. "When I was almost fourteen. In my freshman year."

Though I wasn't even born at that time, I had heard how she boarded in town because when she went to high school there was no transportation, and the eight miles from our farm was too far to walk each day.

"I stayed with Myrtle Lorrey who lived on Erie Street just east of the school." She let her hand drop down to the arm of the chair. "I got free room and board with her because she needed someone to stay with her. She often had nightmares, and she wanted me to wake her up when she had them."

Leaning forward slightly, she took a sip of her caffeine-free soda on the little table beside her chair. She swallowed and laid her head back on the pillow.

Not knowing what to say, I kept silent, waiting for her to continue. Seeing that I was attentive, she said, "But I didn't wake her up."

"Why not?"

"I was terrified. In the middle of the night, I woke up to hear her screaming and making terrible noises. I never heard anyone screech and wail like that. Even the pigs when Papa and I caught them to put rings in their noses didn't make such sounds. And she was thrashing around on her bed. That is her body and legs were flailing and her head rolled back and forth. But her shoulders seemed pinned to the bed as if someone were holding her by the neck to keep her on the bed." She paused for me to absorb what she said. "But nobody was there."

"How could you see? You said it was night."

"I didn't get out of bed, but our rooms were situated so that I could see her bed across the hall. The moonlight coming through her window lit up her silhouette. She was alone. The bed jumped around on the wooden floor and the springs squealed from all her exertions."

"What did you do?"

"Nothing. I just pulled the covers over my head and clamped my hands over my ears. I was petrified with fear. Even if I'd wanted to, I couldn't move or get out of bed." She played with the oxygen tubing again, flipping it to straighten out the loops that lay across the floor. "And I killed her."

"How on earth could you have killed her? You said you didn't get out of bed. Did she die from that fit?"

"No, not that time. She finally woke up. In a little while she came into my room. She pulled back my covers. I was scared to look at her until she asked in her normal voice, 'Why didn't you wake me? I let you stay here to wake me up when I have those nightmares.' I pretended that I just then woke up and told her I didn't hear anything.

"Then her voice got hard and determined. Sort of angry yet fatalistic. 'If you don't wake me next time,' she said, '*It* will kill me.'"

"What was she talking about? What would kill her?"

"That thing in her nightmare. She said to me, '*It's* coming more and more often, and if I don't wake up in time, *it*'ll kill me.' I guess that first time I heard her, her own screams woke her up. She made me promise to wake her the next time. Not only would it kill her, she said, but it would eventually get into my dreams and kill me too. Maybe not for years, but sometime for sure."

I laughed, thinking she was putting one over on me. Even sick as she was, her sense of humor was alive and well. "Yeah, sure." I grinned at her to show I appreciated how she'd taken me in. "It's been . . ." I stopped to figure up, making a big joke of it. "It's been seventy-seven years since then and you're still here."

Audrey didn't smile as she always did when any of her siblings teased her. Being the oldest of a large family, she got lots of ribbing and took it good-naturedly.

Her expression was serious, almost tragic. The wrinkles in her neck seemed even deeper and her colorless face was drawn with worry. She took a couple of deep breaths, wheezing, almost gasping.

"What happened next?" I asked when she didn't respond to my unsuccessful levity.

"Nothing for a few weeks. I should have told Mama about it. I know now that I should have, for she would have moved me out of Myrtle's house right away. But by the weekend when I went home, everything was quiet at night. It stayed that way for a long time. I was busy with schoolwork and I went out for the basketball team. I made new friends and forgot all about Myrtle's nightmares.

"Then just before Christmas vacation, she had another nightmare. This one was even worse than the first. The bed shook so much that I could feel the vibrations across the hall. I don't know why the neighbors didn't hear her, because her shrieks were piercing. Her arms waved wildly, her hands moving from her neck to the air above her. Like she was hitting something that was floating just above her head. She gave several strong screams and then she'd gasp or gurgle until there was very little sound. Just when it seemed everything was over, her screech filled the room. She tried to say some words, probably calling to me, but all that came out were guttural sounds like a hard 'ghk, ghk, ghk.' And then wailing sounds I couldn't bear to hear. Her hands would come back to her neck as if trying to beat off or loosen something."

Audrey looked straight into my eyes. "There wasn't anything there. The moonlight streamed across her bed. From my bed I could see her silhouette very clearly. Once again I buried myself in the covers, put my hands over my ears, and rolled up into a ball to wait it out. Even muffled as I was, I couldn't block out her screams.

I can't describe my terror. It was even worse than the first time."

I was surprised that screams from an old woman's nightmare could frighten Audrey so badly because she was always a daredevil. Not heights, high speeds, nor deep water ever fazed her. She even liked snakes, and once when I was with her in the southwestern desert she didn't run as I did from the nest of tarantulas we trod upon. She traveled alone in inner cities and in Asian and South American capitals without a second thought to any danger. During her many adventures, she faced African rhinos and was in a balloon that crash-landed. None of those real dangers even flustered her.

"I've never known you to be scared," I said.

"I never have been since," she said so softly I could barely hear her.

Perhaps her youth explained her fright of the nightmares. That was the first time she had ever been away from home alone.

"What happened then? Did she wake up like the first time?" I asked.

"The screams just stopped. All at once, almost in mid-shriek. She quit thumping around. Her arms fell to her sides. The bed stood still. I expected her to come in and scold me for not waking her again, but she didn't. I was glad that the nightmare was over. I forced myself to quit trembling and willed myself back to sleep."

"Did she say anything to you the next morning?"

"No." Audrey's eyes had a haunted look to them as she stared at me. Her hands rested quietly in her lap.

There was a long pause. I had to say something. "I'm surprised that she didn't, considering you were there specifically to wake her up when she had the nightmares."

"She was dead." Audrey continued to stare at me. "And I killed her because I didn't wake her up."

"Aw, Audrey, that's nonsense."

"No, that's what happened." She was very serious.

I asked, "What did they say she died of?"

"The doctor said that she strangled herself in her sleep. There were indentations on her neck as if she had been strangled. He knew about her nightmares and how violent she became when she was having one." Audrey took her eyes from me to look out the window past the hummingbird figurine to the row of oak trees across the lawn. "But I was the one that killed her."

I tried to imagine how terrible it must have been for a young girl to witness a death like that. And the guilt she must have felt. "No, you weren't. You didn't kill her. Don't think of that anymore."

She glanced back to me with a half smile. "Yes, you're probably right. It doesn't seem so fearful now that I've talked it over with you."

"Did you worry about what she said about it getting into your dreams if you didn't wake her?" My tone was half serious, half teasing.

She raised up in her chair and looked at me as if I were becoming senile. She made some sounds down in her throat that I couldn't understand and then glanced out the window to the comforting line of trees. "It really was my fault. I killed her. If I'd awakened her, it wouldn't have happened. I've felt guilty about that all my life. You're the first one I've ever told."

Neither of us said anything for several seconds. She seemed to be waiting for me to say something.

"Have you ever had any dreams like Myrtle had?" I asked, a bit uncomfortable under her penetrating scrutiny.

Her eyes darted from me to the autumn view out the window and then back to me. The line of her mouth softened as she leaned forward to reach my hand. In an uncharacteristic gesture for her, she patted it and held on with more strength than I thought she would have. "I'm really glad you're here. Wake me up if I . . ." Then she leaned back as she began to pant just slightly from her movement. She closed her eyes. In a few minutes the muscles in her face relaxed. Her mouth slackened and her head rolled slightly to the right. Her breath returned to easy rhythms.

Her strange manner disturbed me. How could my university professor sister even consider such superstitious rot? I eased her hand from mine and laid it in her lap. Careful not to step on the oxygen tubing on the floor, I tiptoed across the room and opened the door to step outside onto the patio. I sucked in the invigorating air. The stolid trees beckoned me. Reality reassured me. I glanced back to see that Audrey was quietly sleeping, her right hand holding lightly the oxygen tubing, her left hand still in her lap. I took a walk.

The woods were beautiful, vibrant and alive. Two fox squirrels chased each other through the trees. Monarch butterflies flitted from aster to chicory to Queen Anne's lace. I heard the distant call of the mourning dove. Renewed, half an hour later, I returned to Audrey's apartment.

The space around her chair was in disarray. The two tables flanking her chair were turned over. Her water jug and Coke glass were upset and dark liquid spotted the carpet. Current magazines and get-well cards, as well as the circle-the-word puzzle book, were all strewn over the floor. On top of them was the floor lamp to which was tied the emergency pull cord for calling the resident nurse of her apartment complex. Shards of the broken light bulbs were against the wall. Nearby, dangling from the arm of the couch hung the cannula from the oxygen tubing. Drops of blood were on each of the two prongs that had been inserted into her nostrils.

Curled up into a ball on the floor on top of the crumpled newspaper lay Audrey. Her slacks were twisted and the buttons on her blouse were torn off. She was quiet. No movement at all. Her bulging eyes, filled with terror, were open and stared unseeing out the window. The skin on her face was slack and loose, and her tongue hung out of her opened mouth. Blood oozed from her nose.

Both hands clasped the loops of plastic tubing that were twisted several times around her neck.

The oxygen machine gurgled and buzzed and hummed as it continued to produce oxygen and send it through the yards of shining tubing across the new aqua carpet and around and around her neck. From the open end of the tubing where the cannula was broken off, pure, life-giving oxygen poured out into the room.

I gasped, unable to get my breath. A hard band tightened around my throat.

ELLEN GRAY MASSEY BIOGRAPHY

Ellen Gray Massey, Lebanon, Missouri, has taught for forty-three years in public schools and colleges. She currently teaches Elderhostel classes in Branson, Missouri, and in Potosi, Missouri, at the YMCA of the Ozarks. As a teacher, speaker, and writer, she promotes Missouri and the Ozarks. She was inducted into the Writers Hall of Fame of America in 1995 because of her own writings and her work from 1973-1983 with her high school students in Lebanon, Missouri, in publishing forty issues of *Bittersweet, the Ozark Quarterly*. She has received several first place awards from the Missouri Writers Guild: for her biography, *A Candle within Her Soul   Mary Elizabeth Mahnkey and her Ozarks*; a musical play, *A Life I Can See*; for four novels; and for several short stories and articles. She was twice finalist at Western Writers of America's Golden Spur Award. Her most recent books are an historical novel, *The Burnt District*, Hard Shell Word Factory; *Family Fun and Games: a Hundred Year Tradition*, co-authored with her sister, Carolyn Gray Thornton, Skyward Publishing; and a picture book, *The Bittersweet Ozarks at a Glance*, Skyward Publishing. www.runningriver.com/emassey/

*Bored with the "killing" at the reenactment of the
Civil War battle at Pea Ridge, Arkansas, she wan-
ders over the grounds. Her friend Henry says that
her curiosity will get her into trouble. But not this
time.*

THE MAN WHO CRIED "DAVID"

by Radine Trees Nehring

The constant booming of hundreds of muskets—
from this distance at least—could be endured.

Even the thunder of cannons wasn't so bad. After
all, I listened to rock drummers, and the louder they
were, the better.

Nope, noise wasn't the problem. What was getting
to me was the black powder smoke, especially in this
heat. My T-shirt was stuck to my back, my forehead
was dripping. I'd had enough smoke, enough war.

And now there was a dead body lying right in front
of me. That bothered me most of all.

In other places, war was real. Here they called it
acting out history. It was also called fun.

Out on the field, men were playing at dying. I could
hear their cries and moans above the other noises of
battle. They were certainly realistic about it. Just a few
minutes ago a sharp *crack* made me jump, and I heard a
male scream sounding something like the name, David.
Odd, his crying out a name. Odd too—hearing a crack
instead of the boom of a fake shot exploding from a
musket. Someone on the field was shooting blanks from
a sidearm.

After the crack, a Union soldier not thirty feet
from me jerked, his body arching backwards. Then he

stiffened and fell flat on the ground, way too real-
istically.

Crazy man, falling like that. He could have broken
his head open.

The play-dead man lay very still, his blue uniform
cap tilted sideways over his eyes. He was in full sun—
probably risking heat stroke. Playing war wearing wool
uniforms in July was beyond stupid. It might be
authentic, but it was stupid.

At least we were sitting in the shade. Henry, his
daughter Susan, and I came early this morning, hoping
to find a place for our folding chairs under a shade tree.
The large oak we chose soon drew a crowd, and there
was a big puddle of spectators all around us now—some
on blankets, some in lawn chairs. The puddle shifted as
the sun moved through the sky. Clustered bodies added
to the heat, and whenever the breeze died and the smoke
faded, I smelled sweat.

Out on the battlefield most of the casualties were
choosing to fall in the shade of the pasture's other trees.
The man who cried "David" hadn't. Maybe his captain,
or general, or whatever the idiot running this re-
enactment was called, told him not to.

I almost let a giggle escape as I wondered what
would happen if every single soldier here decided to be
shot at the same time, and the whole army fell over.
What a sight! Wouldn't some of them have to get up,
say "Oops," and begin fighting again?

A puff of wind blew more smoke over us and
snatched the straw hat off my head. A young man sitting
in a lawn chair behind me leaped to his feet and grabbed
the hat. Very young man. Eighteen, maybe? Well, he
could be older. He looked as young to me as I probably
looked old to him. Gray hair did it with anyone under
thirty. I knew what they were thinking.

After saying "Why, thank you, young man" in the
best granny voice I could manage, I mashed the hat back
on my head, wiggled my behind in the green canvas

chair, and turned toward Henry and Susan. They had their heads together and were staring out on the field, probably trying to locate Susan's husband. He was one of the hundreds of men taking part in this battle. Those two wouldn't care if I left. Might not even notice.

I could walk over to the sutlers' camp. I didn't want any 1860s style merchandise, but the sutlers and their battlefield supply camps were a part of Civil War history too, and they had to be more interesting than watching soldiers play at dying in heat and smoke.

Besides, seeing the close-up soldier lying so still was getting to me, and the cry, "David," kept echoing around and around inside my head. Soldiers dying across the field could be ignored. This one was too close to ignore, and his image had begun to join with memories of real war casualties I'd seen on television.

Henry, my dearest friend and closest neighbor in Blackberry Hollow, would understand if I left. In fact, he might be wishing he could leave too. He told me only yesterday that his military service and long career in the Kansas City Police Department cured him of any interest in gun battles, including those copying the Civil War.

Even when the two of us get involved in what my son calls "Ma and Pa Kettle detective work," Henry rarely carries a gun. He says he'll leave firearms to the licensed law.

Henry had come today only because Susan was here. Her husband, a Civil War re-enactor, helped organize this re-staging of the 1862 battle of Pea Ridge, Arkansas, so of course he was out there somewhere, playing soldier with the rest of his men.

I touched Henry's arm. "I'd like to get away from this, think I'll walk over to the sutlers' camp. Come along?"

He looked down, smiled, laid his hand over mine and squeezed. Gray hair or not, that did something to me.

"Go shopping?" he said. "No, thanks. I'll stay here with Susan. You won't get lost? There must be several thousand people here."

"The program says the battle will last another hour and a half, so I can be back before the end. See you in an hour or so." I puckered my lips to send him a secret kiss and left the shade of the oak.

The coarse pasture grass smelled of heat and dust—and, faintly, of cow. I thought back to the rows of soldiers marching across here early this morning. It was amazing how many bellies bulged against uniform buttons, and there were quite a few heads with hair as gray as mine and Henry's. All men of course. No woman would be silly enough to dress in wool and play soldier in this heat.

Still, if they wanted to . . .

Women, masquerading as men, had fought beside brothers and husbands on real Civil War battlefields. But now? Susan's husband said most re-enactment groups were dead set against admitting women as soldiers. It was hoops and calico for us, or nothing.

It might be fun to see if I could pass as a soldier, in cooler weather at least. But my springing gray curls would ruin it, as well as . . . I looked down at the two generous bumps pushing out the front of my "MOM FOR PRESIDENT" T-shirt. They'd show.

Ah, well, on to the sutlers' camp. Playing war was for younger, slimmer women.

If they wanted to, of course, they should be welcomed. Today, men and women from the United States serve side-by-side in the military. Why not here?

Discrimination. As usual it made me want to paint a sign and go march somewhere.

We're far from having it made, including in this male-devised game of re-enacting, I thought.

Ahead of me two rows of white supply tents stretched for more than a block on each side of a makeshift grassy street. Women in traditional 1860s dress floated everywhere, looking like enormous turned-over flowers. Children in overalls and straw hats, or miniature full skirts and bonnets, played with balls and hoops and rag dolls, filling the street with color, motion, and happy shouts. A few spectators, evidently bored with the fighting too, were roaming about. This was certainly going to be better than what was behind me on the battlefield.

I poked along from tent to tent, looking at canned goods with 1860s labels, iron cooking pots, blankets, guns, and trappings for horses. One tent displayed women's period clothing, fabric, patterns, and some amazingly nice antique buttons and jewelry. My resolve not to buy any 1860s merchandise almost broke down when I saw the jewelry.

Next to the clothing supplier was a tent, smaller than most, with a closed flap. Of course that made me eager to see inside and I pushed against the flap, meeting resistance from fabric probably fastened at the back. Maybe if I waited . . . the sutler might be taking a needed break.

I looked back down the dusty street toward the whirls and bounces of color created by the playing children. Of course there had been no families and no peddlers at the real Pea Ridge Battle in March of 1862. The men fighting here then had marched for days through sleet and snow. They had little food. Most of the Confederates were teenaged southern farm boys, poorly dressed for winter in the Ozarks. Some wore shoes with holes, others had no shoes at all, just rags wrapped around their feet. When they could, Civil War soldiers stole shoes, coats, and food from the dying and dead—whether enemy or comrade.

I shut my eyes and thought of those long-ago boys. An icy day. Little or no sleep. If they rested, there was only frozen ground with patches of snow. Nothing to eat. The Confederate supply line had been stretched too thin.

I shivered, in spite of the heat.

Someone touched my arm. "You feeling faint, lady? Is it the sun? Come in my tent and sit."

I jumped at the touch and turned to see mournful blue eyes behind round, brass-rimmed spectacles. His overalls had a strap twisted over one shoulder—he'd dressed in a hurry. A sutler. He pointed toward the small tent with the now-open flap.

"Goodness, I'm all right. I was just thinking back to that day in 1862, imagining . . ."

He nodded. "Oh, yes. Gets to you. You can understand why sometimes the re-enactors are so carried away they hurt each other. Medics at battles like this have treated wounds from bayonets, swords, knives. Thank God they don't have real bullets out on the field. All those guns . . ." His voice faded, and his eyes seemed to be watching something miles away.

I thought I'd never seen a sadder man, and looking at him made me sad too, though I had no clue to the source of his sorrow—or mine. It felt like something deeper than this war.

His dreamy look vanished and he waved an arm in the direction of the battle noise. "Did you know there was a woman like you here then? Mary Whitney Phelps. Only woman at the Pea Ridge Battle, other'n a teenage girl hiding in the basement of Elk Horn Tavern. Used the tavern for a hospital. It's said blood dripped through the floor boards all over that poor girl."

For a moment sadness returned to the gentle eyes, but the mood passed. I nodded encouragement, and he went on.

"Mary Phelps came south from Springfield with a wagonload of supplies for her husband's company. He was Colonel John Phelps, leading the Twenty-fifth Missouri. Later he'd be Missouri Governor Phelps.

"How Miz Phelps made it here with supplies, coming through all those bands of loose soldiers and guerilla warriors that roamed the Ozarks back then, only she could tell us. But she did it, then got cut off here when Van Dorn's Confederates attacked from the north. She stayed right in the thick of things. She could shoot. It's said she fought, nursed, passed out food and supplies from her wagon. And she tended her own husband. He was one of those wounded."

"Mary Phelps," I said, savoring the name, feeling a surge of pride flow into me because of a long-dead heroic woman I'd never heard of until now. "I guess I shouldn't be surprised that a woman was here, fighting beside the men."

I stopped, watching him, testing his reaction, but he was staring into space again.

"Um, what did Mary Phelps wear here?"

The question surprised him and brought his eyes back to me. "Oh, well, I don't know. No pictures of her have been found, if any ever existed. Guess a mid-length plain skirt. No hoops, of course. Probably dressed pretty much like the nurses did. Jacket like the men wore, and men's pants under the skirt, maybe even men's boots."

"What happened to her?"

"She began a children's home for war orphans in Springfield. Sheltered those from both North and South. She was one who couldn't see any difference. Earned a commendation from the United States Congress. She died early, though. It's said she took pneumonia while caring for others when she should have been caring for herself."

I hesitated for a moment, then I asked, "So there weren't, as far as anyone knows, other women who fought here?"

The man's expressive eyes said he didn't like my question. "Well, I wouldn't know about that, would I?"

"And today? Do you think there are any women masquerading as men in the battle today?"

His reply was immediate. "No."

I wondered how he could be so certain, but setting curiosity aside, I changed the subject.

Waving my hand toward the shelves of magazines, books, and paper goods in his tent, I asked, "You do this as a business?"

"Only on weekends and during the summer. I'm a high school history teacher from St. Louis. My wife kept up our stock—before she was killed last winter, that is. Guess I'll be closing this down soon. Because of that, you know."

"I'm so sorry." I seemed to upset this man every time I opened my mouth.

The blue eyes disappeared behind closed lids. "A wreck. She was in a car with a man driving drunk. It spun, went in a ditch, and she was killed."

He went on. "The man had only a few bruises. They took away his license for a year, made him go to some classes, do community service. That's about it. I keep trying to forget, and—" his next words were spoken so softly I could barely hear him, "and to forgive . . . both of them," another pause, "both of them."

Why was he telling me this? The story was none of my business. I didn't want to hear it, didn't want to be drawn into this sadness.

"I'm sorry for your loss, I pray you find comfort and healing."

Maybe I had come here today because, wrapped in surroundings that awakened memories, this man needed someone like me to talk to, a sympathetic, motherly stranger, a woman safely removed from his personal sadness. Maybe it was good I had come to this battle.

Not wanting to walk away from him quite yet, I decided to continue with safer questions about a subject I knew he was interested in.

"Pea Ridge was an important battle?"

"Oh, yes. It had a lot to do with who would control St. Louis and the Mississippi River. If the Confederates had won here in the Ozarks, and they almost did, we might be the Confederate States of America today. Not much between here and St. Louis to stop them at that time."

Two women in wide, swinging skirts came in the tent and asked to see letter paper. Suddenly all business, the sutler nodded to me and turned to help his customers. Our conversation was over.

I stood there a moment, thinking about Mary Phelps, and watching the sutler as he pulled out boxes. He seemed such a kind, sensitive person. What beautiful hair he had. Wavy. Looking at it, I thought of Henry's wavy, gray-streaked black hair. Because I loved touching it, running my fingers along the waves, I noticed other men's hair too. The sutler's was white-blond. Above his ears, the hair was mashed flat in a band that circled his head. Hat hair, Henry called it. Too bad. The brim imprint on the sutler's head spoiled the flow of pale, silky waves. I didn't see a hat anywhere in the tent, but maybe he'd left one in his car.

After a last glance at the sutler, I moved on.

A revival-sized tent stood across the street from the small canvas shelter where the history teacher sold his 1860s paper goods. The big tent's flap was wide open, and wooden forms displaying various military uniforms stood on either side. The forms were fully dressed, even to white gloves. I was now curious about uniforms, and I walked in.

There didn't seem to be anyone minding the tent, so I helped myself, lifting uniforms to look at buttons and trim, inspecting the construction of jackets and pants. A few pairs of pants had modern zippers. I knew purists would reject them, but why did it matter? Surely no one would be unfastening his pants in public! I'd go for convenience every time.

I looked at my watch, saw that I had at least forty-five minutes before the battle ended, and began moving officer's fancy jackets along a rack, admiring gold braid and elaborate metal buttons. I was about to take a jacket down and try it on when I heard someone come in. The clothing rack hid me from the front of the tent, so I pushed hangers aside and peeked through, expecting to see the uniform sutler.

Well, no. It was the sad-eyed history teacher from across the street, and he was laying a Confederate uniform jacket and hat on the counter. That was all the man did. By the time I could take a breath, the paper goods sutler was gone. As he left, a male voice just outside the tent said, "Hey there, David. Good crowd, hmm? Selling a lot?"

David! My spine began a familiar tingling. David and a soldier's uniform? Why?

Henry would point out it was none of my business. He said I was too curious—but then I always had been. Henry said curiosity about things that didn't concern me could lead to trouble I wasn't equipped to handle. I had to admit, to myself only of course, that he was sometimes right. But then, curiosity also led to interesting . . . ah . . . treasure hunts. And I was very good at treasure hunts.

Oh, well, this wasn't the place or time to suppose some kind of mystery. Nothing here was my concern.

Shaking my shoulders to quiet my tingling spine, I left the tent.

There were no sutlers in sight along the street.

I still had time to see the army encampment spread over shaded rolling hills beyond Sutlers' Row. Long lines of small tents covered the area. There were fires for cooking, but the smell of wood smoke was pleasant. Women and a few soldiers were scattered about, sitting quietly on blankets or stools, talking, caring for equipment and guns, or, in the case of the women, doing needlework. Since it was nearing noon, several were bending over campfires, and the aroma of food joined wood smoke in the air. Flags marking the locations of various fighting units fluttered in the breeze.

Children smiled and waved, but for the most part, men and women ignored me, keeping at their work or conversation as if they were actors in a play, which, on a massive scale, they really were. It was easy to get lost in history here, easier than it had been next to the battlefield. Shooting and death in war hadn't changed all that much in the years since the Civil War. There were still guns, and they still killed soldiers. But here history was gentle, a women's type of history that I understood, felt comfortable with. There was a rhythm of living here, relaxed and relaxing, quite unlike the guns and death behind me.

Voices, many of them revealing northern accents, were slow and relaxed too. I paid no attention to words—but was content to move among the soothing murmur. After a few moments I passed out of the busy area into rows of smaller one- and two-man tents that were obviously empty. Probably the various groups of male re-enactors stayed here and all of them were taking part in the morning's battle.

A fair-haired soldier came through the trees bordering the battlefield and hurried down the row of tents. He looked preoccupied and seemed not to see me as he brushed past and ducked into a tent at the edge of the family camp.

Well, of course he'd ignore me. I had on today's dress. Soldiers playing a part didn't speak to women in "MOM FOR PRESIDENT" T-shirts. But his hurry was such a contrast to everything else in the camp that I turned around to watch him. Just before he ducked in the tent, he took his gray cap off to expose white-blond waves with a hat-hair halo.

I strolled to the end of the row, turned around, started back. There was motion inside the soldier's tent. A swishing of fabric. The tent flap parted and a woman looked out, ducked back in. She wore a sprigged blue dress, and white-blond waves covered her head. I continued walking, thinking about the blue dress and the blond hair.

Now I was back among the cooking fires, playing children, and women with their needlework. I heard a swish of fabric behind me and the woman in the blue sprigged dress hurried past, headed toward the sutlers' tents. Her hands held her skirts up on both sides so she could move more quickly.

My spine tingled again. I imagined Henry telling me to keep my nose out of other people's business.

But I'd be willing to bet this woman—a woman who had been playing soldier–was headed toward the paper goods tent. That in itself was enough to pull me along after her. That, and my memory of the sutler's reaction to my question about women in the battle here.

I'd have won my bet about where she was headed. The woman in blue ducked into the small white tent.

I paused outside for only a moment before I pushed Henry's warnings away and decided I needed some unique letter paper for a Christmas gift. Stepping as quietly as I could I opened the flap and slid through.

The woman had her back toward me, the man was in profile. They were so much alike, I knew they must be twins.

He was saying, "I couldn't do it, Lily, I just couldn't . . ."

She interrupted, her whispered words a harsh rush of air that, whispered or not, sounded like shrieking.

"I knew I'd have to be there too. David, stop fretting. That drunken devil is never going to kill another person. It's done."

"Lily! Oh, no, no, no." The cry was so full of anguish that tears filled my eyes.

Her voice softened, and I could barely hear the words. "It's better that I . . . you're . . . too good for dealing with . . ." She hesitated, spat "him."

Her next words were brittle with rage. "Being with him that night may have been Carol's choice, but he was still a murderer. Don't you ever forget that, David. You must stop grieving. Now the two of us can be happy together like we were before *she* came along."

The man's face was so pale he almost faded into the white tent behind him. He put his hands up in protest and backed away from her, but said nothing.

She followed him, still talking, and he seemed to shrivel as he huddled against the canvas that stopped his retreat.

"Since he didn't die in the wreck and the law didn't take care of him, we had to. No one will ever know. The gun's back in my tent and the matter is closed, David, it's over."

As he turned toward me, the milk-pale man said, "Oh, no, Lily, now it will never be over."

His voice was full of agony, but, in the seconds before I shot out of the tent, he noticed me, blinked in surprise, and then I thought I saw relief flash into those blue eyes.

Ignoring the heat, I ran past the tents toward Henry, toward the soldier lying so still on the ground.

I wondered if real medics had looked at that man yet.

And Henry had been only partly right. There were indeed some things better left to the licensed law. But he'd been wrong about the curiosity part. Curiosity aside, I knew I *could* handle this. I knew what I had to do because, in this case, a woman should not have been in the battle.

RADINE TREES NEHRING BIOGRAPHY

Radine Trees Nehring lives with her husband, photographer John Nehring, in the rural Ozarks near Gravette, Arkansas.

She has received the Governor's Award for Best Writing about the State of Arkansas, Tulsa Nightwriter of the Year Award, and the Dan Saults Award given by the Ozarks Writers League for nature or Ozark-value writing. American Christian Writers named her a Christian Writer of the Year, and Oklahoma Writers Federation, Inc. has given awards to her non-fiction book, *Dear Earth*, and to her mystery novels. *A Valley To Die For* was nominated for a Macavity Award as "Best First Mystery Novel" by Mystery Readers International.

Research for magazine and newspaper features and her weekly radio program, "Arkansas Corner Community News," has taken the Nehrings throughout Arkansas and Missouri. For years Radine Nehring has written non-fiction about unique people, places, and events in the Ozarks. In her mystery novels she adds appealing characters fighting for something they believe in and for their very lives. Her books starring amateur detectives Carrie McCrite and Henry King include A Valley To Die For, 2002, *Music To Die For*, 2003, and *A Treasure To Die For*, 2004, all from St Kitts Press.

In real life, Dr. Massey, a veterinarian specializing in theriogenology, has treated and written about some unusual animals. But Mr. Darley's companion, Louie? Oh yes, this is fiction.

ARTIFICIAL INSEMINATION WITH SHIPPED SEMEN IN AN UNUSUAL SPECIE

by Dr. Ruth Ellen Massey

"Dr. West, your one o'clock consultation, Mr. Darley, is here." My receptionist escorted a small elderly gentleman into my office. Mr. Darley timidly sat on the edge of the chair.

"I have an unusual problem," he began. His voice fit his stooped appearance, soft and slightly apologetic. "I understand you are a board certified theriogenologist." His use of the word theriogenologist startled me. Except for veterinarians, very few people have ever heard the word, let alone know that it means one who specializes in the study of reproduction in animals. That's why my business cards read, "Board Certified in Animal Reproduction."

"And you consult on any specie of animal?" he continued more as a query than a statement.

"My main interest is horses," I answered, "but I do consult on a variety of farm animals. Also, I have done some work with exotics."

"Good, good. You see, I have a, uh, well, a rather exotic, and unusual, companion." Mr. Darley paused. Then he took a deep breath as if he had finally made up his mind, and blurted, "Louie is an endangered specie. In fact, most people think he is extinct. Obviously, Louie is not extinct. He is very much alive and wants to become a father. But very few of Louie's kind are still alive. He finally located a compatible lady friend, but, well, this is where our problem lies."

Great, I thought to myself. People like Mr. Darley are why I left private practice. The Florida retirement community I practiced in had too many of these lonely retirees who centered their lives around their pets. Their pet became a surrogate spouse, "making" decisions for them. I empathized with their loneliness and under-stood the anthromorphization of their pets. But, as I was approaching forty myself, and single, I was afraid I was looking at myself in another thirty years. So I moved back home to Springfield, Missouri, and began a reproductive consultation practice. I had built a good practice and was now dating an old classmate from vet-erinary school. I did not want to get involved again with elderly people and their animal companions. I decided to end this consultation as quickly, but as gently, as I could.

"Mr. Darley, do you have a permit for Louie?" Many exotic and endangered species can be owned only with a special permit. If Louie was owned illegally, I could be in trouble if I treated him without notifying the proper authorities.

"Oh, no," he hastened to answer. "I don't need a per-mit for Louie. He's not on any endangered specie list. As I said, most people think he's extinct. That is, if they ever even believed he existed in the first place." This last comment was said so softly I wasn't sure I had heard correctly.

"Uh, just what is Louie?"

"Oh, he's very real. But, to our problem. Emma, his lady friend, lives in Argentina and neither can travel. The logistics are just impossible. It's close to Emma's fertile time—in about sixty days, as a matter of fact. Louie and I have read everything we can on the subject, and, as distasteful as Louie finds it, the only solution we can see is artificial insemination with cooled or frozen shipped semen." Mr. Darley was actually blushing, but manfully hurried on.

"The problem is, it's never been done in Louie's specie. That's why I'm here. We saw the program about artificial insemination in alligators on PBS and Louie recognized your name. We had discussed calling you before, but the program made up our minds."

During this speech I was trying to decide how to handle Mr. Darley. He was obviously a confused gentleman. He must have wandered away from the nursing home a few blocks down the street. I decided the kindest approach was to humor him.

"How did Louie and Emma meet?"

"Well, they haven't met face-to-face. They met on the Internet."

"The Internet?" I asked weakly.

"Yes, it's a cyber romance. Louie has trouble typing, so he tells me what to type for him. Emma's friend does the same for her. They are very compatible, and surprisingly, considering how few of them are left in this world, they do not appear to be related for at least five generations back. Louie's pedigree was lost in a fire in the Dark Ages, so we don't know further back than five generations. But, we figure they shouldn't have to worry about any recessive genes cropping up because of inbreeding. We were so worried about that since the number of Louie's kind is so terribly small now."

I could not reply. I was too busy trying to figure out how to get my receptionist to call the nursing home without Mr. Darley knowing it. He took my silence as encouragement.

"That's why that series on PBS about the alligators was so interesting to us. We thought if you could do artificial insemination with shipped semen in alligators, well, Louie said they were totally different, but there were some minor similarities."

"I was only a resident when I worked on that project," I offered only for something to say.

"Yes, but, well, you see our plight. We need somone with experience in unusal species. Louie wants you."

"Uh, Mr. Darley, just what specie is Louie?"

"Oh, dear, didn't I tell you?" Mr. Darley said brightly, too brightly. "Louie's a dragon. Would you like to see a picture of him?" He took a Polaroid photograph out of his sweater pocket and passed it across my desk.

Numbly, I took it and glanced at it. I did a double take and looked more carefully. It *was* a photograph of a dragon. It did not look computer enhanced. It was a very good fake. Suddenly, it all fell together. Mr. Darley wasn't an escapee from the nursing home. He was an actor. And I knew just who hired him. Phil, the former classmate I was dating, loved practical jokes. That explained why Mr. Darley knew the word theriogenologist, and how he *just happened* to see an obscure documentary on late night PBS and *recognize* my name. I decided to play along and see if I could turn the joke back on Phil.

"Mr. Darley, this is indeed an intriguing problem. As you said, artificial insemination, or AI, with shipped semen has never been done with dragons. I don't know if sixty days will be enough time to do all the tests necessary if we are to succeed."

Mr. Darley visibly relaxed. I rushed on. "First, we'll need some way to track Emma's reproductive cycle before ovulation—assuming dragons have a reproductive cycle. I don't know if we can find an ultrasound powerful enough to detect ovulation in Emma. I assume since she is reproductively mature, she is a fairly good-sized dragon. And there's the problem of collecting semen from Louie. We would need to design an artificial vagina for dragons. Assuming dragons have semen, will it freeze and remain viable, or can we use chilled fresh semen like we do with horses and dogs? Also, we have to develop the best semen extender to extend the life of the sperm even before we can see if freezing or chilling will work."

Mr. Darley's face brightened continually during my spiel. God, he's a good actor, I thought. Phil got his money's worth.

"I'm so glad you'll help. I was unsure it was wise for someone outside our little circle to know about Louie and Emma. But Louie said you would help. Dragons know these things. I shouldn't have doubted him."

I decided it was time to end this joke. "Okay, Mr. Darley. First thing to do is to examine Louie and make sure he's fertile. We can make an appointment for you to bring him in. How about nine o'clock tomorrow morning?"

"Oh, no, Dr. West, I can't bring Louie in," he cried. "He's too big to fit through your doors. Besides, think of the consternation if he appeared on the streets. Can you come to our abode? Your business cards do say you make on-farm consultations. Louie was so hoping you could come over today." Mr. Darley gave me a look of such hope and resignation that I found myself on the intercom asking if I had any more appointments for the day.

"Mr. Darley was your last for the day, Dr. West." I swear she had been listening to the entire consultation. She must be in on the joke too, I thought. I'll get even with Phil somehow, I vowed. I had to admit, though, as practical jokes go, Phil had really outdone himself this time.

"Okay, Mr. Darley, give my receptionist directions to your home and I'll meet with you and Louie at five o'clock."

Mr. Darley floated out the door while I tried to get Phil on the phone. His office said he was *on a call*. I figured he must be at Mr. Darley's place to see the end of his joke since he did not make house calls.

I picked up the directions from my receptionist. "Take Route 125 south to Oldfield." I actually became glad Mr. Darley came. The sun was shining, it was in the 70s in mid April, and Oldfield is near Mark Twain National Forest. The redbud trees were just past their prime and dogwood was at full bloom. Pansy violets were starting to bloom and it promised to be a gorgeous drive.

I followed 125 to Highway T and then to a gravel road that followed Swan Creek. I came to a sign that said "Four Wheel Drive Only Beyond This Point!" A dry (most of the time) creek bed became the road for nearly half a mile. My mind had been wandering, thinking about the beautiful day, about Phil and his joke, and how intimate we had been getting lately. But the sign triggered a memory. Phil had spent his summers as a child with a favorite great aunt and uncle that lived in the National Forest. Once he told me their homestead was so remote you could get there only by four-wheeled drive.

All at once, everything made sense to me. Mr. Darley was Phil's great uncle. And Phil was going to propose to me tonight. I sped down the dry creek bed forgetting I did not have four-wheeled drive. It didn't matter. I pulled into Mr. Darley's drive promptly at five o'clock.

His house, invisible from the road, was on twenty acres in a clearing surrounded by huge oak and cedar trees. Mr. Darley was waiting for me at the door.

"I'm so glad you came. Louie is ecstatic, but he's promised to behave. You see, when he gets excited, he stutters. And when a dragon stutters, well, that's why I have all these fire extinguishers." He waved at what must have been twenty in the front room. "Don't worry," he continued, misreading the expression on my face. "As long as Louie doesn't stutter, he can control the flame and is harmless. He's very affectionate."

Mr. Darley's house was old, with high ceilings and wide doors. The ceiling was dingy and looked like the draw on the fireplace had been left closed. Phil had gone all out on realism. I was beginning to

enjoy it, wondering when Phil would appear and propose.

"I told Louie what you said about Emma. He said
that was no problem. We don't need an ultrasound or
hormone tests because she would tell us when the best
time is. He said that's the way dragons have always
done it, since they are solitary creatures. He said he
didn't want to hurt your feelings, but dragons have been
around a lot longer than humans, and centuries ago circumstances had forced them to become expert at knowing when to breed. He does agree that shipping the
semen, either frozen or chilled, may be a problem.
That's really why we need your expertise. In the past,
dragons could always fly at night, but with all the radar
and detection devices now, that avenue is closed to
them. So, we must find a way to ship the semen."

"Why was Louie so interested in the alligator AI
program?" I asked. "I can't imagine dragons are cold-
blooded like alligators. I mean, they breathe fire and all,
but I guess they could be reptiles."

"Oh, they're warm-blooded . . . hot-blooded right
now you might say." Mr. Darley actually winked at me.
"It's that they lay eggs."

"Of course, I should have known."

"But, my dear, how could you have? Ah, here's
Louie."

I turned expecting to see Phil. The next thing I knew,
Mr. Darley was hovering over me with smelling salts.

"Oh, d-d-dear, oh, d-dear. I'm s-s-s-s-so s-s-s-s-s-s-
sorry. I s-s-s-should have g-given w-w-warning."

Mr. Darley grabbed a fire extinguisher and I fought
fainting again. Louie was real. And Louie WAS a dragon.

"Can you stand, my dear? We could go into the dining room for tea. Louie so loves his tea."

We had tea. Louie assured me samples of semen for
trial freezing would be no problem. Don't ask me how.
Louie was very shy and blushed, I think. Copies of

Playdragon? All I know is I got plenty of sperm to work with. His sperm looked like all the other sperm I've studied. There were minor differences, but I could use the same breeding soundness examinations of Louie's semen that I used on horses.

It turned out, in the end, shipping Louie's semen was no problem either. Both egg yolk and skim milk extenders worked, but the egg yolk was superior. I should have suspected that since dragons lay eggs. But, freezing and chilling were another problem. Neither worked. Some species' semen will freeze very well in liquid nitrogen and will keep forever if someone is around to keep liquid nitrogen in the tank. However, dragon semen, at least Louie's, did not survive the cold shock. When thawed, all the sperm were dead.

Next, I tried chilling the semen. Chilling horse or dog semen slowly to 4 degrees centigrade works very well. The sperm will live twenty-four to forty-eight hours, long enough to ship almost anywhere for insemination. But, chilling Louie's semen had the same effect as freezing. None of the sperm survived.

As with so many solutions in science, the answer was found by accident. I was once again trying a new method to chill Louie's semen one Saturday morning when I got called out on an emergency. Since it was a long, complicated birth, I did not return to the lab until Monday morning. I saw the sample still sitting on the counter where I had left it in my haste to get to the emergency. I started to throw it away, but decided to look at it under the microscope. The sperm were still alive, moving sluggishly. They look like chilled sperm, I thought.

"Of course!" I yelled. Room temperature to us is chilled compared to the internal temperature of a dragon. I heated the semen to a temperature that would kill other species' sperm. Louie's sperm looked fantastic, just like fresh semen.

The next day Emma emailed Louie that three days later would be her most fertile time. We didn't exactly tell Federal Express what was in the package.

Louie Jr. was born the day Phil and I married. I never told Phil about Mr. Darley and Louie. He has never seen the photographs of Louie Jr. in my desk. Attached to the photo is a scholarly article ready to submit for publication. But what scientific journal would print an article titled, "Artificial insemination with shipped semen in an unusual specie, *Draco dragoni*"?

Dr. RUTH ELLEN MASSEY BIOGRAPHY

Ruth Ellen Massey, DVM, dipl ACT, is a veterinarian specializing in reproduction. Her favorite specie is the horse. Although Dr. Massey has written numerous articles on veterinary medicine for scientific and lay journals, this is her first mystery story. She lives near Springfield, Missouri, with three cats, four horses, and a donkey.

Lucky and Teeka show the Bachelors Four how grave the funeral business really is when they and Teeka take out a you-can-take-it-with-you insurance policy.

LUCKY STIFF

by Jane Hale

Lucky Mahoney's memorial service was held in the small chapel of Brousard's Funeral Home in Springfield, Missouri. Lucky's wife, Teeka, requested the service be closed except for funeral directors, Garland and Billy Joe Brousard, and me, Mino Caretta. We were the remaining members of our exclusive club, "Bachelors Four." Born, bred, and educated in the Queen City, we traveled far and wide, but like homing pigeons, we always returned to the Ozarks.

When Lucky married Teeka Logan, a curvaceous blonde model he met on a cruise last year, "Bachelors Four" narrowed to three. The "Bachelors" thought as "we," so each of us, in our own way, fell in love with Lucky's bride.

Billy Joe, always the wishful thinker, was Teeka's shadow. More than once, he said, "Hey Lucky, if you get tired of Teeka I'll take her off your hands."

"Billy Joe," Teeka said, "I'm not Lucky's 'girl of the moment'—he married me."

"Wish I'd married you." Billy Joe put into words what his brother and I also felt. We figured we hadn't lost a bachelor—we'd gained a wife.

Teeka became our *lucky charm*. Weekends, the five of us piled into Garland's black Escalade and escaped to

St. Louis or Kansas City to visit the casino boats. Sometimes, Lucky booked us on tours through his travel agency when both Brousard brothers could get away from their funeral business. Give me a laptop, access to online, and the world easily became my insurance office.

Billy Joe liked to quip, "Anywhere Mino goes he takes a 'piece of the rock.'"

"Bachelors Four" and a Carman Diaz doll like Teeka created quite a stir traveling together. Lucky and Billy Joe were mistaken for Mel Gibson more than once although each swore they didn't look alike. Garland could have been a stand-in for the young Cary Grant.

And, me, well, there was the night in Branson when the guys fixed me up with a blind date and passed me off as Robert Redford. A dizzy blonde kept calling me Jay Gatsby. "Oh, Jay," she gushed, "The Great Gatsby is my favorite movie."

Lucky and Billy Joe were rolling on the floor before the night was over.

Even Garland's composure ruffled when a spotlight lit up our table and the band leader announced, "Ladies and gentlemen, we are privileged to have in our midst tonight the one, the only, Robert Redford, and his lovely lady of the evening, Bebe Astor."

Bebe rose, dragging me up with her, smiling and waving to the room at large.

"Is your name really Bebe Astor?" I asked.

"As sure as yours is Robert Redford, Jay." She stood on tiptoe, plastered herself against me, and delivered a kiss hot enough to make Hollywood blush.

The crowd went wild. My friends hooted and yelled. A bottle of champagne arrived at our table, compliments of the house. People stopped by all evening asking for my autograph. Bebe pouted because I wouldn't give out autographs. Finally, she flounced off to the lady's room.

"What'll I do?" I asked Garland. "I can't forge Redford's name."

"They'll never know the difference the way you scrawl your signature. Go ahead," Garland advised, "do it."

Billy Joe handed me a bright red pen. "Use this, Mino. It'll last two days, then the ink disappears. No evidence, no crime."

"Billy Joe, you're a hoot!" Teeka scribbled her name on her cocktail napkin with the red pen. "Go ahead, Mino, autograph my napkin."

"Anything for you, Teeka." I scrawled my name next to hers.

She examined my signature. "You're right, Garland. It looks like Robert Redford to me." She folded the napkin and tucked it in her beaded bag.

Bebe returned. She was delighted when I began signing autographs. Sure enough, no one questioned my scrawl, Mino Caretta.

"I've got to have a pen like that." Teeka's eyes danced with excitement.

Billy Joe placed an arm around Teeka's shoulder, reached into the bodice of her dress, and pulled out another red pen. "Your wish is my command!"

"Billy Joe, what am I going to do with you?" Teeka dimpled.

Garland drawled, "I bet Billy Joe can think of a thing or two."

"Wish I'd said that," Billy Joe said, "but, for now, I'll settle for a dance with Lucky's charming lady."

Our "lucky charm" seemed infallible until Lucky hit a bad streak. He tried to ride it out but his luck went from bad to worse. When the casinos cut him off, he borrowed from us. He got in so deep to me he moved his prize '57 Thunderbird to my garage. I protested when he gave me the signed title to hold.

"Think of it as hedging your bet, Mino."

Teeka whispered, "That car is his life. I'm surprised Lucky didn't leave me in your garage instead of the Thunderbird."

"You're my life, baby." Lucky hugged her. "Mind if I take my personalized license plate and my Bruce Springsteen CD, Mino?"

"Be my guest. What would I do with a L-U-C-K-Y license plate? Take Bruce with you too." The CD was Teeka's favorite, and I already had one. "Your Thunderbird will be back in your garage soon."

Lucky caressed the smooth white surface of the Thunderbird. "My luck's gotta change." Gambling was his life and he'd bet on anything.

Two months before Teeka's brother, Will, had flown up from Texas to help celebrate his sister's first wedding anniversary. Atop the world, we hosted a party for the Mahoneys from the dizzy heights of Hammons Towers. My date for the evening was Sweet Stephanie, a loan officer at First State Bank. Garland and Billy Joe flipped a coin to see who had to stay at the funeral home. As usual, Garland lost.

"How come you always win the toss, Billy Joe?" Teeka asked.

"Promise you won't tell?" Billy Joe smoothed a blonde curl from Teeka's face and pulled a coin from inside her ear. He flipped the coin. It came up heads. He turned it over. It was a two-headed nickel.

Teeka dimpled. "Where's your date, Billy Joe?"

"No time to dig one up."

Teeka's brother, Will, was a mortician too, and he nodded solemnly. "The funeral business is a grave undertaking."

Billy Joe winked. "Pretty stiff competition, eh?"

Lucky glowered. "These jokes will be the death of me."

Teeka scoffed, "I bet I'll die first."

"Betcha!" Lucky claimed her bet.

"How much?"

"The whole insurance policy."

"Right, Lucky. If we had insurance. And how would we collect?"

"The insurance man's right here." Lucky threw an arm across my shoulder. "Mino can write insurance on us. The first one to go will have the whole bundle buried with them. Who says you can't take it with you?"

"Wish I'd thought of that." Billy Joe sighed.

Several bottles of champagne later Lucky made the bet official. "Mino, you write a million dollar life insurance policy on each of us with the surviving spouse as beneficiary. If either of us dies, you pay the policy to an account in Stephanie's bank for cash to bury with the deceased. Our friendly undertakers, the Brousard brothers, will get the body."

Teeka held up a hand. "Will's a mortician too."

"Sorry, Will."

Billy Joe upped the odds. "Lucky, if you go first I'll console the widow. Too bad she won't have her million to sweeten the pot."

Lucky considered the wager. "Okay, since it's our anniversary, you three can pay the premium on the policy for a year. Mino can double the indemnity. We'll each get a million. One to go, the other to sweeten the pot. How's that, Billy Joe?"

Billy Joe raised his glass, "Hey, wish . . ."

We all chorused, ". . . I'd thought of that."

I wrote the insurance policies. Billy Jo, Garland, and I chipped in for the year's premium. The documents were put in the safety deposit box at First State Bank. The dumb bet was forgotten.

I was out of town the next month with insurance business. Billy Joe, Garland, and I played phone tag. I stopped in Branson on my way home from Little Rock for dinner and a show with a client. Later, in my room, I sorted through my phone messages and dialed Brousard's Funeral Home.

"Garland Brousard. We're here in your time of need."

"Mino here."

"Are you in Springfield?"

"No, Branson."

"We've got to talk. Lucky owes the casinos! He's used us as references. They've been calling. It's damn embarrassing. What're *we* going to do?"

"Calm down. Let me do some checking. I'll call you."

On a whim I phoned Teeka.

"You have reached the Mahoney residence. At the tone leave a message. You might get Lucky."

"Mino, here. I'll be home tomorrow. Call me."

At home, I checked my answering machine. The only call I returned was Teeka's.

"Mino, at last you're home! Can I come over?"

I mixed a pitcher of martinis, turned on Bruce Springsteen, and lowered the lights. Bruce was wailing, "I'm on fire," when I heard her blue Corvette pull into the drive.

I answered the door and Teeka fell into my arms, sobbing. I'd dreamed of this moment. But, not like this.

Nestled together on my couch, she told me what I suspected. Lucky was a high roller and he'd got in over his head.

"Where is Lucky?"

"He's running scared. A man in Kansas City made an offer on our travel agency. Her voice dropped to a whisper. "Lucky's there closing the deal. He's using my maiden name, T. Logan." She edged closer. "I'm scared."

"I'll take care of you, Teeka." I hugged her closer.

The picture window shattered behind us.

She screamed.

I pulled her to the floor. My security alarm's shrill cry joined the screech of tires burning rubber outside. I turned off the alarm—911 was the last thing we needed.

"It's been this way since Lucky left," she whimpered. "If I answer the phone they threaten me. If I leave the house they follow me. I'm scared they'll break in and kill me."

"Sweetheart, I'll run decoy in your Corvette. My car's in the garage. You take it. Here's the key to my office. Sleep on the couch. In the morning leave my car at the office and take a cab home. I'll return your Corvette later."

She gave me a quick kiss. "Mino, I should have married you."

I yearned to pull her close and never let her go. I reminded myself she was Lucky's wife. I reached to take her car keys. Her fingers caressed mine, lingered a moment, and pulled free. She smiled and headed for my garage.

Later, back home, I parked her Corvette in my garage. After boarding up my window, I took a cold shower and spent the night tossing, turning, and dreaming of Teeka.

The next day I met Garland for an early breakfast.

He had a cruel surprise for me. "Lucky's on the casino's list. He owes me. He's been betting the horses and the bookies are out for blood. Teeka and I are going away together."

"Jesus, Garland. What makes you think Teeka will go?"

"She planned it."

I promised Garland I'd get back to him. I'd lost my appetite.

My car was at the office, Teeka wasn't. Her fragrance remained on the couch. She wasn't home when I returned her Corvette.

That's the last "we" heard from Teeka until she called me a week later. "Lucky's dead, Mino." She muttered nonsense, "Bookies . . . they learned about the anniversary insurance policy."

"Teeka, slow down, honey . . ." I shouted into the receiver, "I'll come . . ."

Her voice dropped to a conspirator whisper, "No, Mino! They'll kill you too." There was a soft click on her phone.

I thought she'd hung up. "Teeka?" Alarmed, I yelled, "Teeka?"

"Mino, they gave me a week to pay our bills." Her voice broke, "Or, they said . . . they said, I'd join Lucky."

"Teeka, darling. Where are you? I'll come and get you. We'll go to the police . . ."

"No-o-o!" She screamed. "I'd die if anything happened to you, Mino."

"Nothing is going to happen . . ."

A man's voice came on the line. "Mino? This is Will, Teeka's brother."

"Thank God, Will. What's going on? Is Teeka in Texas with you?"

"Be careful, Mino." He hesitated.

"Will, are you there?"

"Listen, this phone may be bugged. I don't have much time. Lucky's body is at my funeral home. Teeka wants to bring him to Springfield Friday for a memorial service. She'll settle their debts. That'll get the bookies off her back."

Teeka was back on the line. "Mino, today is Monday. I'll send the death certificate ahead so you can file the claim. Will and the attending physician signed it. I'll fly in on Friday with the body. I can get things in order and fly back that night for the burial Saturday."

"Are you sure you don't want me to fly down and come back with you?"

"Mino, I've already talked to Billy Joe. He's flying down to help me bring Lucky's body back to Brousard's."

I imagined that weasel, Billy Joe, consoling my lady. "Teeka, let me take care of the bookies and casinos. That will make it safer for you when you return with Lucky."

Teeka gasped. "Oh Mino, I couldn't . . ."

"I don't want to hear any more. You fax me the amounts and where to send them. I'll have it all taken care of when you arrive. Then, you can pay me back with the insurance money."

"Are you sure you have that much money?"

"I can take out a loan on the strength of your insurance money." I hung up whistling, "Anything you can do, I can do better." I dialed my insurance office to start the wheels spinning.

Friday, Garland and I met Teeka and Billy Joe at the airport at 2 p.m. The Brousard brothers flipped a coin to see who would take Lucky's body to the funeral home. For once Billy Joe lost.

Teeka dabbed at her eyes. "There's so much to do, Mino. Did you deposit the insurance money at Stephanie's bank like we decided?"

I handed her my clean handkerchief. "Yes, honey. The money is all there, two million dollars. I sent cashier checks to the addresses you faxed to cover the bookies and casino debts."

Teeka leaned against me. "I knew I could count on you, Mino." She straightened as though steeling herself for the tasks at hand. "Lucky left the notes telling how much he owed to everyone in our safety deposit box at First State Bank. I've got to get there before closing time. Garland, can you get me a cab?"

"Nonsense. I'll drive you." Garland put a reassuring arm around her shoulders.

"Let me, Teeka." I moved closer.

She stepped back. "No! They might be watching. I don't want to put either of you in danger."

"Teeka, nothing is going to happen, I promise." I said.

"That's what Lucky said." She dabbed at her eyes again. "Mino, just write a little note urging Stephanie to help me. I'll call when I finish my errands. We'll all have dinner together before the services at seven." She patted my arm. "I've got to do this last thing for Lucky, alone."

I scribbled a note and signed it.

"Oh, Mino, I've still got the key to your office." She rummaged in her purse.

"Don't worry about it, honey. I'll get it later."

At dinner, Teeka was a vision in black. We fought like schoolboys to see who sat by her. Teeka gave each of us a check for the amount Lucky borrowed. She gave me a check to cover the loan I'd taken out to pay the casino and bookies.

It was time to go to the chapel.

Teeka approached the casket.

Billy Joe, somber in his pinstripe suit, lifted the casket lid.

Out of respect for the widow we remained seated. Teeka fell across the body, sobbing. Her blonde hair cascaded across the still profile of Lucky Mahoney. At length, she straightened.

Billy Joe handed her the packet First National Bank had prepared. A million dollars in large bills. Laying it inside, Teeka paid her debt. Billy Joe closed the casket lid for the last time.

I nudged Garland and whispered, "I hope wherever Lucky's going they don't have casinos."

Garland nodded.

Teeka distanced herself as the grieving widow. She gave us all a chaste hug and promised to call.

Billy Joe and Garland flipped a coin to see who would fly back with Teeka to Texas with the body for the burial. Billy Joe won.

Teeka never called.

Billy Joe never returned.

Our checks on Teeka's account came back, account closed.

Stephanie told me she'd helped Teeka transfer her million to an offshore account after they put the million she owed Lucky in the bag. Stephanie didn't question it since Teeka had my note.

Garland summed it up. "Teeka played us for suckers. Lucky's gone. Billy Joe's taken his place."

Belatedly, Garland checked the funeral directory for The Logan Funeral Home and found nothing. "Who signed the death certificate?"

I searched my files for the copy I'd made of the document. It was gone! I called the home office. The main document had to be there. I breathed easy until I heard a gasp, "Mr. Caretta, the paper is blank. There's nothing on it. But, you saw it. I saw it. Oh God! Two million dollars. We're in big trouble!"

Visions of Teeka's red pen floated across my brain. "Damn!" I was in more than trouble. I owed the First State Bank two million dollars and the insurance money was gone. Billy Joe and Teeka had called my hand and won.

I ran an ad in the antique car magazine Lucky left behind in the Thunderbird. I needed cash for the car, quick!

The most promising bid was a telegram from Dallas. "Name your price. Stop. I've got to have the white '57 Thunderbird."

I smiled—and began to whistle under my breath. I didn't list the color.

I called the Texas number. Bingo! The deal went down.

The next day a stranger arrived with cash and picked up the car.

The "Bachelors Two" followed authorities, who trailed the Thunderbird down the turnpike through Oklahoma. They radioed ahead to the Texas police for help as we neared the Texas border.

East of Dallas, the Thunderbird turned off at Will's Point and headed out of town. We eased up as our car topped a slight rise. Ahead lay a cemetery. I got out my binoculars and squinted into the last rays of sunshine.

A blonde woman knelt in the cemetery beside a raw mound of dirt arranging flowers. A blue Corvette was parked beside the white '57 Thunderbird. A tall, dark-haired fellow was exchanging the license plate.

I focused on the new license. L-U-C-K-Y.

Garland grabbed the binoculars. "Damn you, Billy Joe. His woman, his car, and now, his license plate."

I reclaimed the binoculars just as the blue Corvette sped away. The blonde returned to the Thunderbird, got in, and the car roared off.

The Texas authorities closed in. Bruce Springsteen was blaring "Born in the USA" as we joined the party.

Teeka stepped out the passenger side of the Thunderbird.

The driver unfolded and crawled out. We looked for Billy Joe, but it was Lucky Mahoney standing there, big as life!

"Gentlemen." He lifted his hand in a mock salute.

"You'll never die, Mahoney, you lucky stiff," I muttered.

Garland eyed Lucky. "We should have known something was wrong when Billy Joe lost the coin toss and stayed with your body. If I'd stayed we would have known you weren't dead. The only time I won a coin toss from my brother and it was rigged!"

"You have the right to remain silent . . ." Lucky and Teeka were handcuffed and led away.

"Teeka . . ." Garland called.

She turned. Her eyes were moist and luminous with hope.

"Where's Billy Joe?"

Teeka's glance darted toward the cemetery. "Garland, I'm so sorry. I wish . . ."

Garland interrupted, "Wishing and wanting, that's what started this whole mess. Teeka, join your husband. You're two of a kind."

The Thunderbird had enough cash stashed in the trunk to pay the national debt.

Will was picked up in Dallas and joined Lucky and Teeka in the Texas jail.

The grave site in Will's Point Cemetery had been purchased by T. Logan. Garland received permission to exhume the body and take it back to Missouri. Billy Joe Brousard had wished himself into Lucky's casket. Beside him was an empty bag marked First State Bank. In his folded hands was a check for one million dollars.

Garland whispered, "Billy Joe. Let's go home. I guess you found out it's not much fun to be Lucky Mahoney."

If you listened closely you could almost hear Billy Joe say, "I wish I'd said that."

JANE HALE BIOGRAPHY

Jane Shewmaker Hale resides in Buffalo, Missouri. She and her late husband, Bob, have four sons and ten grandchildren.

She is an active partner in family business, Hale Fireworks and Sportswear. She helped establish the Dallas County R-1 Alumni Association and has served as president since 1971. She is a member and 1997 vice-president of Springfield Writers' Guild; Ozark Writers League; Missouri Writers' Guild, vice-president and conference chairman, 2004; Ozark Writers, Inc., president.

She owns and operates Rainbow Publications/Toys, which promotes and distributes her *Land* series of children's holiday mystery books and line of Mollycoddle animals. Books are approved by Accelerated Reading for schools. Recycling Reading is a promotion/distribution program used to benefit her company and area schools.

Her series includes *Wonderland*, 1997; *Heartland*, 1999; *Foreverland*, 2001; and *Boomland*, 2003. Two more will complete the series, *Spookyland* and *Homeland*. Mollycoddles is the collections of plush animals designed and manufactured as book companions.

Every Day Is Mother's Day, the first book in the *Every Day* series of gift books, was published in 2003 by Skyward Publishing.

Her books can be found online at Amazon.com or can be ordered by most bookstores. They are also from her website www.firecrackerlady.com.

AFTERWORD

In the preceding pages are nineteen stories from the Ozarks of southern Missouri and northern Arkansas. The authors, from the Missouri River to the Arkansas River and from the Mississippi River to the Kansas state border, write about many aspects of the area. All love the rugged, wooded hills, clear spring-fed streams, and resourceful people. These stories are only a sample of the hundreds available from the talented writers of the area.

More will come in *Mysteries of the Ozarks, Volume II.* Look for it.